For Mika, Alex and Meagan

Dark Secrets

STAR Academy

Dark Secrets

EDWARD KAY

DOUBLEDAY CANADA

Library and Archives Canada Cataloguing in Publication is available upon request
ISBN: 978-0-385-66707-4

Issued also in electronic format.
ISBN: 978-0-307-36815-7

Text and cover design: Jennifer Lum
Cover image: © 2011 Lindsay Ward

The author wishes to thank the Canada Council for the Arts for their economic support during the writing of this book.

Printed and bound in the USA

Published in Canada by Doubleday Canada,
a division of Random House of Canada Limited
Visit Random House of Canada Limited's website: www.randomhouse.ca

10 9 8 7 6 5 4 3 2 1

CHAPTER 1

AMANDA GAZED UPWARD, her eyes following the rocket's progress as it climbed higher and higher into the evening sky. She mentally calculated the angle of its trajectory and the speed an object of that size, weight and shape would have to reach to achieve escape velocity from Earth's gravitational pull. Amanda had to squint to follow its trail as the vanishing projectile rose into the darkening heavens. Just as the rocket became too small for her to see anymore, the sky was wrenched open by a blinding flash. Fiery orange and yellow tendrils shot out in every direction from where it had been, solid and resolutely on course only an instant before. But now the missile was blown to smithereens by the explosive force of the very material that had given it its power and upward momentum. A sonic boom like a cannon blast followed a moment later. Amanda felt the thump of the shock wave in her chest, and her eardrums popped. Backlit by the fading burst of light, tiny burned fragments of the rocket's casing began floating down toward Earth, giving them, thought Amanda, the ironic appearance of blackened snowflakes.

On cue, a slightly out-of-tune marching band began to play "Hail to the Victors." It was a type of music known as a "war song" and was performed at games where the Downview Danes, her school's football team, were competing. The aggressively energetic nature of the rhythm and melody was designed to rouse both fans and players. However, Amanda didn't have much interest in surrogate gladiatorial combats, so the music did not have the intended effect on her. Instead, its frenzied tempo and roller-coaster melody made her think not of champions but rather of an old slapstick silent movie. The type where some unfortunate man on a railway handcar was pumping frantically to avoid being mowed down by a speeding steam locomotive. Or perhaps he was running around a circus ring with the seat of his pants on fire, frantically trying to extinguish the flames by flapping his hands over his posterior while being chased by a tiger that had escaped from its cage.

Meanwhile, awed by the finale of the fireworks display, the large crowd of Downview residents who had gathered for the occasion cheered and applauded heartily. The roar of their approval reverberated around the square in front of Downview city hall, mingling with the discordant strains of the music and the last echoes of the fireworks explosion as the acrid odour of burnt gunpowder wafted down onto the assembled throng.

The marching band then lurched into action, high-stepping through the square in a choreographed routine so carefully rehearsed for this celebration that the movements of the players were very nearly in sync. Each one knew that the eyes of the world were upon them, because tonight they were performing to celebrate something far more momentous than a victory by the Downview Danes. They were here to honour the girl who had saved them from becoming mindless slaves to alien invaders from a distant planet. Some of the sousaphone players, overcome by the magnitude of the occasion, began to blow harder and play faster. The fluctuation in tempo gave the music the characteristic of a sonic rubber band, stretching and contracting as if it existed in some parallel universe where the rules of space and time no longer applied. The increasingly wobbly music made Amanda think even more of the man in the circus ring, looking for a water bucket in which to dunk his flaming derrière while he ran away from the escaped tiger. She began to giggle.

"Honey," said her mother, Wendy Forsythe, "don't laugh like that. Everyone will think there's something wrong with you. For once, nobody thinks you're some kind of . . . you know, *weirdo*. So don't blow it. Just wave to the crowd. They've all come out to honour you, after all."

Amanda was used to her mother worrying that other people would think there was something wrong with her. She had known this ever since the age of two, when she had begun laying out her coloured building blocks in sequences that her mother recognized as patterns, though she could not break the code. In fact, Amanda was so accustomed to her mother's insecurities about her that despite having saved the world from alien invasion, all she said now, as she stood in the place of honour, was "Yes, Mom."

Besides, Amanda *was* genuinely honoured by this outpouring of thanks from the people of her hometown, even if their way of expressing it was unintentionally comical. So, not wanting to insult anyone, she did as her mother suggested. She waved to the crowd, tried to ignore the ridiculous music and did her best to put the slapstick image out of her mind so her smile wouldn't break into a belly laugh. But the more she tried to block out the picture she saw in her mind's eye, the more the marching band's music seemed to speed up and slow down. Soon, she could hardly see anything but a mental image of the wild-eyed man in the silent movie, running around in circles and flapping his hands to try to put out the fire on his butt, all while avoiding getting eaten by the tiger. Standing there on the raised platform—exposed to the crowd and surrounded by her family, the mayor of Downview and a gaggle of local dignitaries—Amanda felt a nearly uncontrollable burst of laughter building inside her.

Her mother gave her the evil eye. "Don't you dare, Amanda. Do you hear me? No laughing. I mean it."

Finally, Amanda was able to force the movie image out of her mind. But that was only because it had been replaced by a real-life image that was even stranger than the one she was picturing. As the marching band tottered like a drunken centipede toward the reviewing stand, she could see that two of the majorettes were proudly holding up a banner. The banner was intended to represent the event that had made Amanda famous all over planet Earth (and no doubt beyond it as well). However, it was possible to guess this only because it read "Thank you, Amanda Forsythe!" Nothing else depicted on the banner, mused Amanda, bore any resemblance to either her or the astonishing events that had changed her life—and allowed everyone else's lives to stay the same.

"Look, sweetie, there's even a picture of you on the banner," exclaimed her father, Jack Forsythe, gesturing toward a crudely if enthusiastically painted portrait of Amanda.

Amanda wasn't vain by any stretch of the imagination, but she couldn't help noticing that on the banner, her nose was needle-like and pointed inexplicably to the right, and her eyes were lopsided.

"How come your eyes are crooked?" asked Amanda's younger brother, Daniel. "You look like that type of fish with the two eyes that move from one side of its body to the other."

"You mean a flounder," replied Amanda. "But actually, only one of the flounder's eyes moves. When the fish matures and starts swimming on its flat side, one eye migrates over to the other side of its body. Not both eyes. The other one is already there."

"Whatever," replied Daniel.

At nine, Daniel was two years younger than Amanda and had yet to acquire social graces or exhibit any evidence of his sister's intelligence.

"Anyways," he continued, "that's the kind of fish you look like on that banner. Except that it doesn't have a pointy, crooked nose like you do in that picture. Did the aliens do something to you to make your eyes move across your face like a halibut's? Did they make your nose all pointy and crooked like that so it would be harder for you to fight them?"

"You mean flounder, not halibut," replied Amanda. "And no, I don't think that making my eyes look like a flounder's or my nose look pointy was part of their plan for world conquest. It's just a bad portrait of me, okay?"

Daniel's comment was particularly annoying because a mutating flounder is exactly what Amanda thought she looked like in the banner that was now being paraded before the inhabitants of her hometown and camera crews from around the world.

"Well, it *must* be a bad portrait, then," said Daniel, "because you've never looked much like a fish in real life. Except for when I jumped out of your equipment cabinet last week dressed like one of those spidery aliens and scared you. You should have seen your face!" Daniel laughed so hard he lost his breath and almost choked. "Your mouth opened wide and your eyes went all giant and bugged out, sort of like a surprised codfish that had been goosed or something! Like this!"

Daniel made his eyes bulge out and his mouth gape open in a pantomimed expression of fright.

"Well, if you'd gone through what I've gone through," said Amanda, "you'd be a little jumpy about having people leap out at you too."

Amanda still had nightmares about being chased through the basement of the STAR Academy by her professors after they had reverted to their alien forms. She could see the exoskeletal bodies bearing down on her as they tried to catch her and stop her from escaping and alerting the authorities to their plan to conquer Earth. So Daniel's little "practical joke" of jumping out of her equipment cabinet dressed as a spider was not one that she appreciated.

"If you ever pull a boneheaded stunt like that again," continued Amanda, "I will formulate some terrifying way to surprise you in retaliation. It will be something entirely non-violent. Yet it will be the most unimaginably frightening thing that can be done to someone of your specific psychological type—which, by the way, I have analyzed using state-of-the-art techniques."

"What psychological type am I?" asked Daniel, not so cocky now, voice registering alarm.

"I'm not telling," replied Amanda. "But I've studied you

closely, and I know precisely what it is and what your deepest fears are."

"Maw-mm!" bleated Daniel like a frightened sheep. "Amanda says she knows my precise psychological type, but she won't tell me what it is. And she says she's going to use it to think up something to scare me if I try to scare her again!"

"Well, then, don't try to scare her," said Wendy Forsythe, attempting to ignore her son and enjoy the festivities. Her head bobbed uncertainly as she tried to keep time to the erratic rhythm of the music.

"So," continued Amanda, "no more of your dumb stunts, okay, Daniel? Because if you force me to devise a means to scare you, whatever I create will make you jump out of your skin so far that you'll look a lot sillier than a surprised cod. And I'll record your reaction on a webcam and post it on the Internet so your classmates can all see it and have a good laugh."

"Maww-mmm!" whined Daniel.

Amanda smiled slightly.

"Oh, Amanda," interjected her mother, "just ignore your brother. He's only trying to get you going. As for you, Daniel, don't upset your sister. This is her big night, and I won't have you spoiling it. It doesn't matter how bad her picture on that banner is, or how much you think she looks like a tuna. It's the thought that counts."

"Not a tuna, a *flounder*, Mom," said Amanda. "And anyway, the 'thought' is the most disturbing part. Nothing at the STAR Academy happened anything like the way they're showing it. They're making it look so stupid!"

In the rest of the scene on the banner, the Amanda with the lopsided, mutating flounder eyes was firing two laser pistols like a gunslinger at some evil-looking aliens. Their plans of Earthly conquest thwarted, the once-smug invaders cringed. Their bugged-out eyes now looked fearful as they beat a retreat back to their spaceship, dodging Amanda's laser blasts, which burned gaping holes through their unluckier accomplices and incinerated others altogether.

"I like the way you zapped a hole right through that one's back!" said Daniel. "Think you could teach me to shoot like that?"

"No," replied Amanda, "because I've never shot anyone, with a laser or anything else. I didn't defeat the aliens by blasting them with laser beams! It's like I told the reporters—we never had to harm any of the aliens. We just outsmarted them. And the one named George actually helped me stop the other ones."

"Sweetheart," said Amanda's mother, "people don't really care about the details. They're just thrilled that you saved them from alien invaders."

At this, Amanda's father, who had been preoccupied with entering numbers into a calculator, spoke up. "Your mother's right. And besides, I'm in the middle of negotiating a very lucrative deal for those Amanda-blasting-the-aliens banners. For every one that is printed after this parade, we get twenty cents. So if we sell a million of them . . . well, you're the genius, you do the math."

"If there are a million of those banners with my face on them, looking like a flounder with a crooked nose, I'll kill myself," said Amanda.

"Honey, don't talk like that," said her mother. "People will think you're serious."

"I *am* serious," said Amanda. "I don't want you to sell any of those banners, Dad. Not a single one."

"You just don't understand business," said Jack Forsythe. "We've got to make hay while the sun shines. People might be dying to spend money on a banner with your picture on it *this week*. But by next month or the month after that, there will be someone more famous than you—a boy who survived an accidental ride in a balloon, a kid who can make a dummy talk while standing on his head and drinking a glass of water. The money from this banner would be really good. For *all* of us."

"Sorry, Dad, but it makes me look like I'm insane. I don't want you to sell them."

"I'll cut you in for 10 percent of the profits—after expenses, that is," said Jack Forsythe.

"No," said Amanda.

"You drive a hard bargain," said her father. "Okay, 10 percent of the gross. That means 10 percent of all the money I take in before expenses."

"I know what gross profit means," replied Amanda.

"So do we have a deal or do we have a deal?" he asked.

"Jack, can we talk about this some other time?" said Wendy Forsythe. "Can't we just try to enjoy the music and the fact that Amanda is being honoured, and not being thought of as an oddball anymore?"

Jack Forsythe nodded glumly as he mentally calculated how much money he *wouldn't* make if he didn't sell a million banners bearing the laser-slinging, flounder-eyed likeness of his daughter.

The marching band concluded its rendition of "Hail to the Victors" with an off-key flourish. The crowd applauded wildly. News crews moved in and aimed their cameras at Amanda. Principal Murkly, who just months earlier had mocked Amanda's science fair project in front of the entire school, stepped up to the microphone. He beamed at the crowd.

"And now," he proudly announced "the Downview Public School kindergarten class would like to present a play that Mrs. Wheedlbum and I wrote ourselves in honour of that special student whom we nurtured into what she is today."

"*They* nurtured?" said Amanda with disbelief. "All they ever did was make fun of me."

"Shhh," said Wendy Forsythe. "It's better for your public image if people don't remember that."

Amanda turned to her mother to protest, but as she opened her mouth to speak, she was drowned out by Principal Murkly bellowing through the PA system, "The play is entitled *How Amanda Forsythe and Those Three Other Kids Saved Earth from Space Aliens*."

"'Those three other kids'?" gasped Amanda. "Evelyn, Derek and Sanjay are going to be so upset when they see this on the news. They might think I had something to do with naming the play."

Amanda's mother laid a hand on her daughter's arm, dismissing her concerns. "I'm sure your friends won't mind. It's just a kindergarten play."

The lights on the reviewing stand dimmed. The news cameras turned to face the stage, which had until now been swathed in darkness. An eerie green glow faded up, revealing a dozen five-year-olds dressed as aliens emerging out of dry-ice fog. They wore bulbous-headed grey rubber masks with big red eyes and grey rubber gloves that had long, spidery fingers tipped with suction cups. The tiny actors stalked menacingly about the haze-enshrouded stage, waving the extra arms that had been sewn on to their costumes to mimic the crab-like aliens.

“Prepare to be conquered, Earthlings!” shouted one.

“We aliens are going to take over your planet!” screamed another.

They began to snicker arrogantly at their impending feat of world domination. But just then, a spotlight picked out four Earth children rushing from the darkness toward the invaders. The girl leading the charge sported a wig of long, wavy hair and wore a purple top emblazoned with a stars-and-planets motif, just like the one Amanda had worn at the science fair the previous fall.

“Oh, look!” said Amanda’s mother proudly. “The girl in front is playing you.”

The “three other kids” on the stage were supposed to represent Derek Murphy, Evelyn Chiu and Sanjay Dosanjh, Amanda’s three closest friends at the STAR Academy. In real life they had helped her, with a combination of bravery and intellectual brilliance, to defeat the aliens’ attempts to take over Earth. All four of the actors representing Amanda and her friends wielded cardboard tubes painted in bright colours that were supposed to give them the appearance of laser light swords.

The girl playing Amanda raised hers threateningly and issued a warning. “Aliens,” she announced, “I am Amanda Forsythe. And these are my trusty friends, Eric, Devlin and Sandhu.”

“I can’t believe it,” said the real Amanda to her mother. “First they leave the names out, and then they get them wrong. Derek, Evelyn and Sanjay will be so insulted when they see this on the news.”

“Now, Amanda,” replied her mother soothingly, “you’re concerning yourself too much with the facts. The only fact you should be concerned with tonight is the fact that no one thinks you're . . . you know, *strange* anymore. Just try to enjoy all that approval."

Despite all the recent fame and adulation she was receiving, Amanda was still smarting from the incident at the Downview Public School science fair the previous September. That was when Principal Murkly and Mrs. Wheedlbum, Amanda's former grade six teacher, had made fun of her exhibit on photon-sail interstellar space travel because they didn't understand it. Their mockery had made Amanda the target of teasing from her fellow students, who already tended not to relate to her because she was what they called an "egghead." And in the unimaginative, uninspiring backwater that was Downview, nobody knew what to do with an egghead except try to make it crack. But that was all then. This was now. Far from considering Amanda a freak, they now idolized her for saving the world against all odds—even if they didn't have a clue how she did it.

On stage, the girl playing Amanda shouted, "You have tried to conquer our planet by tricking us kids at the STAR Academy into helping you with our scientific discoveries! But we have uncovered your evil scheme, because we're smarter and better than your species. You have five seconds to surrender or we will destroy you!"

Despite the threat, the aliens just continued stalking about menacingly, mocking the actors depicting Amanda and her friends.

"Aliens rule! Earthlings drool!" shouted one.

"Hey, Earthlings," taunted another, "if you had IQs of twelve, you'd have to grow two more fingers to be able to count that high on them!"

The rest of the aliens blew spitty razzberries—that is, until the Amanda character shouted, "Have it your way, crab breath. Time to open up a can of butt-whup, Earth-style!"

Then she and the children playing Derek, Evelyn and Sanjay counted down together: "Four, three, two, one, put the eight-leggers on the run!"

With that, the four Earth children chased their alien classmates and whacked them with their cardboard light swords, laughing and cheering triumphantly as the vanquished extraterrestrials ran screaming in terror off the stage and into the dark. However, one of the actors portraying an alien was slower than his classmates and had become disoriented. He now found himself separated from the pack, trapped on a corner of the stage. The four Earth children encircled him and began to flail away at him with their cardboard light swords, drawing cheers from the spectators.

The kindergarten teacher waded into the fray. "Okay, that's enough!" she called out as she began pulling the four Earth children off their squealing victim. "It's your classmate Robbie, remember? He's just *pretending* to be an alien. So don't hurt him. You would only hurt him if he was a real alien, like the one Amanda and those three other kids blasted."

Amanda's father turned to her on the reviewing stand and looked at her proudly. "You've made a real impression on everybody."

"Yes," said Amanda. "Though not nearly as big an impression as they're making on each other with those cardboard tubes."

"Oh, Amanda," said her mother. "Relax. They don't mean any harm. They're just a little overexcited by the drama of the brave thing you did. They admire you."

"But we never beat on anybody with sticks," Amanda explained. "That looks more like a turf war between a bunch of cavemen."

"Maybe so," said Amanda's father, "but I've sold more than two hundred of those cardboard Amanda Forsythe Laser Swords this week alone. Even at twenty bucks a pop, the kids are buying them faster than I can paint 'em."

Amanda's father, as he eagerly told anyone who would listen, was the eastern regional sales manager for the Achilles Bunion Remover Cream Company. He was proud of having built his sales territory into the most successful one in the country, and he liked to consider himself a self-made man and a shrewd entrepreneur who knew when to seize a money-making opportunity.

"Yessiree," he continued. "Who'd have thought people would pay that much for a wrapping-paper tube that doesn't even have any wrapping paper on it anymore? I don't like to brag," he bragged, "but this was definitely one of my brighter money-making ideas."

He smiled at his own cleverness and patted his wallet.

Supported by the kindergarten teacher, the boy in the rubber alien mask limped weakly off toward the stage exit, trying not to trip over the extra legs that now trailed between his two feet. The crowd, which apparently thought this was part of the act, applauded as he tottered, crying, into the darkness. The four Earth children raised their light swords over their heads for one last huzzah, shouting, "Hooray for Homo sapiens! Annihilation for aliens!"

"Can we go home now?" asked Amanda's brother, Daniel. "*Mutant Z Death Cage Match* is on in half an hour, and I don't want to miss it."

CHAPTER 2

THE NEXT DAY at a prearranged time, Amanda sat down at her computer and typed in the command to link up for a videoconference. She and her best friends Evelyn, Derek and Sanjay had worked out this weekly routine as a way of staying in touch when the Academy was closed down following the hasty departure of the aliens. Amanda and her friends had to resort to this, because despite all the publicity the Academy had received as a result of their exploits, no human government or corporation saw any value in continuing to operate it. Developing the minds of the world's most promising children was apparently not a high priority for them. Consequently, the Academy was now locked up, silent and empty, with no occupants other than the spiders in the basement and the pigeons under the eaves. So the four former classmates had to make do with this means of communication until they could find some other learning institution that would offer them what the STAR Academy had: a chance to be with other kids who had wildly creative, brilliant minds. But the four friends also shared a dark secret. Although they were lauded as saviours, it was their own scientific research on human brain synapse blocking, which they had naively provided in the course of a class assignment, that had given the aliens a key weapon in their quest to take over Earth and enslave humanity.

Amanda tapped a key, and her monitor split into a three-panel arrangement. Her pulse jumped with excitement, and she experienced the giddy anticipation of knowing that in a few moments, she would be able to see and speak to her three best friends, even though they lived thousands of kilometres and many time zones away from one another. The first of the three panels to light up revealed Sanjay, in front of his computer in Mumbai, wearing a jeweller's eyepiece over one eye. He was holding an incredibly tiny nanobot—a miniature robot no bigger than an apple seed—at the end of a mechanical arm with a tiny tweezer-like apparatus on its tip. In a moment, the second panel lit up, revealing Derek in the workshop he had set up in the garage behind his parents' house in Newent, a town in Gloucestershire, England, a couple of hours' driving time from London. Behind him, a giant globe slowly rotated on its axis. Derek was fascinated by optics and satellite technology, and the globe was his masterwork. With its shimmering blue bodies of water, green and brown patches of land, gossamer clouds and thin veneer of atmosphere, it was an astoundingly accurate real-time projection of Earth. A few seconds later, the third panel began to light up, indicating that Evelyn was now coming on line from San Francisco.

A red light flashed on everyone's monitor and an automated voice said, "All conference members now present."

But Amanda was puzzled to see that instead of Evelyn's face on the monitor, there was just an image of what appeared to be a large tank of water.

"Anybody home?" asked Amanda.

Suddenly, Evelyn's head bobbed up into the frame.

"Oh, hi! Sorry about that," said Evelyn with a shy grin. "I'm still getting the hang of this outfit." She was wearing a full diving suit and helmet, and the others could now see that she was inside a huge aquarium that also held carp, tilapia and lobsters, which were all warily keeping their distance from her.

"Okay," said Amanda to Evelyn, "I think you just won the award for Most Dramatic Entrance of the Week."

"Definitely!" agreed Derek, his English-accented voice taking on a playful tone. "I know that things have been a bit slow since the STAR Academy closed down, but have you been reduced to working in a water park?"

"No, silly," said Evelyn through a microphone inside her diving helmet. "My parents' restaurant has gotten so much business because of all the publicity around the Academy that they've expanded. This is the new aquarium, where they keep the live fish."

"I hope there are no eels in there," said Sanjay. "I hate eels!"

Evelyn smiled. "Don't worry, no eels. But it does hold twenty thousand cubic litres of water. They let me use it for my research outside business hours. I've been trying to duplicate the patterns of the North Pacific Gyre."

"'North Pacific Gyre'? Sounds like a poem by that guy who wrote 'Jabberwocky,'" said Derek.

"Scarier," replied Evelyn. "It's an ocean current that has been gathering a huge amount of floating garbage into a gigantic island twice the size of Texas. Watch this." Evelyn squeezed a dropper of blue vegetable dye into the water. Soon, Amanda and the others could see a swirling pattern that had previously been invisible.

"Not to sound critical, but I think you should use a colour other than blue," said Derek. "Looks like you're inside a giant toilet."

"Well, I'm afraid that makes it all the more appropriate," said Evelyn. "See the way the currents are converging in the centre? That's how the biggest garbage dump on Earth ended up floating in the Pacific Ocean."

Sanjay shook his head. "Sometimes I find fractal theory easier to understand than the behaviour of supposedly sane adults. Why would they dump garbage into the ocean or let oil spills go on and on, leaking into the water, knowing that they're creating a huge problem for us kids to deal with someday?"

"I know," added Derek. "Makes you wonder if they're all bloody daft or just selfish."

"I'm not sure which," responded Evelyn. "But if I can duplicate the ocean currents, I might be able to figure out where the garbage is coming from so something can be done to stop the guilty parties."

"Brill," said Derek. "I've been doing more work on my satellite optics. Maybe we could use it to study the currents. I've got the memory and resolution more developed now than it was at the Academy. If you could give me a ballpark idea, as you Yanks say, of where the garbage is coming from, we could record a couple of weeks of footage from the satellite. Then we could put the imaging in reverse and track individual bits of waste as they enter the ocean. That way, we'd know exactly who the culprits are."

"Sweet," said Evelyn. "But to really figure out where it's coming from, I need far better facilities than I have here at the restaurant. MIT has a really good ocean engineering course . . ." Evelyn paused and then rather hesitantly added, "And actually, they've offered me a scholarship."

Amanda looked alarmed. "But I thought we were going to find a university with programs that suit all of us, so we can all be together again come September!"

Sanjay looked down uncomfortably. "That was a nice idea, but speaking strictly for myself, I'm running out of options. Most of the universities with decent nanobot facilities are in Japan. But as you know, the Japanese are not all that big on space travel, at least not yet. So there wouldn't be much there for you, Amanda."

"And Cambridge has the best facilities for optics," added Derek. "Besides, you're becoming such a big celebrity, why would you want to go to school with 'those three other kids' anyway?"

Amanda heard a certain tightness in Derek's voice that betrayed his smart-alecky comment, and she could sense that behind his cheeky grin, he was hiding some other emotion. Jealousy? Hurt, perhaps? Or a sense of betrayal? She couldn't quite make it out. But whatever it was, it unnerved her. Derek and Amanda had disagreed about things in the past, but there had never been any tension between them like there was now.

"'Three other kids'?" asked Amanda uncomfortably, doing her best to pretend she didn't know what he meant.

"Now don't get coy on me," said Derek. "I saw that ceremony in Downview on telly this morning."

Amanda blushed, a little nervously. "You mean they broadcast that ridiculous show all the way over in England?"

"Never mind England," said Sanjay. "They've shown it three times already on the national news here in India."

"Wow!" said Amanda, trying to sound surprised. "Hard to believe the international media would make such a big deal over something that happened in a place as unimportant as Downview."

"Not really," said Evelyn. "As the local newscaster here joked, it was a momentous event, what with the entire world being saved from aliens by 'Amanda Forsythe and *those three other kids*.'"

Amanda felt her face getting hot. She hated that feeling, because she knew how red her face would be in a few moments. Nearly two months had passed since the real-life events that had inspired the distorted epic portrayed by the Downview Public School's kindergarten class. It had all started the previous September, when Amanda's presentation at her school's science fair, despite being mocked by Principal Murkly, made a highly favourable impression on Headmistress Oppenheimer and Professor Leitspied of the Superior Thinking and Advanced Research Academy. Reputedly given unlimited funding by anonymous philanthropists, the staff members of the STAR Academy, as it was more commonly called, were entrusted with finding the two hundred most intellectually gifted children on Earth, an elite group that included Amanda. Oppenheimer, Leitspied and George, the Academy's chief engineer and student project adviser, were responsible for putting these two hundred children through an accelerated, all-expenses-paid program, nurturing their extraordinary talents so that the full power of their creative gifts could be brought to bear on helping humanity solve its most urgently pressing problems. It had been a wonderful experience for Amanda. For the first time in her life, she had friends, real friends who understood her and her ideas. But after just a couple of pleasurable and mentally stimulating months, when they had been given free rein to develop their pet science projects, Amanda, Evelyn, Derek and Sanjay had discovered that the faculty were not merely the uncommonly brilliant and supportive academics that they at first appeared to be. They were something quite different indeed: aliens from a planet more than sixty light years away, who had been sent to Earth on a goodwill mission to establish friendly contact with the natives. At least that was the plan, until Headmistress Oppenheimer and Professor Leitspied took such a great liking to Earth, in the wrong sort of way, that they decided they very much wanted to become its supreme rulers. This they had hoped to achieve by tricking the students into using their massive combined intellectual powers to create devices that seemed beneficial to humanity but would, when combined with certain other inventions, allow them to dominate the entire human race.

For her key role in defeating the aliens, Amanda had become a star, the most famous of the four friends. But it wasn't at all how she saw herself.

"Look, I'm sorry, guys," said Amanda now, "but I had nothing to do with that play. My school principal and my ex-teacher created it. I didn't even know about it myself until the performance."

"That's okay," continued Sanjay, just a little sarcastically, "the Indian media were just thrilled that one of their own people was involved in helping save the Earth from aliens. Except I will have to change my name to Sandhu if I ever want to be famous for it."

"Well," said Amanda, "now you know why I wanted to get out of Downview in the first place. So let's not start fighting among ourselves over something as fleeting as fame."

There was a moment of silence between them.

Then Amanda continued, "We were a team at the Academy. Look at how much we accomplished together. It would be a shame to lose that."

"You're right," said Derek, his voice softening as he looked at Amanda. "I wish I had a solution. And I do want for us to be together. But it just seems like some kind of unsolvable problem, all of us getting together to study."

"We'd have to create a new institution," said Sanjay.

"Or reopen the Superior Thinking and Advanced Research Academy," said Evelyn.

"If only we could," said Amanda.

Derek grinned wryly. "Yeah, that's the story of our lives. If it's not one thing, it's another. If they cater to nanobots, they're weak in astronomy. If they're good with oceanography, they're lacking in optics. If they've got it all, it's run by aliens secretly planning to take over the world."

Amanda heard her father downstairs, treading heavily around the living room.

"Amanda?" he called.

"Just a minute," she responded.

Then she looked at Derek, Evelyn and Sanjay.

"Sorry, guys, I've got to go. I promised my dad I would do something with him today."

"Like go with him to a ticker-tape parade?" asked Derek.

"No, smarty-pants," replied Amanda. "Not anything so interesting. Anyway, listen: can we promise that none of us will sign up at a university until we've at least *tried* to find a way to study together?"

Amanda's three friends, the first friends she had ever had in her life, looked at each other uncomfortably. Then Derek spoke.

"Yes, I promise. I'd really like to work with you three anoraks again too. But we can't put it on hold forever. We'll have to figure out something in a hurry or we'll miss the deadlines for the September semester."

Evelyn and Sanjay nodded their heads in resigned agreement.

Then they said their goodbyes, and as Amanda's monitor went dark, she wondered if it was really possible that after all they had been through, the four of them would never be together again.

CHAPTER 3

"AMANDA!" CALLED her father. "Come on downstairs. Someone important will be here in a few minutes, and I want you to meet him."

Whatever difficulties Amanda and her friends were having finding a university that could accommodate all four of their specialties, she was receiving no shortage of media attention over her role in foiling Oppenheimer and Leitspied's attempts to enslave the human race. She was also receiving no shortage of offers from companies willing to pay to use her image to sell their products. This excited Jack Forsythe tremendously—so much so that finding product endorsements for Amanda had become as obsessive a quest for him as finding new markets for Achilles Bunion Remover Cream. As he never tired of telling Amanda, "You know, it wouldn't hurt our family to have a few million bucks set aside for a rainy day. I bet that Bill Snootman character has more than one offshore bank account. Why should we be any different than his family?"

Having experienced Eugenia Snootman first-hand—her jealousy, her snide comments, her bullying, her hideous gene-manipulation experiments—Amanda could think of plenty of reasons not to copy the behaviour of that particular family. Still, she tolerated her father's constant pursuit of endorsements because she hoped that with the money from the deals, she could find a way to get her friends back together. This, she believed, might be possible by donating the money to whichever university came closest to suiting all their needs, on the condition that the school use it to upgrade its facilities to make it a good fit for all four of them. However, as Amanda was about to learn, the endorsement offers tended to come with a heavy price tag of their own.

Jack Forsythe stuck his large head through the doorway into Amanda's bedroom. She noticed that his skin had taken on an orangey hue as a result of his recent heavy use of suntanning creams. Amanda's mother was worried that her husband might be exposing himself to dangerous chemicals because of his new habit. But Jack had brushed aside her concerns, explaining that "in business, if you want to be a winner, you gotta look like a winner. If people think I spend half my time on a yacht in the Caribbean, then they won't think I'm in any hurry to make a deal with them. Which will make them want to make a deal with me even more."

Amanda was eventually able to calm her mother by reading the label of the suntanning cream and discovering that the active ingredient was carotene. This, Amanda explained to her terrified mother, was a colouring agent derived, as its name suggested, from carrots. So it was harmless, except in the aesthetic sense.

Amanda's father now gave her a broad, toothy smile.

"Showtime!" he said in an excited stage whisper.

His smile became fixed in an even broader and toothier mask, the skin crinkling around his forehead and lips. Amanda suspected that this was his professional salesman smile, because she had never seen him smile like this before. And yet he looked quite at ease with that expression on his face, as though he had stretched his lips like that so many times over the years that if you laid his smiles end on end, they'd go to the moon and back. She guessed this was the smile her father employed to convey optimism and dynamism to his customers. But, thought Amanda, it had a certain manic quality that, when combined with the orange hue of his skin, gave him the appearance not of someone who lived on a yacht in the Caribbean, but rather of an overexcited jack-o'-lantern. She knew better than to try to tell him this, however.

"Amanda," he said, "hurry up. He's here. It's our first official endorsement offer. The guy from the Scrunchy Snack Food Company. And between you and me, I think we've got a whale on the line!" he said jauntily.

The Scrunchy Snack Food Company, Amanda knew, made everything from deep-fried pork rinds to deep-fried artificial cheese. They had branch operations on every continent in the world, except Antarctica. And there were industry rumours that even *that* would change once Scrunchy's food scientists found a way to make their experimental Scrunchy Penguin Chips taste less fishy.

Amanda's father ushered her into their living room, where the man from the advertising agency that made commercials for

Scrunchy Snacks was waiting. He stood up as she entered, shook her hand and gave her a broad, toothy smile that was remarkably similar to the one she had just seen on her father's face.

"Art Cozen's the name. And I can't thank you enough, because if it wasn't for you stopping those aliens and their synapse blocker, everybody on the planet would be walking around unable to remember our advertisements, and they'd forget their craving for a Scrunchy Snack!" he said, joking. "We'd be out of business!"

"Ha, that's a good one!" said Amanda's father. "Get it, Amanda? If the aliens had blocked out everyone's synapses with that gizmo, nobody would remember the ads. Ha!"

Amanda nodded and smiled, though she couldn't bring herself to muster a toothy, face-stretching one like her father's or Mr. Cozen's.

"Now," said Mr. Cozen, "everybody everywhere knows how much you love space and space travel. So this campaign will really play on that. The idea is to have a gigantic fleet of helium-filled airships—blimps, in other words—each one two hundred metres long. They will fly above thousands of cities all over the world every night. And on the bottom of each blimp will be a giant video screen featuring a huge image of you. The blimps will be painted black," continued Mr. Cozen, "so they'll blend right in with the night sky. That way, it will look like the giant moving image of you is floating in space right over everyone's heads. You'll be wearing a spacesuit and a helmet, and you'll be holding Scrunchy's newest taste sensation. It's an exciting product that combines our two most favourite snacks in one delicious combo: deep-fried cheese puffs with a deep-fried pork rind ring around it. Check it out."

He pulled a sample out of his briefcase and held it in the air for Amanda to see.

"No other snack food has ever had such a great look! Or such a great taste," he declared. "But it doesn't just look and taste great. It's got a great name too: Saturnalia! Got a really festive *ring* to it, if you'll pardon the pun!"

"You mean the festival the ancient Romans had to honour the god Saturn? The one where they would celebrate by stuffing themselves to the point of nausea, then vomit up everything they'd eaten so they could make room for even more food?"

Mr. Cozen looked perplexed. "Er, that's the one. But we're hoping that most people wouldn't have your degree of knowledge on the subject. That stuff about the vomiting is a little off-putting and kind of spoils the fun, festive feeling. Anyway, the name has a double meaning, because each Saturnalia cheese puff has a pork rind ring around it, just like Saturn, see?" He traced his finger around the circumference of the snack.

"Fascinating," said Amanda with a small grin. "I didn't know that Saturn's ring was made of pork rinds."

Mr. Cozen laughed indulgently. "Well, no, it isn't. But if it was, we like to think it would taste as good as one of these puppies. So picture this: there's a giant video image of you on the blimp, floating in the night sky like you're doing a spacewalk. People look up and see you there, brighter than a full moon, blocking out everything else in the heavens. You flip up the visor on your astronaut helmet, pop one of these babies into your mouth and over loudspeakers, say, 'Scrunchy Snacks Saturnalia! I'd cross the universe to get one!'"

"Actually," said Amanda, "if you opened your helmet in

space, your head would explode because of the difference in pressure between your body and the vacuum outside it."

Mr. Cozen pondered that for a moment. "Again, that's a detail that we're hoping most people aren't aware of," he said. "People are just thrilled that you saved them from alien invaders. They don't really care about the details."

"Yes, I'm hearing that a lot," replied Amanda.

"But here's *one* detail that I think you'll both be very interested in," said Mr. Cozen.

He wrote a figure on a slip of paper and handed it to Jack Forsythe, whose eyes and smile got so big that he looked like a jack-o'-lantern that had just been told that from now on, every day would be Halloween.

"Holy Dinah!" he exclaimed. "Amanda, look how much they're offering!"

"That's right, Mr. Forsythe—it's a lot of money. And why not? Because with Amanda filling the night sky, telling everyone about Scrunchy Snacks, billions and billions of kids who normally wouldn't eat deep-fried cheese and deep-fried pork rinds will be dying to try them. There will barely be enough pigskin to keep up with demand."

"Hmmm, that's got to affect the price of footballs," said Jack Forsythe. He took out a digital voice recorder. "Note to self—buy up all existing supplies of footballs, as prices are sure to go up because of demand for pigskin for Scrunchy Snacks."

"I like the way you think, Jack Forsythe," said Mr. Cozen.

Amanda, however, did not. But she looked at the number on the paper anyway. It *was* a very large sum. With that money, she would be a step closer to her dream of building a learning institution that would enable her, Evelyn, Derek and Sanjay to continue their research together. Then she noticed that Mr. Cozen's fingertip was shiny with grease where he had rubbed it around the circumference of the deep-fried snack.

"Mr. Cozen, do you know how many calories there will be in a Saturnalia, or what percentage of it will be saturated fat?" asked Amanda.

"I don't know," replied Mr. Cozen uneasily. Then he brightened. "But as our client likes to say, Scrunchy Snacks are *part* of a balanced diet."

"Really?" asked Amanda. "Which part?"

"I'm not sure," replied Mr. Cozen with a wry smile. "But I'm sure about this: you're witty and fast on your feet. You'll make a *fantabulous* spokesperson!"

"I'm sorry," said Amanda, "but blocking people's views of the stars and planets with my image would be hypocritical, given my interest in astronomy. And I'm afraid I couldn't encourage other children to cross the universe to eat a high-calorie, high-fat snack that would eventually give them heart disease."

Her father looked stricken. "But, *Amanda* . . ." he said, pointing to the number.

"Sorry, Dad," she replied. "I just can't do it."

The next offer came from the manager of a rapper named Emcee Squared, who had written a song dedicated to Amanda. It was called "Yo, Amanda." The manager, whose name was Mr. Z, arrived at the Forsythes' house in a long pink convertible with zebra-striped seats and a Jacuzzi with a shark in it. Mr. Z was an intense man who had diamonds set into his canine teeth.

He was accompanied by his assistant, a rotund man named Darius whose head was shaved bald. Darius wore a lime-green leather tracksuit, orange running shoes, lots of bling, and he carried a boom box.

"Amanda," began Mr. Z, "first let me say that this is an incredible honour. It's just amazing."

"Thank you," responded Amanda. "That's very kind of you to—"

"I mean," continued Mr. Z, "to have a rapper of the stature of Emcee Squared write a song about you. Wow, that is one *incredible* honour, an amazing honour." He stabbed the air with his index finger for emphasis. "Up to now, he's only ever written songs about himself. But he's really taken a shine to you over your saving the human race from aliens. It means a lot to him. So he's written a song about you. Take a listen. Hit it, Darius."

Z's assistant pressed the Play button on the boom box. A heavy bass line and drum track thudded from its speakers. Amanda couldn't decipher the words in the verses, but she was able to make out the repeating choruses, which went like this:

Yo, Amanda! Yo, Amanda! You bomb-diggity in tota'.
You be more boo-ya than Darth Vader and Yoda.

Mr. Z waved an index finger to signal Darius to hit the Stop button.

"Is it amazing or is it amazing?" he exclaimed. "You must be just blown away to have Emcee Squared write a song about you. I know I would be."

"It's a first," replied Amanda.

"And it gets even better," said Mr. Z. "Squared would like *you* to co-star in his video. He's *never* allowed anyone to co-star in one of his videos before. It's an incredible honour!"

"What happens in the video?" Amanda asked.

"Well, you're dancing on a podium in a disco, getting down. But suddenly, you realize that everybody there except you is an alien pretending to be a human. You're trapped on the podium, aliens all around you. Until . . . in charges the cavalry: Squared to the rescue, crashing right through the wall behind the wheel of his gold-plated Hummer."

"What about my friends Evelyn, Derek and Sanjay?" asked Amanda. "They helped defeat the aliens too. Can we cast them in the video?"

Z looked apprehensive. "Just having Emcee Squared share the spotlight with you is an amazing honour. Putting three more kids on stage with him might be pushing it a bit. But we could work your peeps into the crowd scene. They could be zombies."

"You mean aliens?" asked Amanda.

"Right. Aliens. But space zombie aliens," replied Z. "Darius, show Amanda what I'm talking about."

Darius lurched into action, lumbering around the Forsythes' living room, legs stiff, arms outstretched, looking like Frankenstein's monster—or at least what Frankenstein's monster would have looked like had he been a rotund bald man wearing a lime-green leather tracksuit, orange running shoes and lots of bling.

"There are hundreds of space zombie aliens," continued Z, "trying to climb onto the podium where you're trapped so they can eat you alive. But Squared isn't scared, 'cause he's totally street!" Once more, Z jabbed the air with his finger for emphasis. "He just plows that Hummer right through them, pedal to the metal like it's rush hour in Alpha Centauri, and signals you to jump on the roof. That's how he rescues you."

"*He* rescues *me*?" asked Amanda.

She didn't know what to say. It was incredible, but not in the way that Mr. Z seemed to think it was.

Darius plodded past the sofa, arms outstretched, face frozen in an expressionless stare.

"Rrrrraaahhhh!" he roared.

Z turned in the direction of the roar and frowned at his assistant. "Darius, what up? Pay attention. We're finished with that part. You can stop all that staggering around now."

"Oh, okay. Sure thing, Mr. Z," Darius replied, shambling to a halt. He was struggling to catch his breath now, and his forehead was shiny with perspiration.

Jack Forsythe jumped in. "This all sounds great. So how much would you be willing to offer my daughter to appear in the video?"

Z scrunched up his face and nodded slowly, like he was hoping that the honour of appearing in the video would have been enough. Then he reluctantly took a piece of paper out of his pocket and showed it to Amanda's father.

"Wow!" Jack Forsythe said, rubbing his hands together. "Take a look at this, Amanda."

"Sorry, not interested," she said without looking at it.

"But you haven't even seen how much they're offering," said her father.

"I don't care how much they're offering. Last time I checked, I still had my frontal lobes, no thanks to Oppenheimer and Leitspied, so I'm going to have to say no."

The day after that, an executive from a film studio came round, wanting to buy the rights to Amanda's life story and make a movie out of it.

"It was an amazing thing you did, Amanda," said the man from the film company.

"That's my daughter," said her father proudly.

"And that," said the man from the studio, "is why we're prepared to offer you one million dollars for your life story."

"A million dollars. Wow!" bellowed Jack Forsythe.

Amanda saw how excited her father was. And since the money would both help her family and allow her to give some funds to a science academy, and it didn't seem to involve endorsing anything other than her own life, she encouraged the man to continue.

"People seem to have really distorted ideas about what happened," said Amanda. "I'd love for them to know the true story."

"Abso-tively," replied the man. "And that's exactly the story they'll hear. Of course, we've only got an hour and half, so we'll have to streamline it a little."

"Totally understandable," said Amanda's father. "Don't you think so, honey?"

"Yes," replied Amanda thoughtfully. "I suppose that makes sense if you have to squeeze a few months into ninety minutes."

"Good!" exclaimed the man. "You're a smart girl, a pragmatist. So I think you'll understand me when I say that for most people, it's not really believable that a group of children could actually defeat aliens single-handedly."

"But your movie will set them straight, is that right?" asked Amanda.

"You bet," replied the studio exec. He went on to explain that to help ease the audience into appreciating the story, the studio wanted to cast a certain Hollywood husband-and-wife duo, frequently touted as the most beautiful couple in the known universe, in the roles of the chief and deputy of the Gallwater police.

"They'd bicker and snipe at each other about little things, like who left the milk out and who is the better detective," said the man from the studio. "But you'd know that beneath it all, they did it only because they were so in love with each other. And that would really come through when they were in danger and had to go after the aliens to rescue the vampire kids in the orphanage."

"Vampire kids in an orphanage?" asked Amanda, thinking she had heard him wrong.

"Right!" said the movie executive. "People love orphans in children's stories. It gives kids watching it a chance to act out independence fantasies without actually putting themselves at risk. It's what's called a trope. And vampires are very, very big at the moment. Why, you can't swing a stake without stabbing a vampire movie! And no wonder—our research shows that kids prefer vampires to other humans by nearly two to one. Three out of four children say they'd rather have vampires for parents than their real parents. Four out of five kids say they'd prefer a vampire to a human as a boyfriend or girlfriend, even if it bit them. So like I was saying, when those good-looking police detectives come and rescue you vampire kids from the orphanage—"

"The police didn't rescue us," interrupted Amanda. "We rescued ourselves. Evelyn and I only brought the police as backup, in case our plan A didn't work. And they were useless. They couldn't even figure out how to unlock the cage that Derek and Sanjay were in."

"Right," said the man. "That brings me to another point. Our market research department did focus group tests with audiences, asking if they found it believable that a girl, or even two girls, could save the world from aliens. They said no. Even if the girls were vampires. So we would reverse the roles. You would be the girl locked in the cage. Then we would get a guy with smouldering good looks to play a vampire version of Derek. He would rescue you from the aliens and save the world. What do you say?"

"I say that makes me look like some helpless vampire girl," replied Amanda. "It sounds absolutely ridiculous, and I wouldn't go along with it for twice the amount of money you're offering."

"Got to hand it to this daughter of yours," said the man to Amanda's father. "She's no pushover when it comes to making a deal. Now, Amanda, we've established that you wouldn't say yes for twice one million. I know you're a math whiz, so if I'm reading you right, that means you're looking for a number along the lines of $2.5 million?"

"No, it doesn't mean that," said Amanda. "It means—"

"You're one tough cookie. Okay, let's say three million for your life story and call it even. How does that sound?"

"Sounds like more fun than a barrel of money—er, I mean *monkeys*!" said Jack Forsythe, rubbing his palms together, his big orange face breaking into a toothy smile.

"Good!" said the exec. "Now, the last detail to work out is that part about the alien called George. We're gonna have to change it so that when that good-looking Gallwater police couple have sent in the cavalry—fighter planes, tactical bombers, the works—George knows his goose is cooked. So he takes off in his spaceship. But it's only a temporary reprieve for Earth. Because when George gets back to his home planet, he will scare up a whole horde of aliens to try to take over another day."

"But George wasn't evil," said Amanda. "He helped me. And he left only to get rid of the bad aliens so they couldn't try to take over the Earth ever again. Why would I want to make it so the aliens might invade a second time?"

The man looked at Amanda with a self-satisfied expression. "I've got a one-word answer to that, young lady: sequel! And nothing says sequel like a bunch of aliens who try to take over Earth, get temporarily kiboshed, but can come back to fight another day. Helps you spread your advertising budget out too. And besides, people like sequels."

"Imagine that," brayed Amanda's father. "That would mean two movies about you!"

"Well, now, Mr. Forsythe," said the man, "I can't guarantee the sequel would involve your daughter. We might cast it with Sylvester Stallone playing an ex-soldier who everybody thinks is nuts because he's convinced there are aliens among us disguised as people—but then he saves the Earth by blowing all the aliens to bits."

"You mean all the aliens but *one*," added Amanda's father with a sly wink. "Sequel number two!"

"Jack Forsythe, I like the way you think!" said the man. "Now I know where your daughter gets her smarts. And don't worry, Amanda, even if your character isn't in any of the sequels, you'll still get a percentage of the sales and the spin-off merchandising—dolls, comic books, lunchboxes, all that good stuff that kids like to buy. As for product placement, Mr. Forsythe, we can work some of that Achilles Bunion Remover Cream into one of the Stallone scenes. After all, he's no spring chicken. It's gotta be hard on your dogs to run around in combat boots all day at his age. So what do you say?"

The man from the movie studio was just as dumbfounded by Amanda's response as Mr. Z and Mr. Cozen had been when she told them she wasn't interested in lending her name and image to their products. Amanda's father was equally disappointed. Over the past few weeks, he had become highly skilled at mentally calculating percentages of gross sales—and equally skilled at fantasizing about what he would do with all that money.

Amanda was in a bit of a funk herself after the disappointment of the endorsement proposals. Although she thought they were degrading and idiotic, she did wish she could find a way to help her parents out with their living expenses. And of course, she dreamed of finding a school like the STAR Academy, where she, Evelyn, Derek and Sanjay could hang out, have fun and make incredible inventions together. But she decided it would have to be done without compromising herself or harming others, even imaginary others.

By now, Amanda had all but given up on the idea of working on an existing space program in any significant capacity, a situation she found absolutely maddening given the advanced projects she'd created at the STAR Academy. After witnessing the lunkheaded Murkly and Wheedlbum try to take credit for her achievements, and hearing ludicrous pitches to lend her name to movies, video games, breakfast cereals, snack foods, pimple creams, toenail polishes and a host of other questionable products, Amanda thought she had seen everything. But as many people who think they have seen everything soon discover, she had not.

CHAPTER 4

AMANDA WAS UNCOMFORTABLE with the strange way the world was evolving around her since she had involuntarily acquired fame. So she was especially filled with relief when she sat down at her computer and saw the familiar faces of Evelyn, Derek and Sanjay in the three-way split screen, ready for their weekly videoconference. True, these long-distance get-togethers weren't as much fun as hanging out together in her dorm at the Academy, making popcorn, telling stories and working on inventions all evening. But the calls had become an oasis of sanity, friendship and intelligent conversation ever since she'd returned to Downview. And after the strange events of the past week, an oasis of sanity was something she was in particular need of.

Derek, as usual, was the first to speak. And also as usual, his opening words took the form of a friendly insult delivered with a cheeky grin. "You anoraks split any atoms lately? I haven't seen any more parades in your honour, Amanda, so I presume you've been busy with your photon-sail project?"

"No," admitted Amanda, "I've barely done any work on it at all. The week has been kind of a washout."

"How so?" asked Sanjay, looking up from a nanobot that he was tinkering with.

"My father's obsessed with trying to get endorsement offers for me, so I've been taking a lot of meetings."

"'Taking a lot of meetings'? You sound like a business tycoon," said Derek.

"Yes," added Sanjay a little tartly. "We can say, 'We knew Amanda Forsythe when . . .'"

"Give me a break," countered Amanda. "It's nothing like that. You know what my father's like. It was all totally lame stuff."

"Like what?" asked Evelyn.

"Just silly things," replied Amanda, "like appearing in some dumb Emcee Squared video."

"You were asked to be in an Emcee Squared video?" asked Derek, surprised.

"Um, yeah," replied Amanda, a little sheepishly.

"Wow! I mean, he's a total prat," said Derek. "All his lyrics are about himself, and all his tracks are sampled from other people's songs. He's about as original as reverse-engineered North Korean spy technology."

"I wonder if you could get roles for us in it?" asked Evelyn. "I wouldn't mind being in one of his videos. It could help me raise money for my oceanography research."

"Yes, and it would help me with my nanobots," added Sanjay.

"Sorry," responded Amanda. "I already asked, but they were only willing to give the three of you bit parts as space zombies, so I said no."

"Well, that's a relief," said Derek. "I've never seen myself as the space-zombie type. Sanjay and Evelyn maybe, but not me."

Derek delivered the joke with his usual lopsided grin, but his voice had a slight edge to it. It was so subtle that if Amanda didn't know him well, she might not have noticed it, but it was unsettling.

"So what sort of other 'lame' endorsement offers have you had?" asked Sanjay.

"Um, well, there was one from the Scrunchy Snack Food Company," replied Amanda.

"Scrunchy Snacks?" said Sanjay. "My God, they're the largest snack company in the world."

"What did they want you to do?" asked Derek.

"Oh, really nothing much. It was pretty dumb," said Amanda, trying to dodge the subject.

But Derek persisted. "Come on, what kind of dumb?" he asked.

"Well, they wanted to build a fleet of black airships," replied Amanda, "and put a giant video image of me in a spacesuit on them. They were planning to fly them over hundreds of cities every night, advertising Scrunchy Snacks."

"Crikey, Amanda, you're a celebrity!" said Derek. "All I got was an offer from a company in Birmingham to use my likeness on special packets of crisps–that's potato chips to you North Americans—that come in a little plastic cage. With the slogan 'Be Like Amanda Forsythe: Rescue Some Derek Brand Crisps Today.' It was so embarrassing, I wasn't even going to tell any of you. Meanwhile, there you are up in space, floating around, your face plastered all over the night sky throughout the world."

"You don't think I would let them ruin the night sky with my image just to sell a bunch of junk food, do you?"

"I don't know. Fame can make people do strange things."

"Yes, evidently it can," retorted Amanda. "But I don't care about being famous. Or rich. All I wanted was to raise enough money so we could continue our experiments together somehow. But I'm not willing to do it by selling junk food or idiotic music or some stupid video game."

"Someone wanted to make a video game about you too?" asked Sanjay.

"Yes, Samsara Electronics did. But I turned them down."

"How come you didn't tell us about it?" asked Derek. "They might have been interested in having us involved in developing a game."

"Because they did focus group tests, and according to them, you don't have enough name recognition, so they weren't interested. Sorry."

"Right—'those three other kids,'" said Derek sourly.

"Look, can we forget about that stuff? I'll go nuts if I stay here in Downview much longer, listening to stupid endorsement offers from companies selling junk and having the school board think they're giving me a break because I get to take grade ten physics instead of finishing grade six. And on top of that—"

Amanda heard the doorbell ring.

"Hang on a second—there's someone at the door."

"Probably just a network executive coming to offer you your own Amanda Forsythe reality show," jibed Derek sarcastically.

"Already turned that offer down," retorted Amanda, sticking out her tongue at him. "And by the way, it was worth over a million dollars. Now will you stop being such a goof?"

Amanda headed to the front door. She looked through the security peephole and saw a courier holding a package and keying some information into a handheld computer.

Amanda opened the door. He began to speak before looking up.

"Hello! Package for a Miss A. Forsy— Hey, you're that girl who saved Earth from the aliens! You and those three other kids. Wow! Nice to meet you."

"Thanks," said Amanda.

"I just need your signature for the delivery confirmation."

Amanda signed his electronic signature pad.

"Could I get an autograph too?" asked the courier, holding up a paper and pen.

"Sure, no problem," replied Amanda.

She signed her name on the slip of paper, then handed it back to him.

"This is so cool!" said the courier, looking at it. "An actual autograph from Amanda Forsythe, the girl who saved the world. Wicked! I'll get a *ton* of money for this on eBay. Thanks, and have a nice day."

"Yeah, sure. You too," said Amanda, shaking her head in disbelief as she watched the courier walk back to his truck, holding the autographed scrap of paper aloft, then kissing it.

However, Amanda forgot all about the courier and his boorish financial interest in her autograph when she looked down and saw who the package was from. On the envelope was the corporate crest of Snootman Global Enterprises Inc., a company owned by Bill Snootman, the world's most famous software developer and, not coincidentally, also its richest man. His company made software of every type, from programs to run robots that can dispose of bombs to ones that mine data for marketing companies, helping them analyze credit card purchasing patterns to determine, for example, what kind of book a particular child likes to read. But that wasn't the reason Amanda felt a leaden lump hardening in her chest when she looked down and saw that the package had come from the office of none other than Bill Snootman himself. No, that lump was because Bill Snootman was the father of Eugenia Snootman. *The* Eugenia Snootman, as people were wont to say of the famous former student at the STAR Academy. *The* Eugenia Snootman, Amanda's nemesis and, by virtue of being the daughter of Bill Snootman and his wife, Charleze, a former Miss Universe, the wealthiest eleven-year-old in the world. *The* Eugenia Snootman, budding society girl and fully blossomed sociopath, extremely intelligent but even more vain, self-centred and jealous of Amanda's scientific brilliance. *The* Eugenia Snootman, so manipulative that manipulating everyone who came into her orbit was not enough to satisfy her. No, she had to manipulate the very building blocks of life itself, splicing together the genes of dissimilar animals to create monstrosities that mother nature in her wisdom had seen fit to avoid. *The* Eugenia Snootman, who became so enamoured with the aliens' superior if warped intellects that she took some of Headmistress Oppenheimer's DNA and grafted it into herself in the hope of becoming even smarter.

Unfortunately for *the* Eugenia Snootman, she was unaware that although the aliens projected a human form to deceive any people who made their acquaintance, they were in fact large, spider-like creatures, repulsive beings, at least to human eyes. As a consequence, *the* Eugenia Snootman's most notable scientific accomplishment had been to accidentally morph herself into a stomach-turning, eight-legged freak that was more alien than human. *Fortunately*, the kindly alien known as George had found her just in time and injected her with a biological blocker to stop her misguided plans. *Unfortunately*, by the time he discovered her, the only visible part of Eugenia's original self was her head, mute without the vocal cords, perched atop her exoskeletal body and capable only of panicky bleats. Not a good transformation for a vain girl with ambitions of one day being the doyenne of all socialites, a fixture in such places as St. Moritz, Monaco and Aspen. For Amanda, just receiving a letter from the rich and powerful father of that highly unpleasant former classmate was enough to fill her with an overwhelming sense of dread and send a jolt of adrenaline through her system. So it was with more than a little foreboding that she broke the seal on the envelope, removed the document it contained and cast her eyes upon it.

"Dear Miss Forsythe," began the letter. "We have not met, but I expect that you may be familiar with my name via my business ventures and technological developments. Additionally, you were a student with my daughter, Eugenia, at the Superior Thinking and Advanced Research Academy. I am aware that you and my daughter were not the best of friends, but—"

Amanda paused, mulling over the fact that Bill Snootman had anticipated her reaction to the mere mention of his daughter's name. The phrase "not the best of friends," thought Amanda, was an understatement—as much an understatement as if someone had said, "I am aware that you may not be comfortable with the idea of a large colony of black widow spiders and king cobra snakes living in your mattress, waiting for the optimal moment to strike you dead, but—"

It would have been more appropriate, thought Amanda, for him to say, "I am aware that my daughter was insanely jealous of you, and while at the Academy, tried to bully and torment you at every turn. Not just with her little taunts and insults, but in far more sinister ways, such as threatening to have you blacklisted for life if you didn't hand over your research to her so she could use it to beat your team in the intramural science competition in front of the entire school. And I am aware that she so badly wanted your scientific discoveries (the ones she was not intelligent or imaginative enough to come up with on her own) that she tried to intimidate you with the prospect of being attacked by Tinkerbell—a vile creature, half reptile, half ferret, that my daughter's warped, manipulative mind drove her to create for the express purpose of terrorizing you. And yes, it's true that she ratted you out to the aliens to ingratiate herself to them and secure for herself a better position once they had taken over our planet and enslaved the human race, including, in all likelihood, her own mother and father . . ."

The reality, recalled Amanda, was that Eugenia had been jealous of her from the moment they met. In fact, Amanda was now completely distracted, thinking of the galaxy of ways in which she and Eugenia were "not the best of friends." There were so many that by the time Amanda had remembered them all, she'd lost her train of thought and had to go back to Bill Snootman's letter from the beginning of the last sentence she had read.

"I understand that you and my daughter were not the best of friends, but it is likely that she had a healthy respect for your intellect and scientific creativity. However, I cannot know this—and a multitude of other things concerning Eugenia—for certain, as she still suffers major side effects from the DNA transfer from the alien known as Headmistress Oppenheimer. For example, Eugenia has not recovered the use of her voice, despite an ambitious speech-therapy program. I have employed the foremost geneticists in the world—those not already under contract with the defence departments of various governments, both rogue and legitimate—to try to return Eugenia to her normal human state. To date, there has been no progress. Therefore, my daughter lives in a constant state of distress."

Amanda wondered where this rambling letter was going. She didn't have to wait long to find out.

"I understand that you were involved in some sort of experiment that involved blocking my daughter's memories. There is no use denying it, as my lawyers have affidavits from a number of witnesses who have sworn that you demonstrated such a device on my daughter in front of the entire faculty and student body, cruelly humiliating her. The psychological stress of this embarrassment alone is upsetting for a father to hear and would be enough to provoke a fervent response under normal circumstances. But what is even more disturbing to me is that this disruption in Eugenia's normal brain patterns may ultimately have caused my daughter to make the decision to insert the alien DNA into her body, placing her in the dire predicament in which we now find her. From media reports, I understand that it was the aliens, and not you, who created the core technology for the synapse-blocking device."

Amanda breathed a small sigh of relief when she realized that even Bill Snootman had fallen for the cover story she had created around the synapse-blocking device. In fact, the aliens had nothing to do with masterminding it, other than assigning it as a project for the students. The synapse disruptor had been a key part of the aliens' plan for world domination. Headmistress Oppenheimer and Professor Leitspied told Amanda and the other kids that their task was to build a device that would help unhappy people forget bad childhood memories. It sounded like a good idea, the way Leitspied explained it to them. "Some may have been chosen last for sports teams," she said. "Others may have wanted to be class president but were never elected. Some may have wished for a pony but lived on the third floor of an apartment building with restrictions regarding pets. Others may have wanted brilliant parents who looked like Hollywood movie stars, but had to settle for mothers and fathers who were dull-witted and plain. These bad memories can make grownups very, very unhappy." But as Amanda, Derek, Evelyn and Sanjay found out—almost too late—the project was a secret part of Oppenheimer and Leitspied's plan to take over the world. By beaming the synapse-blocker ray throughout the world, they hoped humans wouldn't be able to remember anything, and so could be turned into mindless slaves. The evil scheme had been hatched by the two rogue aliens disguised as staff members of the STAR Academy. But the technology itself was entirely the work of the team that Amanda was in charge of, Team Prometheus. Because of the incredible complexity of the task, Amanda had allocated small units of research to each of her teammates. She then combined their results to design the final synapse-blocker prototype, which had proven so effective that when it was demonstrated on a skeptical volunteer—Eugenia Snootman—the test subject could not even remember her own name. Amanda had unwittingly provided Oppenheimer and Leitspied with the key piece of technology that they needed for their plan of world conquest.

After Amanda and her friends had foiled the aliens' plan and they had been returned to their home planet, the government and military—having heard about the synapse-blocking device from the other students—showed intense interest in finding out more. Fortunately, because no one but Amanda, Derek, Evelyn and Sanjay knew exactly how it worked, she was able to concoct the cover story that the aliens had really engineered the device. Thus, she and her friends avoided coming under pressure to disclose the synapse blocker's secrets to any government, corporation or criminal element, which they knew would undoubtedly find some sinister use for it. However, the fact that their cover story was so convincing was no help to her in this situation, as Amanda soon discovered.

"Therefore, I do not hold you solely responsible for my daughter's condition," continued the letter. "Rather, it is my opinion, and that of my legal counsel, that you, along with the aliens known as Headmistress Oppenheimer, Professor Leitspied and George, are all legally responsible for Eugenia's current state. Consequently, I am suing the four of you collectively for $100 million in damages. Furthermore, evidence suggests that you enabled the three aliens to flee the planet before the authorities could intervene and arrest them. So although they are named in my lawsuit, there is no chance of them paying their share of the damages, thanks to you. It is for that reason that my lawyers will be focusing on you exclusively in seeking on my behalf damages in the amount of $100 million. I will cease legal action if you remit a cheque for that sum to me within the next forty-eight hours. Otherwise my lawyers shall begin filing court orders to seize your assets and those of your parents. Should you have any questions, please feel free to contact me directly. Yours sincerely,

William Snootman, Chairman and President, Snootman Global Enterprises Inc."

Amanda felt faint. Her heart pounded and her hands began to perspire. Her chest felt tight, like it was being squeezed by a giant fist. She couldn't breathe. She hadn't even felt such panic when Oppenheimer and Leitspied reverted to their alien forms and chased her through the basement of the STAR Academy. She would have gladly traded the experience of being pursued by aliens for the horrifying situation in which she now found herself. At least you could outsmart aliens and school principals. The richest man in the world and his grasping hordes of litigation lawyers were another story, however. She had about as much chance up against Snootman as she would wrestling a two-hundred-kilogram gorilla in a phone booth. There was no escaping his wrath, Amanda knew, unless she actually built that spaceship she had always dreamed of and left planet Earth, never to return.

Amanda gagged as the realization struck her that her life was over. Done. Finished. What Eugenia had failed to accomplish, her father was about to achieve in spades. On top of that, the lives of Amanda's parents, who were legally responsible for her, were also over. They would be left penniless by Bill Snootman's lawsuit. Worse than penniless, thought Amanda. They would be left indebted for the rest of their natural lives. Even Daniel's life would be destroyed. She pictured her family living in a shelter for the indigent. This thought unleashed a wave of anxiety through her—though she had to admit that a day or two in a homeless shelter would no doubt do Daniel some good in the humility department. But an entire childhood spent in such a place would be devastating, and even Daniel, pest that he was, didn't deserve such a fate. What a joke her life was, thought Amanda! Saviour of the world one minute, and destroyer of her own family the next.

Amanda could feel her own pulse pounding in her temples. The walls of the living room began to appear concave. She had read enough about neurology to know that it was just a visual distortion created by the rush of stress hormones through her bloodstream. But that didn't make it any less terrifying. As though she were inhabiting someone else's body, she watched as the letter slipped from her shaking hands and fell to the floor. She had the sensation that she was drowning, unable to breathe, as if the room had filled up with invisible water that was pressing in on her from every side.

Amanda was only snapped back to reality by Derek's voice. His tone was cheeky as always as he called from her computer speakers so loudly that she could hear him all the way down the hall to the front door.

"Earth to Amanda!" he shouted. "Stop plodging about and come back to the videoconference!"

Amanda picked up the letter and staggered to her room, putting a hand on the wall to steady herself. As she sat down at her computer, fingers trembling, she could see the concave heads of Evelyn, Sanjay and Derek gazing at her, their sardonic expressions turning to concern as they saw her anxious face.

"Whoa, what was that all about? You going all whitey on us?" asked Derek.

"Yes, you look like you've seen a ghost," said Sanjay.

"Which, as I believe we scientifically established at the Academy," added Evelyn, "do not exist."

"It's something much worse than a ghost," said Amanda. "Ghosts can't sue you for $100 million."

"Come again?" exclaimed Derek. "What's this about $100 million?"

"Bill Snootman," Amanda muttered, still reeling from the shock. "He just sent me a personal letter saying that I'm liable for Eugenia's decision to splice the alien DNA into her own."

"But that's ridiculous," said Evelyn. "I was there. You didn't give her the DNA. Oppenheimer did."

"I know," said Amanda. "But he says that because of that experiment with the synapse disruptor, the aliens and I are collectively responsible for Eugenia's deciding to transfer Oppenheimer's DNA into herself."

"Suddenly, I'm feeling rather glad just to be one of 'those three other kids,'" said Derek.

"It's ludicrous," added Sanjay. "You helped save the world from being taken over by aliens—aliens who probably would have enslaved Bill Snootman too—and now he's suing you. Talk about ingratitude!"

Amanda frowned. "I'm suddenly seeing my future flash before my eyes, and it's not a pretty sight."

There was a long, uncomfortable silence as they all sat there, not knowing what to say or how to react to this devastating news.

Then at last, Evelyn spoke. "It's very disturbing, I agree. But there's something that doesn't add up about all of this."

"No kidding," replied Amanda. "If anyone had told me a year ago that the end result of my helping to save the Earth from alien invaders would be a $100-million lawsuit, I'd have said they were crazy."

Derek tapped away at his keyboard, looking off screen at another monitor. He studied something intensely, then turned to Amanda. "There *is* something that doesn't add up with this," he said. "I just checked Bill Snootman's net worth online. According to *The Wall Street Journal*, his current business holdings are worth $53 *billion*."

"Great," said Amanda. "That means he can hire as many lawyers as he wants to destroy me and my family."

"Maybe," said Derek. "But maybe not."

"What are you talking about?" asked Amanda.

"Think about it," responded Derek. "If Snootman's worth $53 billion, it means he doesn't really need the $100 million. That represents less than one-fifth of one percent of his total assets. Even if he got it from you, it would be just a drop in the bucket. That's like someone with a hundred dollars suing you for twenty cents."

"That's not logical," commented Evelyn.

"No, it's not," said Derek, "unless it's not your money he's after."

"Meaning what?" asked Amanda.

"Meaning, maybe he's just threatening the lawsuit to get your attention," said Derek. "Maybe there's something else he wants from you. Something that he thinks you would say no to unless you were afraid of losing everything and endangering your family."

"Interesting idea," said Sanjay. "It's like the path of least resistance theory—you know, water will naturally flow around a rock if it can, instead of pushing it out of the way. It's as if Snootman is hinting at some alternative course of action that will ultimately be acceptable for you to take, but only by pointing out a less acceptable alternative first."

"Exactly," said Derek. "And why would he invite you to call him personally when he has all those expensive lawyers on staff to do the talking for him?"

Amanda began to calm down just a bit. She was starting to feel a little curious now, rather than just terrified out of her wits. She looked at the letter and found Bill Snootman's email address, typed it into her computer and added a quick message. "Dear Mr. Snootman," it began. "Received your letter. Please contact me at the following videoconference address to discuss. Sincerely, Amanda Forsythe."

Amanda hit the Send key.

"Just remember," said Derek, "he wants something that you've got."

"Right," said Amanda with a sigh. "Now I'll just have to see if it's less disagreeable than paying out $100 million."

An instant later, her screen flashed, indicating that someone was waiting to conference.

Amanda pressed the Receive key, and her screen was filled with the image of a virtual secretary who looked somewhat like a news anchor, but with even more heavily lacquered hair.

"Amanda Forsythe?" the woman asked.

"Yes, that's me," she replied.

"I have Mr. Snootman standing by for the requested video conference. Are you ready to take the call?"

"I am," Amanda answered, gathering her wits.

"I'll transfer you over to him. One moment please."

A second later, Bill Snootman appeared in the middle of Amanda's screen. She had seen many images of him before. It was impossible not to—he had been on the covers of so many news and business magazines, not to mention the technology journals that Amanda often read. But he looked considerably older now than he had appeared in those photos. Certainly much older than his forty years. His hair seemed to have turned prematurely grey, and he had a sallow complexion. His eyes were sunken and had dark, baggy rings around them.

"Amanda Forsythe?" asked Snootman.

"Yes, that's me," she replied.

"Bill Snootman here. How are you?"

"To be honest, not so good since I received your letter."

"Things haven't exactly been rosy here either since that incident at the Academy with my daughter. Still, I do appreciate that if you and those three other kids hadn't done what you did, I'd probably be sitting here forgetting what I just said, having my synapses blocked by Oppenheimer and Leitspied."

"And Eugenia would have turned into an alien completely, instead of just partially," Amanda reminded him.

"That's also true," replied Snootman. "Which is why I'm prepared to make you an offer."

Derek looked at Amanda and winked.

"I'm listening," she said.

"As I mentioned in my letter, I have had some of the world's top geneticists working on a solution to my dear Eugenia's problem. Fortunately, I have so far managed to keep the paparazzi away from my daughter, so her physical appearance is unknown to the press and the public. If photographs of Eugenia in her current state were ever to appear in the tabloids, the emotional effect on her would be devastating. Given the lack of progress in returning Eugenia to normal, she is becoming despondent, and frankly, I am beginning to question her mental state."

At that last comment, Derek reflexively screwed up his face. He began typing a text message. Amanda tried not to read it as it appeared on her computer screen. "As if her mental state wasn't questionable already! LOL."

Amanda looked away from Derek's face in case he made her laugh. A giggle right now would undoubtedly increase the size of the lawsuit to $200 million, and Amanda knew that no fleet of blimps with her image on them would be large enough to generate the money to pay off those kind of damages.

"You can imagine her distress," continued Bill Snootman. "Despite the help of geneticists, her body remains almost entirely alien. With each passing week, it becomes increasingly difficult to hide her condition. She has had to turn down numerous invitations to such events as birthday parties of the daughters of oil sheiks, runway shows by Parisian couturiers and of course the MTV Awards. The media are beginning to speculate that perhaps the encounter with the aliens traumatized Eugenia so much that she suffered a nervous breakdown. I have had to buy quite a number of these tabloids just to squelch the rumours. But some are so profitable that their owners aren't interested in selling them at any price. And I'm afraid that if these jackals knew the full horror of the truth and printed it, Eugenia would indeed have a complete mental breakdown. This is all particularly hard on her mother. When my beloved wife, Charleze, a former Miss Universe, made plans to enter Eugenia in next year's Junior Miss Universe competition, she never intended the title to be so . . . *literal*."

Amanda shifted uncomfortably in her seat, not knowing how to respond. No doubt there were corners of the universe where Eugenia's current appearance would be considered the epitome of physical perfection. But Earth was not one of them.

"In reality, I feel I am in some small way to blame for this," Snootman continued. "I always encouraged Eugenia to take the same approach to life that I use to run Snootman Global

Enterprises: look for ways to outdo your competitors, and reach new heights by continually reinventing yourself. Clearly these aliens were extremely intelligent, so it's only natural that my dear daughter wanted to be like them."

Indeed they were, thought Amanda. But if Eugenia had wanted to reinvent herself, she had succeeded all too well. Amanda knew that wasn't what Bill Snootman wanted to hear, though, so instead she just said, "I'm very sorry about Eugenia's state. But I don't know what I can do about it."

Which was true. Amanda had no idea where Snootman was going with all this.

"Well, in fact, I believe there *is* something you can do about it," he said. "Allow me to explain. It is a fact of science that all the best work is done by young minds. Einstein developed his theory of relativity when he was twenty-six; Isaac Newton created the mathematical formulae for calculus at twenty-one. Alexander Graham Bell invented the telephone at the ripe old age of twenty-nine."

"Yes," replied Amanda, "I've heard that before." Amanda felt a sense of déjà vu. This was precisely the line of conversation that Professor Leitspied had used on the students that first day at the Academy, flattering them even as she tricked them into creating technologies that almost allowed her and Oppenheimer to take over the world. Amanda hoped it was mere coincidence that Snootman was now using the same argument.

"In that case," he continued, "you've probably also heard the adage that if a young scientist tells you something is possible, he's probably right; if an old scientist tells you something's not possible, he's probably wrong."

"Yes," said Amanda, "I have heard that."

"Good," Snootman replied. "Because that is the reason I have contacted you today. The geneticists I hired to reverse my daughter's condition tell me that it's a hopeless case, that the transformation is permanent. I find that conclusion unacceptable. I want my daughter back, Miss Forsythe."

"That's understandable," said Amanda. Though not to *me*, she wanted to add. But since you are her biological father and have a mammalian brain that directs you to protect your offspring even when it's not in the best interests of humanity, the planet or anything else, it's entirely understandable—if irrational—that *you* would feel that way. Of course, not wanting to fan the flames of an already uncomfortably hot situation, she just said, "But genetics is not something that I know very much about."

Bill Snootman looked strangely intense yet hopeful as he gazed off into the middle distance. "I have a theory that with accelerated training, it would be possible to develop young ultra-geniuses into the world's greatest experts in the field of genetics, regardless of their specific backgrounds. Young minds are fresh, unshackled by decades of convention. Thus they would be able to see the possible where older minds see only the *im*possible. I'm talking about people such as you and your three young colleagues—the ones you think I don't know are listening in on our conversation."

Amanda was trying to mentally formulate a response, but Bill Snootman just smiled.

"Miss Forsythe, I wrote the program for the videoconferencing software that you, Evelyn Chiu, Derek Murphy and Sanjay Dosanjh are using at this very moment. Please do not think me so foolish to have failed to devise a means to monitor who is present during my own videoconferences. I may be old for a scientist, but

I'm still open to that which is possible, however unlikely it may seem." He hesitated for a moment, then added, "I have to be."

On the monitors, Evelyn, Derek and Sanjay looked sheepish but said nothing. Amanda felt a genuine pang of sympathy for Bill Snootman seeing how tired and desperate he was.

Without pressing the point about her friends' eavesdropping, Snootman continued, "As a scientific ultra-genius myself, I realize the loneliness and isolation that this brings. There are so few people with whom one can truly communicate. I know that the four of you must long for one another's company, and for projects you can work on together. That's why you have these videoconferences. So I'm willing to fund the best science-education program in the world for the four of you, at a facility of your choosing, on the condition that you immediately devote yourself to learning as much about genetics as possible, with the goal of reversing Eugenia's condition. If you succeed, I will drop my lawsuit against you."

Amanda noticed that on her screen, all three of her friends were nodding their heads and silently mouthing "yes" to Snootman's offer. However, she had become an expert negotiator after listening to so many endorsement proposals. So instead of saying yes or no, she made a counter-offer.

"That's a good start, but there are a few other things I'd like," said Amanda.

"Such as?" asked Bill Snootman.

"In addition to our education, I want the research and development programs for our pet science interests to be fully funded, the way they were at the Academy. That's my space-travel research, Evelyn's oceanographic studies, Derek's satellite and optical projects, and Sanjay's nanobot development."

Snootman thought this over a moment before answering. "All right. Subject to the usual audit processes to ensure that the resources are being used for their intended purpose."

"Agreed," replied Amanda.

Derek, Sanjay and Evelyn looked at each other on their monitors, fairly bursting with excitement.

"But as we've already discovered," said Amanda, "there is no institution in the world that offers the ideal facilities for all of us. This is true of everyone else who attended the STAR Academy as well. So I want the Academy to reopen. And I want all the original students to be invited to return on full scholarships."

Bill Snootman flinched. "Two hundred children living at the Academy on full scholarships, all expenses paid? That would be very, very expensive."

"Maybe," countered Amanda, "but to solve such a complex equation as a cross-species DNA splice of this magnitude, we will need many more heads than just the four of ours. Think of it: two hundred of the most creative young minds in the entire world, brought to bear on a problem of the utmost importance to you. Funding such an undertaking just makes good sense. It's enlightened self-interest."

Bill Snootman rubbed his chin, considering the idea. Then his hands disappeared from view and she could hear what sounded like very rapid text messaging.

Amanda could feel that her argument was swaying him, so she pressed her point. "The Academy was a wonderful concept. There's no doubt in my mind that we would have created astounding benefits for humanity and the planet as a whole, had our work there not been subverted. With the original 199 students—plus Eugenia, who will become the two hundredth once we solve the problem—there's no telling what we can accomplish. More enlightened self-interest."

Bill Snootman paused, mulling it over. "All right," he said finally, sounding faintly weary. "If that's what it takes. I hope you don't have too many other demands. I'm not sure I could convince my lawyers and accountants that I haven't gone soft in the head if I say yes to much more."

"But what about the Academy itself? Where will it be located?"

Bill Snootman smiled. "I anticipated your request. So during our conversation, I took the liberty of sending out some text messages. I have just, in the last thirty seconds, made arrangements to purchase the original STAR Academy building. It makes sense. The infrastructure for housing and training everyone is already in place. The ownership of the building and grounds reverted to the township of Gallwater, since the aliens, not surprisingly, hadn't made arrangements for the property taxes to be paid after their departure. Apparently, the locals were planning to open it as an alien theme park and museum to try to generate some income. But the offer I made to them while speaking with you just now was evidently more than they had anticipated earning from it as a roadside attraction. We will be in possession of the STAR Academy by this time tomorrow, at which point I shall have a team of technicians inspect the premises and ensure that everything is safe and all systems are functional."

"Who will the faculty be?" asked Amanda.

"I'm glad you asked," said Bill Snootman. "I have arranged for science professors from several of the best universities in the world to be excused from their regular duties for as long as it takes them to teach you everything they know."

"That's impressive," said Amanda. "How soon will all this happen?"

"I'm hoping that by this time next week, the Academy will be ready to receive students," replied Snootman. "I would like you to give the school a final inspection before the others are brought in, to make sure there are no disturbing reminders of its former history. So what do you say, Amanda Forsythe? Do we have a deal?"

Amanda considered it all. She noticed that for just the briefest nanosecond, a look of anxiety and vulnerability flickered across Snootman's face, as if he was genuinely afraid she would say no. Then she nodded. "Yes, Mr. Snootman. We have a deal—subject to my parents' approval, of course."

"Hopefully there will be no need to worry about that," said Bill Snootman with a tired smile. "While we've been speaking, one of my representatives has been in contact with your father and is at this moment making him a very attractive offer."

"What kind of an offer?" asked Amanda, feeling suddenly protective of her father.

Bill Snootman smiled again. "Snootman Global Enterprises purchased the Achilles Bunion Remover Cream Company three minutes ago. That put me in a position to offer him an appointment as sales manager for both the east and the west coasts—if he approves of your coming to the Academy. Of course, being sales manager for both territories is a demanding job." Bill Snootman looked at his watch. "Which is why, in seven seconds, he will be offered a salary of one million dollars a year."

"How much did you say?" asked Amanda, not certain she had heard him correctly.

"Woooooo-hoooooooooo!" came a delighted bellow from downstairs. "Woooooo-hoooo!"

It was Amanda's father's voice.

Bill Snootman smiled slightly. "Evidently he is pleased with the arrangement. I didn't tell him about the lawsuit. I see no need to spoil his big promotion with that kind of news."

"That was very thoughtful of you," said Amanda.

"Enlightened self-interest," replied Snootman. Then he looked at her in a confidential manner. "By the way, are you aware there is no scientific proof that bunions can be removed with cream?"

"Yes, painfully so," Amanda answered. "But my dad doesn't seem to know about that. Or the fact that the name Achilles is associated with the heel, not the big toe. Which, as I gather you know, is where bunions are located. And I'd rather not tell him. I think it would make him feel his whole life has been for nothing."

"No worries," said Bill Snootman. "Your secret is safe with me. Or should I say 'our secret' now that I own 100 percent of the Achilles Bunion Remover Cream Company. Your father will never have to know."

"You seem to have thought of everything," said Amanda.

"I try," said Bill Snootman. "There's no problem in the world that can't be reduced to ones and zeroes. At least that's what I tell myself."

"Right," agreed Amanda, trying to imagine what the world must look like to someone who reduces every problem to a binary form, as if life were a series of on/off switches.

"So can you be ready to travel a week from now?" asked Snootman.

"If the school board gives me the necessary release, yes."

"I think, by now, you can guess the answer to that," said Bill Snootman. "I've agreed to fund a new practice facility for the Downview Danes. Bunch of Neanderthals, if you ask me, but the team seems to be important to the school trustees. Also, they were concerned about not being able to find a new remedial science teacher to replace you. But my people managed to locate someone suitable for teaching Principal Murkly and Mrs. Wheedlbum and those other clods the basics of science."

"Really? Who?" asked Amanda.

"Some retired science professor who was eager for the work. I can't quite remember his name. It's something like . . . uh, Dullwood or Dimwood."

"Hopwood?" offered Amanda.

"That's the one," replied Snootman.

Amanda smiled at the picture of Murkly and Wheedlbum in a confined classroom with her former tutor, a man with such huge colonies of malodorous microbes under his armpits that he smelled permanently of vegetable beef soup.

"I'm sure that Principal Murkly and Mrs. Wheedlbum will have an appreciation for microbiology and quantum math after he's done with them," she said. "Not to mention fresh air."

"I'm not certain what you're referring to," replied Snootman, "but if he sharpens their senses, that's a positive thing."

"Oh, he'll sharpen their senses all right," said Amanda.

"Good. Now, I've got a team of lawyers standing by in a limousine in that park at the end of your street. They will be coming by your house with the contracts within the hour. I'll have a representative contact you shortly with the travel arrangements. Looking forward to meeting you in person."

Amanda knew the polite answer would be "Me too," or something to that effect, but with the lawsuit still hanging over her head, she couldn't quite bring herself to say it, even though she was excited about returning to the Academy.

"Thanks. See you soon," she replied.

"Bye for now," said Bill Snootman. His image, now visibly hopeful, was already dissolving and was soon replaced on her monitor by the Snootman Global Enterprises logo.

Amanda hit a key and the logo faded out, allowing Evelyn, Sanjay and Derek to once again appear at full size on her monitor.

Derek was the first to speak. "That was totally brill, Amanda. When did you become such a tough negotiator?"

"Around the third or fourth time somebody from some company wanted me to make a public embarrassment of myself to sell their junk," said Amanda.

"You were fantastic, Amanda!" said Sanjay. "Well done! Now I can see you guys again and work on my nanobots too!"

"And I can continue my underwater research," chirped Evelyn, "without having to go someplace where I wouldn't get to see the rest of you."

"It will be great to be together again," said Amanda. "But remember, we *will* have to work on getting Eugenia back to normal too. That's part of the deal."

"A necessary evil," said Sanjay.

"Does this mean we'll have to touch her?" asked Derek, in what was only partly mock revulsion.

"Probably," replied Amanda.

"Then we'd better make sure we've got lots of latex gloves," said Evelyn.

"And a few barge poles," said Derek.

"You guys are so bad," said Amanda. "But you'd better get it out of your system now, because once we're at the Academy, we can't talk like this about Eugenia."

The others seemed surprised by her earnestness.

"Except behind her back, of course," added Amanda slyly.

"Phew! I was worried about you for a minute," said Derek. "Thought you'd gone all squidgy on us."

"Well, I actually do feel a little sorry for Bill Snootman," Amanda responded. "But that doesn't make me any more eager to have Eugenia in my life again—in exoskeletal form or otherwise."

"Maybe she'll be so grateful for our help that she'll be nice to us," said Evelyn hopefully.

"Who knows? Stranger transformations have happened," Derek remarked, "as Eugenia has already proven. Though something tells me that it was easier for her to turn into a monster than it will be for her to turn into somebody decent and nice."

"Ditto that," said Amanda. Then she thought about the enormous task ahead of her. "Well, one week is going to pass by quickly. I'd better go offline and start getting packed. See you guys on the other side."

Amanda, Derek, Evelyn and Sanjay said their goodbyes, feeling giddy with excitement but also a little nervous. The next time they saw one another, it wouldn't be on a monitor, but in person once again, at the Academy—a place where not only their dreams had come true, but also nightmares on a scale that they could not have imagined.

CHAPTER 5

AMANDA'S RETURN TRIP to the Superior Thinking and Advanced Research Academy was a study in contrasts to her first journey there. First, a Snootman Global Enterprises private jet had ushered her directly from Downview to the airport nearest Gallwater. It was the same airport where she had met George for the first time, barely six months earlier, when he'd greeted her in the arrivals area in his strangely out-of-date chauffeur's uniform.

But this time, Amanda didn't even have to enter the airport terminal. Instead, the plane's cabin attendant escorted her to a large executive helicopter that would take her on the final leg of the journey. She settled into one of the luxuriously padded leather seats and, a moment later, felt a gentle vibration as the helicopter's powerful twin turbine engines whirred to life. She watched the rotors whooshing around, building up speed until they were just a blur. She was considering the problem of why some things seem to be invisible just because they are going so fast, and what the implications of that might be on the larger scale of life, when she felt a surge of G-forces as the helicopter began to climb.

Soon, the airport was disappearing behind them. At its operating altitude, about three hundred metres above the ground, the helicopter gave Amanda an ideal vantage point: high enough that she could see well into the distance, yet close enough to the ground that she could make out details. The suburbs beyond the airport soon gave way to open countryside. Amanda began to recognize some features of the landscape that she had seen for the first time the previous September. Just a few minutes later, she caught sight of Gallwater, the sleepy village with the even sleepier police chief and deputy who had proven so resistant to Amanda's warnings about the aliens' plot. Then at last, on the horizon, she spotted the Academy itself.

Amanda felt her pulse begin to race. From the helicopter, in the crisp, clear air of early spring, she saw the Academy as she had never seen it before. Not even the 3-D image that Derek had helped create using the aliens' ultra-high-orbit satellites had fully captured its otherworldly appearance. At this altitude and distance, the tall Gothic building on the hilltop looked blatantly out of place amid the lush green countryside beneath it. The Academy seemed to hover over its surroundings as though it might lift off at any moment like George's spaceship. The cemetery encircling it on the hillsides and the walled courtyard behind it gave it an air of secrecy. At the same time, the building loomed so high above the surrounding area that it seemed to dominate it. It occurred to Amanda that the aliens had likely first seen this site from the air, just as she was doing now. She had spent so little time outside the Academy grounds—none, in fact, between her arrival and her escape—that she'd never had an opportunity to notice this before.

Amanda recognized the section of road where George, chauffeuring her to the school that first morning in his 1950 Studebaker Starlight, had become so happily distracted by her questions that he had almost caused a head-on collision. She looked down on the road below and saw the two sets of skid marks, heading straight toward each other and then veering away at the last moment. It was only now, seeing the proof of the near collision, that Amanda realized just how close she had come to losing her life before she even had a chance to set foot inside the Academy.

Seeing that reminder of her near-death experience, and with the Academy now looming large in the distance, Amanda experienced a flood of feelings. Even though her time at the school could be measured in weeks, it was intense and had changed the course of her life. True, she felt some uneasiness about returning to the site of such dangerous encounters—the least of which, it now seemed, was the barely avoided car accident. That little mishap paled in comparison to Eugenia Snootman's threats to destroy Amanda's future if she didn't hand over her scientific secrets, as well as to Oppenheimer and Leitspied's plans to lobotomize all the children after milking them for every useful invention that would enable them to take over Earth. But on the plus side of the equation, there had been incredible discoveries, a mentally stimulating atmosphere and a heady new sense of camaraderie gained from making friends at the Academy. And though Oppenheimer and Leitspied had turned out to have malevolent intent, George had been unfailingly kind, considerate and ethical. Amanda found herself feeling a sharp pang of wistfulness at the thought that the person—or rather, alien—responsible for most of her best experiences at the Academy would no longer be a part of it.

The helicopter began its final descent to the Academy grounds, now so close that Amanda could read the names on the tombstones in the surrounding cemetery. To her surprise, it touched down not in the inner courtyard, as she had expected, but in the large circular driveway in front of the Academy's entrance. With the craft now firmly on the ground, the pilot cut the engine and the rotors swirled gradually to a halt. Amanda had been so caught up in her thoughts that by the time she took notice of the steward, he was already smartly opening the door behind her. He unfolded the stairs, stepped down, then turned to face her.

"Right this way, please, Miss Forsythe. Mr. Snootman is eager to see you," he said, gesturing toward the Academy.

Amanda placed a foot on the top step, then hesitated. Even though she was well acquainted with the Academy, she suddenly felt the same sense of awe she'd experienced when she stepped out of George's car the previous September. The mansard roof high above her was no less impressive for its familiarity. Amanda's eyes were drawn to the Gothic arch of the entranceway, above which the inscription *Maxima debetur puero reverentia*—"To a child, we owe the greatest respect"—still remained. To Amanda's surprise, the large pair of Tesla coils mounted above the entrance like lighting sconces were fully powered up. They crackled as they shot bright bolts of electrical plasma between them, just as they had when George, Oppenheimer and Leitspied had been here. She was so drawn to the sight that at first she didn't notice the figure who quietly appeared in the doorway at the top of the steps. In contrast to the building that surrounded him, this person seemed smaller than life. Or at least smaller than the dynamic, self-confident version she had seen in numerous magazines, newspapers and television broadcasts. His shoulders slouched slightly, in a way that indicated not chronic bad posture but profound weariness. Amanda could see that his eyes were tired-looking too, the lids a little puffy, the skin beneath them tinged with grey. Nevertheless, the figure in the doorway managed a small smile as Amanda approached.

"Welcome back to the Academy, Miss Forsythe," said Bill Snootman.

The richest man in the world—and the father of the girl who had sworn to destroy her future—descended the steps to greet Amanda in the driveway rather than waiting for her to climb the stairs and meet him. It was a detail that she immediately noticed. Bill Snootman seemed much more modest than she had imagined he would be. He reached out and offered his hand.

Amanda stepped forward and politely shook it, noticing that it was perspiring slightly. Was he actually nervous in her presence? she wondered.

"Did you have a pleasant journey?" he asked.

"Yes. Between your private plane and your helicopter, it was much shorter than the last time I came here too."

"I'm glad to hear it," replied Snootman. "I think it's important for people to arrive from a journey as refreshed as possible when there is important work to be done. You can always replace money, but you can't replace time. That—and lost loved ones—are the only things in life you can't ever get back. Hence the private jet and helicopter. Much quicker than a commercial flight and ground transportation—which also would have made you more visible to the paparazzi."

"Speaking of which, why did the helicopter land out here instead of in the courtyard, where no one could observe us?" asked Amanda. "I don't see any of those paparazzi lurking out there. But I know how concerned you are about the tabloids finding out about Eugenia's condition."

Snootman scanned the horizon rather nervously, then turned back to Amanda. "I hope I have been secretive enough that the press haven't yet caught wind of my plans for this place. Still, there is a risk of our being seen. But I felt that risk was worth it in this case. You see, I had the helicopter land out here with you because I want you to have the experience of walking through this entranceway again."

"Why?" asked Amanda, genuinely curious.

"Because both symbolically and practically, this is a new beginning for you," replied Snootman. "When you cross that threshold and re-enter this building, the Academy will be what it should have been all along—a place where your intellectual development, and that of some other very gifted children, will be nourished and nurtured to its full potential. There are no ulterior motives here. I'm not like Oppenheimer and Leitspied. I don't need to take over the world. I already own more of our planet than most people could even dream of. And I have more money than I could ever possibly spend. There's only one thing I want that I don't have: my daughter. And I'm confident that if there's any way to get her back, you, with the assistance of the other students, will find it."

"Thank you for your confidence in me," said Amanda.

She wondered if this would be a good moment to discuss dropping the lawsuit, and was about to raise the subject when there was a loud crackle from overhead. They both looked up in time to see a particularly large burst of blue electrical plasma shooting across the doorway above their heads. Bill Snootman looked at the Tesla coils that were producing the dangerous-looking but beautiful spectacle and smiled.

"Have those been running the whole time we were away?" asked Amanda.

"No," replied Snootman. "But I saw the fixtures and couldn't resist firing them back up again, even though they serve no practical purpose. Tesla coils fascinated me when I was a kid. My favourite was the one in *Frankenstein*."

"Me too," said Amanda. "I built one myself once. Not for special effects or making monsters, but for research."

"Really?" said Bill Snootman, smiling despite his fatigue. "So did I. That was one of the very first science projects I ever undertook. I was nine. Imagine those aliens choosing something as strange as Tesla coils for lighting sconces."

"They probably saw it in one of the old television broadcasts they were monitoring," said Amanda. "But I never got to ask them about it."

"I was so fascinated by those coils that I just had to find out more about the person who created them," said Bill Snootman. "Nikola Tesla. He was a genius. He would be famous even if the only thing he'd ever developed was alternating current."

"I agree," said Amanda. "Imagine how backward the world would be if Tesla hadn't proved that Edison's ideas were wrong, and people were still struggling to make direct current work on a large scale."

Snootman, looking energized himself by this line of conversation, perked up momentarily. "Yes, the things that man invented! Radio-controlled devices, the induction motor, even the spark plugs in that helicopter you flew in on, among others."

Amanda hesitated. "I read that he believed he could harness the power of the ionosphere and create so much electricity that everybody on Earth could have it for free. But he said the utility companies conspired against him to stop it, because they didn't want people getting power from the sky without paying for it."

"Well, I wouldn't put too much store in some of the things he said later in life," replied Snootman. "He got pretty wacky in his old age. Claimed to have invented a death ray too. People said he was crazy. But when you think about it, building a death ray's not that different than using a base station to direct laser beams to power a photon-sail spaceship, is it?" he asked.

Amanda smiled. "So you know about my pet project?"

"Yes, I am aware that photon-sail interplanetary travel is a keen interest of yours. I also know that transmitting energy through the air was one of the technologies Oppenheimer and Leitspied had you kids working on. Eugenia wrote about both those things in her diary."

"I didn't know she kept a diary," said Amanda.

"My daughter is full of surprises," said Snootman.

That was not something Amanda needed to be told. So far, all of Eugenia's surprises had been about as pleasant as finding a scorpion in the toe of your shoe. So she wondered what her diary would reveal.

"That journal is the only way I have of knowing what Eugenia was thinking or experiencing here at the Academy. But from what she wrote, I know that she thought she was on the verge of a breakthrough. According to her diary, there was just one obstacle in her way. But she thought that with a little more effort, she could eliminate it."

Amanda had to bite her tongue. She knew perfectly well that the "obstacle" to which Eugenia was referring was Amanda herself, for her refusal to give up her remote energy transmission research. Eugenia was such a liar and so concerned about posterity, Amanda realized, that she didn't even tell the truth in her own diary.

Amanda looked at Snootman thoughtfully. "We did manage to direct enough energy to power an unmanned scale-model airplane built by the Zurakowski twins. But that's as far as we got before we found out that Oppenheimer and Leitspied weren't planning to use it to send energy to impoverished Third World villages. Once we discovered that they really intended to use it to scramble everyone's brains, we just *pretended* to be working on the problem."

Amanda realized to her relief that Bill Snootman probably knew nothing about the incident in the hall outside Oppenheimer's office, when she and Evelyn had seized the aliens' disembodiment-ray device. Amanda had used the power transmitter and a small version of the synapse disruptor to temporarily muddle Tinkerbell's thought patterns after Eugenia ordered the vile reptile-ferret hybrid to attack them. The only people who knew about it besides Eugenia were Evelyn, Derek, Sanjay and Amanda herself. The four friends had sworn never to tell anyone about it. And in the pandemonium that had ensued as Eugenia began her unexpected transformation into a spider-like creature, she would have been too preoccupied to write about the incident. At least that's what Amanda hoped.

Bill Snootman pointed to the *Maxima debetur puero reverentia* inscription in the archway above their heads. "I decided to leave that up there too," he said. "Even though Oppenheimer and Leitspied subverted the message, it's still a wonderful maxim. Because it's true. We adults *do* owe the greatest reverence to children. For without children, what future is there? I think about that every hour of every day."

Snootman's gaze wandered off into the distance. Then he looked back at Amanda.

"I just wish I'd heard that saying eleven years ago. Maybe things would have turned out differently." He sighed. "Let's go in. I don't think there are any paparazzi lurking about out here, but the less we show ourselves, the better. I wonder why people are so interested in reading about celebrity wardrobe malfunctions and all that rubbish when there so many *real* wonders in the universe?"

Amanda looked at him thoughtfully. "Some psychologists believe it is related to the levels of dopamine in the human brain. Dopamine is a chemical neurotransmitter found in all kinds of animals. In humans, it influences functions such as sleep, attention, learning and mood. Some researchers believe that when people see scandalous images of celebrities, it triggers a pleasure response in chemical receptors in the brain."

"Fascinating," said Bill Snootman. "I never knew any of this. I'm more of a computer and electronics specialist."

"Well, it just so happens that there's an interesting connection to computers," Amanda continued. "Psychologists say this phenomenon has become more common since the development of the Internet."

"Great. The Internet that my research and my software helped build," said Snootman ruefully. "Just goes to show that whatever you create to do good, somebody somewhere can find a way to use it to do something bad."

"I'm afraid I know all about that," responded Amanda, thinking of the inventions that Oppenheimer and Leitspied had tried to use to take over the world.

"Yes, you'd know that better than anybody," said Bill Snootman. His expression was grave for a moment. Then he gestured toward the entranceway. "Shall we?"

Amanda nodded and followed him up the steps. Passing beneath the imposing archway, the Latin inscription and the crackling Tesla coils, she felt the same butterflies in her stomach that she had the first time she crossed this threshold. The outside world receded into nothingness, and her new existence was, once again, the Academy.

CHAPTER 6

THE LONG HALLWAY was dim, the ebony panelling absorbing what little light there was. But as Amanda's eyes adjusted to the gloom, her gaze was drawn upward by lights above her. To her amazement, she saw that hovering just below the ceiling, carefully lit to stand out from the surrounding darkness, was what appeared to be some fantastical sculpture. As big as a blue whale, it ran the length of the hall and consisted of two spiral strands joined together by a ladder-like structure. It rotated slowly, gradually revealing all its facets. It could have been the framework of a space station, thought Amanda, or a transmission tower. But each strand and connector was made up of much smaller pieces of different materials, all bonded end to end. It was something no human engineer would ever make. But it could be something, it occurred to her, that would make a human engineer. It was a giant reproduction of a DNA strand, the building block of life that had become Bill Snootman's obsession.

Amanda walked slowly beneath it, carefully examining its length, awestruck by the beauty of the spiralling structure. Then she noticed that further down the corridor, near the Constellation Hall, there stood a transparent cylinder, two metres across and reaching almost to the ceiling. It was filled with some thick, clear liquid and shimmered with light. Translucent globular shapes rose slowly within it, giving the device the appearance of a towering lava lamp. However, as Amanda got closer, she could see that the globular forms weren't random, but were a consistently similar size and shape. Within each one was a nucleus, and within each nucleus were a number of strands. Outside the nucleus, smaller objects began moving to opposite ends of the sphere. In the centre, other strands were lining up. Each globular shape began to narrow around its middle, until it separated into two globes, each now with its own nucleus. Amanda suddenly realized that what seemed to be just a beautiful light sculpture was in fact a huge representation of living cells dividing within a human body in a process known as mitosis. The two giant models that Snootman had placed in the main hallway were breathtaking. And their mystery and complexity made Amanda wonder for a moment if she was really up to the task.

Then she forced that thought away and became aware of distant sounds from within the building—echoing voices and the clatter of tools and equipment.

"Those are my staff," said Snootman. "They've spent the week cleaning up, building the sculptures that you've just been admiring, getting the electrical and mechanical systems running again, and bringing in food for the cafeteria. I can't imagine how three aliens managed to keep this place going on their own."

"Well, for starters, George, Oppenheimer and Leitspied were unbelievably intelligent and technically advanced," replied Amanda. "George had most of the day-to-day operations automated. Plus they each had eight arms, which must be pretty handy for multitasking." Seeing Bill Snootman flinch slightly, Amanda silently chided herself for her verbal misstep. "Oh, sorry."

"No, don't apologize," he replied. "Your logic is flawless. I'm sure it is handy. It's just that if you're used to having two arms and two legs, and you live on a planet where everybody else has two arms and two legs, it's pretty unsettling to have eight."

"And I will do everything possible to fix that," said Amanda. "I've spent most of the past week getting a basic understanding of DNA. As I mentioned, I devoted most of my childhood to studying physics, engineering and astronomy, so I've still got a lot of ground to cover."

"Well, I hope I've given you sufficient motivation to cover it," said Snootman.

"I wouldn't worry about that," replied Amanda, thinking how horror-struck her parents would be if they ever found out that she, and thus they, were on the receiving end of a $100-million lawsuit.

"By the way, do you know what a polymath is?" asked Snootman.

"No, I don't," confessed Amanda. "But *poly* means 'many' in ancient Greek. And *math* was their word for 'knowledge,' if I'm not mistaken. So maybe it means knowing many things?"

"Close," said Snootman. "A polymath is someone who uses his brain in more than just one discipline. A doctor who understands astronomy, for example, or a physicist who likes to study biology on the side. It's a great habit to get into to keep your thought processes fresh. I, for example, create computer software. But I also love making anagrams—words created by rearranging the letters of other words. You'd be amazed at what you can come up with by reconfiguring the building blocks of language. It's not unlike the way my dear daughter used to enjoy reconfiguring DNA in unexpected ways to make new creatures."

Amanda took pains not to betray any emotion about Eugenia and her disgusting "hobby."

"Take my surname, Snootman, for example. Only eight letters, S-N-O-O-T-M-A-N. But those building blocks can be rearranged to make a surprising number of other last names: Amontson, Tomanson, Santo Nom, San Monto, Montason, Montanso. And those are only some of the possibilities. If you set your mind to it, I bet you could come up with a few more. In fact, I *know* you can, because I've tried. But if I told you all the names you could make out of Snootman, that would spoil the fun. Better that you try it on your own if you want to get the full benefits. Do you see my point?"

"I think so," said Amanda. "You're suggesting that by engaging your brain in such exercises, your intellect stays sharper?"

"Exactly. Keeps the mind limbered up and open to new possibilities. That's why I've tried to make the facilities here as creatively stimulating as possible, so every child will become used to thinking outside the box. Come to think of it, someone should create a more thinking-outside-the-box phrase than 'thinking outside the box.' Hmm, there's an anagram waiting to be made. Well, let's continue our tour, shall we?"

He led her through the workshops, the classrooms and the laboratories. Everything was equipped just as well as it had been when the aliens were running the Academy. In fact, Amanda couldn't help noticing that the biology labs were better than ever. Each workstation had its own high-powered microscope linked to a video monitor to give users an even bigger view of the tiny universes they would be examining. There were a number of large tanks containing nutrient baths, for growing life forms or their components *in vitro*, meaning that they were developing not within a living mother but in an artificial environment that would provide everything required to sustain life. And to remind students of mother nature's slow pace of change when left to her own devices, there was a row of skeletons illustrating the evolution of man. Small monkey-like animals stood next to creatures that appeared to have characteristics of both humans and apes. Following that was the skull of a Neanderthal, very similar to that of a modern human, and finally a Homo sapiens skeleton. And to illustrate what happens to those who cling to the wrong branches of the evolutionary tree, Snootman had also included skeletons of our two closest neighbours, genetically speaking: a chimpanzee and a gorilla.

This emphasis on biology was no surprise to Amanda, given Bill Snootman's motivation for reopening the Academy.

Next, he brought Amanda up to the Academy's attic. This was the mysterious, sealed-off portion of the building where George had hidden his spaceship. It was an area that was normally closed to students. Snootman gestured toward a plain wooden door, the kind that looked like it would have nothing more interesting behind it than a closet full of janitor's supplies. But from the way he became intense as he approached the door, Amanda suspected that there was something far more important to him than brooms, mops and cleaners on the other side. Bill Snootman placed his index finger on a small sensor panel, which lit up in response.

"It's reading my fingerprint," he said. "A security feature to limit who can enter."

Amanda heard the soft clatter of precision tumblers turning inside the door. Then it swung open silently.

They entered a dimly lit corridor, at the end of which was a steel door that looked like the entrance to a bank vault. Except that even bank vaults didn't normally have a towering security guard on either side, like this. Each guard stood two metres tall, and even in their suits, they both looked like they had been chiselled out of granite. They nodded at Bill Snootman.

"Behind that door," said Bill Snootman, "are Eugenia's living quarters."

"Is she there now?" asked Amanda.

"No. She's on her way. She no longer fits easily into any conventional means of personal transportation. So I had a special chamber made for her—something like a shock-proof, transportable bedroom disguised as a shipping container, so as not to attract attention from the news media."

Amanda looked at the vault door and thought about how unpleasant it must be to live under such circumstances, even for someone as nasty as Eugenia Snootman. She felt a moment of angst as she wondered if she was really up to the task of returning her nemesis to human form. But with the threat of the lawsuit still hanging over her, she quite literally could not afford to show her concern.

So instead she said, "You've done an impressive job with everything here, Mr. Snootman. And I'm sure that with the resources you've put into this place, and with all of us working together, we can return Eugenia to the way she was."

Amanda was surprised to see that her simple reassurance seemed to calm Bill Snootman.

"Good. I'm relieved to hear it. Now, your friends will be arriving soon. But first, I've got one last thing to show you. Please follow me."

Snootman led her down to a hallway in the basement. He stopped in front of a pair of large stainless-steel doors, much bigger than the ones at the entrance to Eugenia's quarters.

"There's something I'd like you to see."

Amanda heard the swoosh of hydraulics. The heavy doors slid open, revealing a darkened room so cavernous that the light from the hallway couldn't penetrate far enough for her to see where the far walls or ceiling were.

Snootman gestured toward the doorway.

"After you."

Amanda hesitantly stepped across the threshold into the darkness. Instantly, banks of lights triggered by sensors lit up in sequence, revealing a hangar-like laboratory that, to Amanda's amazement, was now as brightly lit as a summer's day.

"What is it?" she asked.

"This is your personal lab for your space experiments," he replied.

A giant working model of the solar system was suspended from the ceiling, the sun in the centre of the room and the planets in orbit around it, fanning out to the farthest edges. The various moons circled their respective planets. On the walls were billboard-sized backlit photos that she recognized as having been taken through the Hubble Space Telescope. She saw the yellowy-white Orion Nebula, surrounded by wispy clouds of orange, red, purple and green gases. There was the Crab Nebula, the ghostly remains of an exploded star, brilliant white with red tendrils of gas flowing around its edges. On another wall was one of Amanda's favourites, the hauntingly beautiful Messier 101 galaxy, more than twenty-four million light years away from Earth. With its orangey-white centre and shimmering, octopus-like arms, it was twice the width of our own Milky Way. The lowermost of those arms led Amanda's eye to a corner of her own lab, where there was an enclosed workshop with lathes, cutters and mills.

"All of the machining equipment is fully robotic. It can automatically fabricate any space vehicle parts you can conceive of," said Bill Snootman.

In an adjacent climate-controlled room, Amanda could see a supercomputer.

"I designed and programmed that myself," said Bill Snootman with a trace of pride. "It's the most advanced of its type in the world. It will allow you to plot a course to the farthest reaches of the galaxy, or to the most infinitesimally small corner of a living human cell."

Next, Amanda saw a window, several centimetres thick, beyond which was a heavily reinforced chamber that appeared to be vented to the outside.

"That's your rocket engine test lab," said Snootman. "Those windows and walls are strong enough to withstand a direct hit from a bunker-buster bomb, so they'll take the force of any rocket you can create here."

Amanda was already feeling overwhelmed by the magnitude of the facilities when she spotted a cylindrical concrete structure at the far end of the room. There were catwalks around it and several doorways into it.

"That's just the basic shell of your launch silo for now," said Snootman. "But once you start working on your spaceship, my technicians will outfit it with everything you need."

Amanda was speechless.

"I hope your silence indicates approval and not disappointment," said Snootman.

"Approval doesn't begin to describe what I'm feeling. I can't believe this is even real!" she replied. "This facility that you've created is far beyond anything I expected."

"I always keep my promises, Miss Forsythe. But don't forget, you have to spend at least half your time working on my daughter too, looking for a cure."

"Don't worry, Mr. Snootman. It's kind of hard to forget," said Amanda. She thought this might be the moment to renegotiate that delicate financial matter. "Especially with your $100-million lawsuit hanging over me."

But Snootman didn't bite.

"Nothing more than ones and zeroes," he replied. "Just think of it as digital motivation. Now, Amanda, please come this way. I've got one last special surprise."

After seeing the marvels of her new lab, but hearing his refusal to drop his threatened lawsuit, Amanda wondered what more of a special surprise Bill Snootman could possibly have up his sleeve. Judging by his track record, it would be something very, very good or very, very bad.

He led her to a heavy shatterproof window looking into a white room about the width and depth of a squash court.

"Well, what do you think?" he said.

"What do I think of what?" asked Amanda. "I don't see anything but walls."

"Then look up. *Way* up!"

Amanda craned her neck and was surprised to see a figure in a full-coverage helmet and astronaut's jumpsuit floating in midair three storeys above them. The face of the floating figure was obscured by a visor. The person in the jumpsuit and helmet stretched his legs out at a sixty-degree angle in a jackknife pose and performed an impressive yoga stretch. Having completed the stretches, he gripped his ankles, arched his spine and slowly pulled his legs behind him until his ankles touched the back of his helmet. As if by magic, the helmeted figure held the pose for a moment, altitude not fluctuating more than a centimetre. Then he slowly rotated end over end toward the far wall. Amanda watched breathlessly as the figure then reversed the pose, tucking legs and arms in tight to his chest in a cannonball position. With a sudden snap forward, his entire body started spinning on its axis at a dizzying speed and hurtling downward. At the rate he was going, it seemed he would smash into the floor for sure. Amanda grimaced, waiting for the impact. But at the last moment, the figure released his grip and assumed his original spread-eagled position, arms and legs again perfectly symmetrical. Then he began to rise gently toward the ceiling once more. There, he assumed a lotus position and hovered in place, so still that he appeared to Amanda to be meditating. But whoever this was, he was fully alert, because when Bill Snootman waved through the glass, the figure immediately waved back at him, then pressed a wrist-mounted control. At that, the buoyancy of the air within the chamber seemed to decrease, and the person in the jumpsuit began a graceful, controlled dive toward the floor, rolling upright at the last second and landing perfectly on both feet in a cat-like crouch. A moment later, a hatch to his right opened. The figure stepped out and removed his visored helmet. To Amanda's surprise, this was no "he" at all. A mane of dark hair pulled back into a ponytail framed the high cheekbones and angular jawline of a young woman.

"Amanda," said Bill Snootman, "I'd like you to meet Dr. Hypatia Kovalevsky. Dr. Kovalevsky, Amanda Forsythe."

"Pleased to meet you, Dr. Kovalevsky," said Amanda.

"And I'm very pleased to meet you, Miss Forsythe," said the doctor, smiling warmly as she reached out and shook Amanda's hand. Dr. Kovalevsky's handshake was confident yet unimposing, thought Amanda. This was a person with nothing to prove.

"That was amazing what you were doing in there!"

"I'm glad you liked it," said Dr. Kovalevsky. "But it's not nearly as amazing as what you did. I owe you a big thanks. Because if it weren't for you, I'd be walking around like a drooling zombie, doing chores for aliens instead of working on my space projects."

Amanda had a hard time picturing this intelligent, athletic scientist as a drooling zombie. Still, it was in rare moments like this, when a distinguished stranger like Dr. Kovalevsky acknowledged her accomplishments, that Amanda grasped the impact she, Evelyn, Derek and Sanjay had had on people all over the world. It gave her a jolt of pride, but one tinged with humility; she was still not convinced that other eleven-year-olds wouldn't have done just as well under the same circumstances. But knowing that she had touched people's lives made her more excited than ever about continuing to making a positive contribution to the world.

"Dr. Kovalevsky is doing research on long-distance space travel," said Bill Snootman. "But she's the expert, so I'll let her tell you about it."

"I was just testing out this chamber that I designed," said the doctor. "It uses variable-speed fans to simulate weightless conditions. I'm experimenting with ways to keep our bodies from becoming weak during prolonged periods of weightlessness, because muscles eventually waste away from lack of exercise in a zero-g environment. That will be one of the most serious challenges facing humans in interstellar travel—at least until you build a spaceship fast enough to get us to other galaxies in a couple of weeks."

"Or find a shortcut through some wormholes," added Amanda, thinking of the star map that George had given her, and his hint that if she looked at it carefully enough, she would find a few of those "shortcuts."

"Indeed," said Kovalevsky. "But meanwhile, I'm hoping that with this zero-g workout chamber, I can develop exercises to keep us from shrivelling up like space mummies."

"Could I try it some time?" asked Amanda.

Dr. Kovalevsky smiled. "No time like the present."

She opened a storage compartment, took out a jumpsuit and handed it to Amanda.

"I hope we got your measurements right."

Amanda felt giddy as she saw a nametag reading "Forsythe" stitched to the front of her jumpsuit.

"Cool!" she exclaimed.

"If you think it's cool now, just wait till you're floating in there," replied Dr. Kovalevsky.

"Amazing!" was all Amanda could manage to blurt out as she grinned from ear to ear.

"So what are you waiting for?" asked Dr. Kovalevsky, smiling.

Amanda slipped into the jumpsuit, then put on the astronaut boots and full-coverage helmet that Dr. Kovalevsky handed to her. Once she'd pulled the visor down over her face, she noticed a faint hum from a speaker inside the helmet.

"Can you hear me?" The sound of Dr. Kovalevsky's voice came through the speaker.

"Loud and clear," replied Amanda.

"Good. Our helmets have wireless microphones built into them so we can communicate at all times," said Dr. Kovalevsky. "Most people find weightlessness a little disorienting at first, so if you start feeling uncomfortable in there, just let me know."

Dr. Kovalevsky led her through the hatch at the floor level of the chamber. Amanda felt a heady sensation as she looked up to the roof of the brightly lit, silo-shaped room.

"The walls are padded with rubberized mats, so if you lose control, you shouldn't get banged up too badly," joked Dr. Kovalevsky. "And if you get disoriented and need a minute to sort yourself out, there are recessed handholds built into the walls every metre. But I don't think you've got anything to worry about. Are you ready?"

"I'm so ready I think I could start floating at any moment, even without the fans," said Amanda, barely able to contain her excitement.

"Good, but wait for me to turn them on. Trust me, it will make it so much easier," said Dr. Kovalevsky. "Before we start, I'll give you the rundown on how everything works." She pointed to the left forearm of her jumpsuit, which had a tiny control panel with pressure-sensitive buttons built into it. "These are the controls for the fans. You can vary the speed of every fan in the chamber to create effects ranging from low gravity to zero gravity. There are two ways to leave the chamber—through the hatch we just entered, and through the hatch up at the top. The ceiling hatch is there as a backup device, though I've never had to use it. I designed this chamber, and I inspect it all the time. But you can't be too careful in space—because out there, your first mistake might be your last."

Dr. Kovalevsky pressed several of the buttons on her wrist-control panel. Giant fans embedded behind grates in the walls, floor and ceiling began to rotate, soon building to a roar. Dr. Kovalevsky clicked another button.

"Okay, get ready. I'm increasing the speed of the updraft fans. We'll start to rise in a few seconds."

Dr. Kovalevsky tapped the wrist control. Amanda felt the thrilling, unfamiliar sensation of lightness flowing through her body. She began to laugh as her feet rose a few centimetres off the floor.

"You still with me?" asked Dr. Kovalevsky.

"Totally!" shouted Amanda.

"Good, but if you get freaked out at any point, just call into your microphone or go like this." Dr. Kovalevsky made an X-shaped arm-crossing motion above her face. "That will be your signal to me to cut the power. Now, elevator going up!"

Dr. Kovalevsky tapped the control once more, and this time Amanda felt a gentle twinge in the pit of her stomach as she rose toward the ceiling. When they were about two-thirds of the way up, she heard Kovalevsky's voice once again.

"We're going to level off now."

"Roger that!" said Amanda, savouring the thrill of weightlessness.

"For today, we're going to keep it simple," said the doctor. "Just lie flat on your back."

Amanda did so, and she soon felt the most luxurious sensation she had ever experienced. It was as though she was totally buoyant, floating on the surface of a saltwater lake, carried by gentle waves.

"Now to get oriented, start by tucking your head in and leaning forward, nice and slow."

Amanda did as Dr. Kovalevsky asked, but because she was unaccustomed to the free-floating environment, she leaned forward too suddenly. A moment later she was spinning end over end, so fast that she totally lost her orientation and couldn't tell the floor from the ceiling. Amanda felt herself bounce off the wall, then off the ceiling.

"Whoa, slow down there, cowgirl!" Dr. Kovalevsky called through the headphones. "Spread your arms and legs out so you create some air resistance."

Amanda did so and was relieved to feel her speed decreasing. She gradually came to a halt, floating face down and looking toward the floor.

"Out in space, you could never slow yourself down like you did just now, because up there, there is no air resistance for you to push against," said Dr. Kovalevsky. "So this is actually a more forgiving environment. That means it's not a totally accurate zero-g experience. But it's a start."

"It's a *great* start!" said Amanda.

Her head had stopped spinning now, and having regained her orientation, she enjoyed the gentle sensation of floating. She could see Bill Snootman through the observation window three storeys below. He nervously checked his watch, then gave a small hand signal to Dr. Kovalevsky.

"Looks like our time is up," said Dr. Kovalevsky. "Mr. Snootman requires us on solid ground. So I will gradually reduce the upward thrust. In a few moments, you'll feel yourself sinking. Stay parallel to the floor until I give you the signal."

"Will do," replied Amanda.

Dr. Kovalesky tapped one of the buttons on her wrist control, and a moment later, Amanda felt herself descending toward the floor, as gently as if she were drifting off into a dream. When they were nearing the bottom of the chamber, Dr. Kovalevsky increased the updraft slightly.

"Now gradually turn your feet toward the floor for landing. Keep your legs nice and flexible so they can absorb the impact, just as if you were parachute jumping."

Amanda got into position.

"Okay, we're coming in for touchdown," said the doctor.

When they were about half a metre above the floor, Dr. Kovalevsky cut the power. The cushion of air disappeared and for a brief moment, Amanda felt herself falling straight down. But it was a very small drop, and by adopting the same loose-legged parachutist's stance that Dr. Kovalesky employed, she experienced no more impact than if she had jumped off a footstool.

They removed their helmets.

"That was unbelievable!" shouted Amanda. "I've never felt anything like it before."

"Glad you enjoyed it," replied Dr. Kovalevsky. "A few more sessions and you can fly solo."

"How often can I use this chamber?"

"As often as you want," replied Dr. Kovalevsky. "Just remember why you're here. Your primary mission is very important to Mr. Snootman."

"Don't worry," said Amanda. "I don't think I could possibly forget."

She didn't know if Dr. Kovalevsky was aware of the lawsuit, but after such a pleasant demonstration of weightlessness, she didn't want to spoil the occasion with matters of such gravity.

They exited the chamber and found Bill Snootman checking his watch again.

"Thank you for the demonstration, Dr. Kovalevsky. I'm afraid I have to take Amanda away from you now. Her friends will be arriving shortly."

"And I wouldn't want to keep you from them," said Dr. Kovalevsky warmly. "You must miss them. It's been quite a few months since you've seen them, hasn't it?"

"Yes, and until last week, I was afraid we'd never have a chance to get together again." Amanda couldn't help grinning, knowing that in just a few minutes, she would be reunited with Evelyn, Derek and Sanjay.

"In that case, I shouldn't delay you any longer. See you soon!" said Dr. Kovalevsky.

"Definitely!"

Bill Snootman checked his watch again. "Well, you don't have much longer to wait until you're reunited. According to the signalling device in my watch, their limo has just passed through Gallwater. They should be arriving within two minutes."

Amanda felt her pulse racing at his announcement. He saw her excitement.

"I'll leave you to enjoy your reunion with your friends. I just wanted to have a chance to speak with you first, and to make sure that all the facilities meet with your approval."

"They definitely do," said Amanda.

"If you need anything else, just ask one of my staff. I've set up shop in what used to be Oppenheimer's office. I will be there for the next few weeks, until I know that things are running smoothly."

He handed her a cellphone.

"My number is programmed into this. If you require my assistance, you have full authority to contact me at any hour of the day or night. Once the rest of the students arrive, there will be an assembly in the Constellation Hall. In the meantime, go see your friends. If you need me, I'll be in my office."

"Thanks," said Amanda. She turned and bounded up the stairs two at a time, so excited about seeing Evelyn, Sanjay and Derek that she felt as if she were running on the moon.

CHAPTER 7

AMANDA RACED OUT of the entranceway, passing beneath the crackling Tesla coil sconces just in time to see a stretch limousine with tinted windows make its way up the lane. It pulled close to where she stood, then the driver got out and opened the rear door. Evelyn emerged first, followed by Sanjay and Derek. Amanda ran toward the car.

"Hey, you guys!" she called. "How are you?"

"Oh, we're in rough shape," cried Derek in mock exasperation. "I couldn't possibly eat another crisp! Well, maybe just one more," he said, cradling a large bag of potato chips while shovelling candy bars into his pockets.

"Yes, it was terrible," said Sanjay, his fingers dripping with sugar syrup from an orange coil of Jalebi, an Indian sweet. "That's the best-stocked limousine I've ever ridden in."

"What do you mean? It's the *only* limousine you've ever ridden in!" teased Evelyn, who balanced a cherry cola in one hand while licking a trail of melting pistachio ice cream from a cone she held in the other hand.

"True," he replied. "But if they're all like this, I could get very, very used to it!"

"You're all lucky to be alive," said Amanda wryly. "If the Academy was ten kilometres further away, by the time you got there, you'd be suffering from insulin shock."

Behind them, attendants had already made their way out from the Academy and were helping the driver load the children's luggage from the trunk of the limousine onto a cart.

Derek looked over his shoulder to make sure that no one could overhear them.

"So have you seen Snootman yet?" he asked.

"Yes, he took me on a tour of the Academy."

"And?"

"It's pretty amazing. The facilities are even better than when Oppenheimer was in charge."

"Brill!"

"What about Eugenia?" asked Evelyn. "Did you see her?"

"No, she's not here yet."

Just then, a deep rumble rose up in the distance, a low frequency so intense that they did not hear it so much as feel it. Above them, they heard the clanking of gears. They looked up and saw that the roof of the Academy was opening like a giant clamshell to reveal the section of attic where George had kept his spaceship hidden. This was where Amanda had last spoken to him before he returned to his home planet.

The roar of rotors drew near, and the bulbous snout of a huge freight helicopter hovered into view, poking out above the courtyard wall. The section where the pilot sat was made of glass panels set into a metal framework, and it hung down below the fuselage, which was long and thin all the way to the tail, to make room for external cargo. The craft reminded Amanda of a giant primordial dragonfly. Suspended beneath it on thick steel cables was a large metal container marked "Heavy Equipment."

"Heavy equipment?" shouted Derek. "I wonder what sort of heavy equipment it could be?"

Amanda noticed Bill Snootman in the window of his office, intently watching the helicopter and its cargo. As the helicopter lowered the container toward the roof deck, Snootman leaned forward, anxiously following its progress until it touched down safely on the attic floor. From his expression, Amanda knew exactly what it contained.

"It's not heavy equipment," shouted Amanda over the din of the helicopter engines. The other three turned to her with questioning looks. "It's Eugenia."

None of them spoke for a while after that. They just watched as a worker released the cables from the container. Then the helicopter slowly rose, carefully turned 180 degrees and rumbled away from the Academy. The retractable roof of the school began to close up once again. The four of them stood there, watching as it reverted to the benign appearance of a finely restored piece of Victorian architecture rather than what it really was: a secret device with an even bigger secret inside it.

Snootman's series of carefully orchestrated events continued. As soon as the helicopter had disappeared and the roof had closed, a convoy of luxury coaches with tinted windows rumbled through the gate. Amanda and the others watched as the vehicles lumbered up the winding road through the cemetery to the Academy, stopping near the entrance. The doors of the buses opened, and the rest of the former students began to emerge. A dozen security staff from Snootman Global Enterprises appeared, seemingly from nowhere, to greet them. They were extremely polite to the returning students, treating them not like children but as if they were visiting heads of state or movie stars. Like the two security guards that Amanda had seen outside Eugenia's quarters, they were large and muscular looking, with an imposing air. They wore tinted glasses and communicated with each other through wireless earpieces and microphones hidden in their jacket lapels. The security people formed a line on either side of the entranceway. The kids getting off the buses were clearly feeling both excited and more than a little self-important as the towering guards nodded deferentially and said, "Welcome back. This way, please." And, "Straight into the Constellation Hall, if you would be so kind, sir." And, "Right this way, if you would, miss."

Talking excitedly among themselves, the remaining 195 of the original students walked up the steps into the Academy. From there, other security staff politely ushered the children into the Constellation Hall, handing each student a small, plastic-lined white paper bag as he or she entered.

The Constellation Hall was, as its name suggested, the largest room in the entire building, and the primary gathering place. It was designed to accommodate all two hundred students from the Academy's various classes. With its tall, arched windows, it had always reminded Amanda of a cathedral. As a large security guard escorted her and her friends toward the front of the hall, her gaze was drawn to the ceiling. Over a background of deep midnight blue were thousands of stars in gold leaf, painstakingly textured so each one caught the light in a way that made it seem to twinkle. Amanda found the effect as breathtaking as ever.

Looking at this magnificent rendering, she felt as if she could float straight up into the cosmos. Since her first day at the Academy, she had drawn inspiration and comfort from this reminder of the worlds that lay beyond everyday life, often forgotten but always there, waiting to dazzle those who made time to cast their gaze skyward.

From the start, the Constellation Hall had been Amanda's favourite room, despite what seemed to her to be the fanciful placement of the stars; the constellations, she noted when she first laid eyes on the ceiling, were not where they should be in relation to one another. And they were in the wrong parts of the sky. One constellation even had an extra star in it! But what Amanda had assumed was inaccurate sky mapping was in fact, she later learned, one of George's symbolic gestures. The starscape represented the visible universe as seen from the halfway point between Earth and George's home planet. The "extra star" was our sun. George had meant to reveal this secret to humanity as an act of fraternity between civilizations when the time was right. Sadly, that time never came. But as Amanda looked up at the ceiling now and reacquainted herself with the star patterns, she thought fondly of George, both for his imagination and for his idealism.

The security officer led the four friends to the front row and politely waved his meaty hand to indicate where they should sit. It occurred to Amanda that this was precisely where they had sat the morning they demonstrated their synapse disruptor on Eugenia. She wondered if Snootman had seated them there intentionally.

"Here comes the inner circle," said Derek.

The four children who had been members of Eugenia's entourage were escorted to front-row seats on the opposite side of the Constellation Room, just where they had sat during the assemblies and the synapse-disruptor display. Joules, the boy who had always walked sideways like a crab, stuttering as he cleared a path for Eugenia, was among the group. He gazed around expectantly, then took out the inflatable travel pillow he always brought with him to provide a comfy cushion between Eugenia's privileged derrière and any hard surfaces it might be required to rest upon. He blew into the pillow till his face was the colour of an overripe pomegranate.

"I hope there's a doctor in the house," Derek whispered, "because if the exertion of blowing into the cushion doesn't get him, the news about Eugenia will."

Still struggling to regain his breath, Joules scanned the hall, looking perplexed. Then he set the cushion in a place of honour on the bench, in the centre of the group.

"W-w-where's Eugenia?" he gasped to the others. "I-I h-haven't seen her anywhere. Arsinée, Ethyl, have either of you seen her?"

"No, I haven't, Joules," replied Arsinée.

"Me neither," said Ethyl.

Joules turned to the other boy in their group. "What about you, Henbane?"

"Nada," he said. Then he added, "Wonder what these bags are for, anyway? They look like the ones you see in the seatbacks of airplanes."

"Maybe they're to put money in," said Arsinée. "Because when Eugenia does arrive, I hope she will still have that automated teller machine on wheels with her. After all, she promised to give each of us a million dollars if we stayed friends with her till the end of the school year. But we never got any of it."

"Yes," snapped Ethyl. "At the very least, the amount should be pro-rated for the two months we put up with her. Since the school term is forty weeks, we should be paid nearly two hundred thousand dollars even if we never see her again."

Arsinée did some quick calculations in her head. "Actually, it should be pro-rated at $3,571.43 a day, based on a seven-day week. That's more like $215,000."

"So weekend days count?" asked Ethyl.

"Are you kidding?" said Arsinée sourly. "We should probably set a surcharge for having to spend our leisure time with her too. But don't worry, I'll figure it out."

"H-how can you t-talk that way about Eugenia?" asked Joules, turning like a crab to face them. "E-Eugenia was a g-great leader. And a g-genius in her own right."

"As if you wouldn't have taken the million dollars," said Arsinée.

"It was n-never about the m-money," stammered Joules. "You know that."

Just then, Bill Snootman appeared from the wings, only a few metres away from the children. He was far too close not to have overheard their conversation, which may have been why he had an especially pained look on his face. It certainly was the explanation for the suddenly white faces of Arsinée, Ethyl and Henbane, who, like everyone else in the room, recognized Bill Snootman immediately.

"Don't worry, young man," Snootman told Joules in a kindly tone. "I'm Eugenia's father. All your questions will be answered shortly."

With that, he ascended the stairs and walked toward a podium in the centre of the stage. The room buzzed with excited conversation as children spotted him. The chatter grew to a crescendo as he reached the microphone and gazed out at the assembled group. There was a torrent of applause as a giant video wall lit up behind him, revealing his image in real time, larger than life. As he leaned toward the microphone, the entire room fell silent. No one wanted to miss a single word from the world's richest genius.

"Good afternoon. My name is Bill Snootman, and I'm here to welcome you all back to the Superior Thinking and Advanced Research Academy. It's an honour for me to stand here today before the brightest young minds on Earth. I know that many of you, possibly all of you, will become the household names of tomorrow—the Newtons, the Einsteins, the Teslas, the Bantings, the Bests, the Hawkings and the Curies. The STAR Academy will at last be a major part of helping you achieve those goals.

"As each of you has personally experienced, the work of scientists can be misused by those intent on power. But this is done not just by visitors from other planets. Far from it. Many, many times in the past, the knowledge gained by scientists has been misused by our so-called leaders, both in politics and in industry. This has led us to harm our fellow humans and the other creatures that share this planet with us, instead of helping them. But we have an opportunity here to change all that. Although this institution was led astray by your former headmistress, Dr. Oppenheimer, and her colleague Professor Leitspied, I believe that the original aim of the people who sent them here to educate you was a noble one. And not only a noble one, but a critically important one. With all the calamities that humankind faces—climate change, overpopulation, pandemics, the end of fossil fuels and on and on—we scientists have a more important role than ever to play as custodians of the planet and the life forms it supports. And it is only through scientific co-operation that we will find the answers to those problems. Make no mistake: your research here is vital to the entire planet. The work we do now and in the years to come will determine whether future generations will inhabit a world that is a living hell or a paradise on Earth. I am determined that together, we shall make it the latter and not the former."

At that, the students broke out in applause. Bill Snootman smiled.

"Before I go any further, I should point out that all of you owe a debt to a certain young woman for persuading me that it would be worth the expense of bringing you all here to solve the problem that is before us. Amanda Forsythe, would you stand up, please, and take a bow?"

Amanda rose rather shyly and waved to the crowd. The students broke out in cheers and applause—though she did notice that Eugenia's clique was somewhat less enthusiastic, and she thought she saw Arsinée and Ethyl whispering to each other, snide expressions on their faces. Amanda ignored them, bowed to her fellow students and took her seat.

"Way to go," said Evelyn, tapping her on the shoulder.

"Nice work!" added Derek.

Sanjay leaned over behind him to nod agreement and gave her the thumbs-up sign.

Bill Snootman smiled at Amanda, then continued.

"As under the previous STAR Academy administration, you will be given the resources to develop your individual projects. But you will also work on an assigned project. For this, you will not be attempting to create synapse disruptors or energy transmission beams, but rather will be studying DNA and helping solve certain vexing scientific puzzles. This is an area of study that is of particular interest to me, and it is the reason that I have agreed to pay all your living expenses and fund your research while you are here. It is my hope that with help from your new professors, you will form something never before seen on Earth: a huge brain trust functioning like one vast super-mind. The intelligence that collectively exists within this room will then be brought to bear on a problem that is of particular urgency and importance to me—the nature of which I am finally about to reveal."

There was a murmur of anticipation throughout the hall.

"I must therefore now remind you that as stated in the agreements you and your parents or guardians signed, you will not now or at any time in the future divulge what I'm about to reveal to anyone outside the Academy—media, friends, relatives, even your own mothers and fathers. Anyone violating that agreement will, as you are all aware, be faced with a $100-million lawsuit. And just to show you I am sincere, I'll now introduce the gentlemen from the legal firm that represents me: Barratry, Hentchman and Goldstiel."

A spotlight faded up on three serious-looking men in suits standing to Snootman's right. The first lawyer, Barratry, attempted a smile. But his facial movements made him look like a shark pulling back its lips and baring its teeth as it prepared to strike. Hentchman didn't even acknowledge the children, and instead picked at some dead skin on his fingertips, apparently unconcerned with the social niceties of being presented to a group of two hundred people. Goldstiel, a thin, balding man with severe wired-rimmed glasses, methodically scanned the crowd, his frosty blue eyes seeming to memorize each child's face. Amanda felt an uncomfortable chill when his gaze settled on her for a moment—taking her in as if filing away her details to use against her later.

"These three men have amassed the most impressive record in the world for successfully litigating dubious lawsuits," continued Snootman. "For example, they were responsible for having an innocent farmer convicted of theft after genetically modified seeds belonging to their client, an aggressive agribusiness, blew onto the farmer's field, took root and killed off his existing plants. Not coincidentally, the damages awarded to their client were precisely equal in value to the farmer's lands and machinery, forcing him to sell the farm that had been in his family for five generations, leaving him penniless."

Barratry and Goldstiel gave each other a wink and a little smile as they playfully pointed their fingers at each other and bent their thumbs like they were each pulling the trigger on a pistol.

"You *bad*!" mouthed Barratry.

"No, *you* bad!" came the mimed response from Goldstiel.

They grinned like schoolboys.

"These gentlemen," continued Snootman, "also brought about the downfall of a democratically elected Third World government when it tried to ban a known cancer-causing chemical manufactured by another company they represent. Additionally, they bankrupted a family-owned dry-cleaning business for losing a pair of pants belonging to one of their most litigious clients. The parents are now living on welfare and were forced to put their youngest child up for adoption."

The kids in the Constellation Hall were beginning to look bewildered.

"Now," continued Snootman, "you may think it unethical that these three gentlemen brought about the ruin of hard-working, honest people for what seem like mean-spirited and frivolous reasons. So do I. In fact, I think what these men did is absolutely despicable. But that is *precisely* why I hired them. I recognized in them an absolutely reptilian disregard for the common good, a concern for only the narrowest interpretations of the law, rather than the remotest consideration for the intent of the law itself. On top of that, these three men know that I find them repugnant. Yet they do not care, so focused are they on their fiduciary duties, no matter how inhumane those duties may be. You may be the smartest children in the entire world, but I assure you that where lawsuits are concerned, you are no match for the world's three most sociopathically devoted litigation lawyers. So listen to me very carefully . . ."

Some of the children were now white-faced with fear. Others trembled. One was breathing into the bag he had been given.

"Break your oath with me, and these three men will ensure that you, your grandparents, your parents, your children and your children's children will be reduced to living on the streets, sleeping under bridges, wearing rags and eating out of garbage cans."

Bill Snootman let the silence hang for a long moment, allowing the children to shift nervously in their seats, giving their bright, imaginative minds time to fully envision the grim consequences of crossing him. Then the spotlight on the lawyers dimmed and they faded from view.

Snootman continued his speech. "I mention this not to terrorize you but to remind you that we have a contract that is not to be broken. If you abide by it, you and your families will have nothing to fear. Indeed, if you keep your promise, each of you can look forward to a future of stellar success and wealth. I will personally guarantee it."

The room breathed a collective sigh of relief.

"And now," said Bill Snootman gravely, "on to that secret I promised to reveal. I confess here and now that enlightened self-interest lies behind my decision to reopen the Academy and invite you all to it on full scholarships. I truly do care about all those pressing issues I mentioned. But the matter that is of greatest personal importance to me concerns my daughter, Eugenia. Some of you were her colleagues in Team Alhacen. Others were her friends."

As he said the word "friends," Bill Snootman turned his gaze onto Arsinée and Ethyl. Both girls stared down at the floor, shamefaced. They squirmed in their chairs, no doubt thinking about Barratry, Hentchman and Goldstiel and wishing that they'd never uttered their caustic comments about Eugenia's money.

"So you may wonder," continued Snootman, "why you do not see her sitting here among you. Well, the reason is that in the hour before the aliens fled the STAR Academy, there was an incident involving Headmistress Oppenheimer, Professor Leitspied and my daughter. As you will recall, Eugenia had a keen scientific interest in hybrid life forms and a gift for gene splicing. She was very impressed by the aliens' intellectual powers. Wanting to gain some of their mental prowess, and unaware of what they looked like when in their true alien form, she procured some of their DNA and—with their aid—spliced it directly into her own body."

A murmur rose up from the 195 children in the room who did not already know about Eugenia's ill-considered attempt at improving on what nature had given her.

"Consequently, Eugenia began to take on the physical form of the aliens. The transformation would have been total were it not for the intervention of the alien you knew as George. He was somehow able to halt it before it became complete. But in his haste to avoid capture by Earthly authorities, George had to flee in his spaceship before he was able to carry out whatever bio-reversal process would have returned Eugenia to her original state."

There were more whispers throughout the hall.

"So without further ado, I would like each of you to turn your gaze to the video wall behind me. There, you shall see the result of the gene splice. I preface this by saying that if you were not about to be directly involved in the effort to restore Eugenia to her normal condition, I would never subject you to what you are about to see. I warn you: it is a disturbing sight. But it is why you have all had your scholarships paid for. Now, is everyone ready?"

Some students quietly mouthed a nervous "yes." Others sat there stone-faced. A few crossed their arms, looking cocky, as if there was nothing in the universe that could possibly surprise them.

"Very well, then," said Snootman.

Derek leaned in close to Amanda and whispered, "I think some of these brainiacs are about to figure out what those white bags are for."

Bill Snootman walked offstage so everyone would have a clear view of the video wall. On cue, the Constellation Hall was plunged into darkness. The video wall at the back of the stage pulsed with light, and an image began to fade up. At first, the students strained in their seats, trying to make out the dim picture.

Then, as the giant monitor grew brighter, gasps of disbelief and revulsion filled the hall. The face on the screen was unmistakably that of Eugenia Snootman. Her hair, as always, was perfectly coiffed. And her professionally applied makeup created the effect of beauty—or as close to that as was possible on a girl whose eyes were small and too close together, who had a pointy nose and a sharp chin, and whose thin lips seemed perpetually ready to stretch into a sneer. The gasps were caused not by Eugenia's carefully art-directed face, however, but by what it was attached to from the chin down: a hideous, eight-legged exoskeletal body that looked something like that of an Alaskan king crab. The unearthly mutant version of Eugenia stood as tall as a man on its spindly legs and was thrashing around a padded room. Catching sight of her reflection in the camera lens, what was left of Eugenia gazed out beseechingly, her expression uncharacteristically vulnerable. Every student in the room, including Amanda, Derek, Evelyn and Sanjay, winced at the sight of that marooned face staring sadly into their own. Then the video image of Eugenia opened her mouth as if to speak. But instead of words, all that came out was the terrifying shriek of two high-pitched and horribly discordant notes, like those of an air-raid siren. Overwhelmed by the sight of her own hideous reflection, the mutant Eugenia burst into panic, thrashing around the padded room on her eight legs, banging into the walls and screeching as she flailed about.

Derek was right. It didn't take the ultra-geniuses long to deduce the purpose of the white airsickness bags. And that was a good thing, because a number of them had to put the accessory to immediate use.

In the front row, meanwhile, Joules rose from his seat and

threw himself toward the stage, crying, "Eugenia! N-no! No! It c-can't be so!"

Sinking to his knees, he tore at his lab coat and wrung his hands, pounding his fists on the floor.

"Oh, Eugenia," he wailed, "I'm s-sorry I never told you that I l-l-love you, and that I worship the ground you walk on. I do. I *do*! I was just too . . . *afraid* of you to t-tell you!"

Arsinée stood up. "Joules, for heaven's sake, get up off the floor," she hissed. "Your behaviour is totally unscientific and irrational. Pull yourself together or people will think you're intellectually normally abled! And that will reflect badly on all of us."

Her admonition did nothing whatever to calm Joules, who now clambered onto the stage and staggered to the video wall. He gently caressed the giant image of the eleven-year-old girl's face and said, "Oh, Eugenia! If only it could have been m-me instead of y-you!"

Joules shook from the sobs, tears running down his face.

"Stop it, you big ninny!" snapped Arsinée, her voice dripping with disgust.

Bill Snootman quickly emerged from the wings and nodded to an unseen technician. The image on the video wall faded to black, and the room lights came up. Snootman put a consoling arm around Joules's shoulder. The boy suddenly realized that he was the centre of attention and turned an even deeper shade of crimson than he had been when blowing up the cushion.

"It's all right, son. No need to be embarrassed," said Snootman. "In fact, your devotion gives me hope. Anyone who feels the way you do will surely give it his all. I'm certain there are many, many people in this room who love Eugenia just as much as we do. And we all want the best for her."

Amanda noticed a tiny grin creeping onto Derek's face. It was the kind of grin that always crept onto his face right before he made one of his trademark wisecracks.

She gave him a warning glance. "If you make me laugh, I'll splice some tapeworm DNA into you when you're asleep."

"I didn't say a word," said Derek, grinning even more.

Meanwhile, on Bill Snootman's command, a towering security guard gently led a sobbing Joules back to his chair.

"That's a good lad," whispered the guard. "Mr. Snootman appreciates blind devotion."

Bill Snootman stepped to centre stage once again and addressed the students. "I realize that was very disturbing, but it was necessary in order to convey to you the scope of the problem. Now, I think that after the stress of your trip and what you've just seen, you all deserve a break. You can have the rest of the day to get settled in. You will occupy the same dormitories that you had in the past. Your baggage has been taken to your rooms, so please feel free to settle in. Dinner will be served at 6:00 p.m. in the cafeteria. For those of you who would like some entertainment, we will be showing several very exciting films in the Constellation Hall at 7:00 p.m. After that, it will be off to bed and lights out. You've all had a big day, and you'll have a big day tomorrow too as you begin your studies. So I want to make sure you get your rest. Thank you very much."

With that, Snootman walked offstage. The students applauded considerably more weakly than they had when he took the stage ten minutes earlier.

Derek turned around in his seat and took in the view of the stunned crowd. "Crikey, look at all those shell-shocked faces," he said.

Sanjay nodded. "I don't know what shook them up more—seeing an eight-legged Eugenia, or that bloodthirsty pack of lawyers Snootman's got working for him."

"I think either one of them would be enough do the trick," said Amanda.

"Oh, well," said Evelyn. "Movies always help me forget my worries. I hope it's a good one."

"Me too," said Amanda, though she didn't think there was any movie in the universe that could take her mind off the magnitude of the problem that lay before them.

Derek slouched in the beanbag chair next to the fireplace in Amanda and Evelyn's dorm, a lopsided grin on his face. "Well, dinner wasn't too bad, though certainly not as good as when George was in charge of the kitchen."

"I know," added Sanjay. "I have to say, I miss the in vitro meat. And it's strange to see people working behind the counter after getting used to George's automated system. But it was not too shabby nonetheless." He shook his head incredulously. "That movie was another story, though."

"Yeah, can you believe that?" said Derek. "It's amazing that even someone as strange as Snootman would consider a film with a title like *Deoxyribonucleic Acid and You* to be 'entertainment.'"

"Perhaps it got more interesting after the first forty-five minutes," said Evelyn.

"I very much doubt that," replied Sanjay.

"Maybe there's something good to watch here," said

Amanda. "Snootman told me that he stocked each room with a library of five hundred movies."

"Good. See if there's some science fiction," said Derek.

"Science fiction? Why?" asked Evelyn, her nose crinkling as though someone had just conducted an experiment with skunks and rotten eggs in their dorm. "The people who write those stories never know anything about science. You have to constantly suspend your disbelief."

"That's precisely the point," said Derek. "I *want* to suspend my disbelief. I want a story where an author who knows nothing about science writes about it in some totally whacked way that couldn't possibly happen but is entertaining nonetheless."

"That sounds foolish," said Evelyn, turning her gaze to her pet mouse, Lelie, who was back in the aquarium by the night table. "I'd rather look at Lelie frolicking in his oxygenated liquid environment than subject myself to some silly story that breaks all the rules of science."

"Well, in that case, I think you're going to get your wish," said Amanda, glancing through the list of titles. "Here are some of the movies in our library: *Double Heroes of the Double Helix: The Men Who Unlocked the Secret of DNA*."

"Argh!" said Sanjay.

"How about *Perplexing Polyplexes*?" asked Amanda.

"Next!" called out Derek.

"Anyone for *Oligarchy of the Oligonucleotides*?"

"Oy, that's not entertainment," said Derek. "That's not even a diversion. That's mental torture, that is!"

Amanda scanned the list. "Well, I'm afraid it doesn't get any better—unless *Thrilling Thymines* grabs you." She gazed at her friends' befuddled expressions. "I'll take that as a no."

"If that's Snootman's idea of relaxation," said Derek, "he must be out of his mind already."

"Or desperate," said Amanda. "Very, very desperate."

The others paused to consider that. Then Evelyn broke the silence.

"Who's for some hot cocoa?"

This suggestion went over much better than the choice of films, so she went to their small kitchen and began preparing it. Meanwhile, Amanda set about lighting a fire. She took some kindling, a bit of scrap paper and a couple of logs and had it going within seconds. By the time Evelyn was finished making the cocoa, the room was bathed in a comforting orange glow from the fireplace.

Evelyn smiled, enjoying the warmth from the hearth. "I'd forgotten about your uncanny skills with combustion. How do you manage to light those fires so easily?"

"It's just physics," said Amanda, "and an understanding of the fire tetrahedron: fuel, heat and oxygen, and the chemical chain reaction they produce. Most people remember the fuel and the heat but forget the oxygen. You've got to have lots of split kindling so the air can get in around the fuel. It's simple, really. Similar principle to a jet engine."

Evelyn laughed. "'Similar principle to a jet engine,' she says. I'm so glad we're all together again. I've missed our conversations."

"Me too," said Derek, lifting his mug of hot cocoa. "I propose a toast. To Amanda, for having the smarts to take a bad situation and turn it into a way of bringing us all together again at the STAR Academy."

"Yes, to Amanda, for bringing us together again," said Sanjay.

"Thanks, guys," said Amanda. The four of them clinked their mugs together. They all took a sip and savoured the sweet, rich cocoa.

"But really," she said, "it's Eugenia who is responsible for us all being here."

"That's true," said Evelyn, "but I can't quite bring myself to drink a toast to her."

"Me neither," added Sanjay. "I'd never have thought in a million years that we'd have anything to thank her for."

"Well, back in England," said Derek, "there's an old expression: even a broken watch on one of the eight legs of a mutant alien girl with a bad attitude tells the correct time twice a day."

"Derek, that's *so wrong*!" said Amanda. Then she smiled slyly and added, "But so right."

From there, the conversation of the four reunited friends evolved into a pleasantly meandering discussion of underwater cities, medical nanobots, space-based optical devices and interstellar manned spacecraft. Then they decided to make it an early night so they'd be ready for their first day.

As Derek and Sanjay stood in the doorway preparing to leave, Amanda and Evelyn bid them good night. "And if you lose any of your nanobots," said Amanda, "don't come running back here with stories of Bill Snootman being an alien. I'm too tired to deal with it till tomorrow."

"Me too," said Evelyn. "I'm so tired I think it would be wonderful if someone *did* shut off my brain."

"Careful what you wish for," said Sanjay.

And with that, the two boys sauntered off down the hall toward their own dorm.

Amanda closed the door so she and Evelyn could get

ready for bed. Amanda changed into her favourite pajamas, the ones with the stars and planets on them. Then the girls slipped into their beds and, tired after their long day, were soon both fast asleep.

CHAPTER 8

As AMANDA WALKED INTO her old homeroom class the next morning, she experienced a strange sensation. It felt like one of those dreams where things are familiar, but nothing is quite the way it's supposed to be. Gone were George's incredible moving holograms of endangered animals. The sheets of glass upon which they had appeared were still there, but they were opaque and lifeless. And gone too, of course, was Professor Leitspied, who had inspired so many students with her lectures but turned out to be so cunning that Amanda hadn't wanted to believe the truth about her until it was almost too late.

Now occupying Leitspied's place at the front of the classroom was a small, elderly man in a tweed jacket. He wore large glasses with thick lenses that magnified his twinkling eyes. His pleasant face was framed by a mop of grey hair that gave him the appearance of a grandfatherly lion.

As Amanda sat down with Evelyn at a workstation, she noticed that the students had divided themselves into two groups. On one side of the room was the former Team Alhacen, and on the other was the team that Amanda had led, Prometheus. It was the intramural fault line that Oppenheimer and Leitspied had created to spur the students to work harder by competing for academic honours. Amanda hoped it was only force of habit that made the students divide themselves so, and not some underlying distrust created by their former rivalry. As the last of the students settled into their seats, the elderly man spoke.

"Hello, and welcome to my classroom. Or I should say, welcome back to *your* old classroom. My name is Dr. Okina, and I'm here to teach you the basics of DNA, the building blocks of life. It will be your challenge to use the knowledge you gain here to save a girl from a terrible fate."

Save *two* girls from a terrible fate, thought Amanda.

"To aid in your quest, you have thousands of helpers," said Dr. Okina.

Amanda and the others were puzzled. Some of the kids looked around, as though they expected to see technicians appearing out of the woodwork. Dr. Okina smiled.

"No, I don't mean human assistants. It is my belief that everything you need to know about this vast subject, you can learn from these tiny creatures." With a flourish, he removed a cloth cover from a clear tank. Amanda saw that it was swarming with fruit flies feeding off small heaps of what appeared to be rotting mangoes, oranges and something so putrid that she couldn't even guess what it had once been.

"Cor, it's like garbage day at New Covent Garden Market," whispered Derek.

"Gross! They're everywhere!" said Evelyn, covering her mouth as she retched.

"Yes, they *are* everywhere," Dr. Okina replied. "And I have come to value them like flying treasure. Because humble though they may be, these creatures share 90 percent of our genes. And despite their tiny size, they have huge chromosomes, so they're easier to study than other species. An entire new generation can be produced every sixteen days. So using these creatures, one can study the effects of gene manipulation with a speed that would be impossible in any other higher organism. Allow me to demonstrate."

Dr. Okina opened the lid of the tank and reached in with a tiny butterfly net in pursuit of a single specimen. However, there were so many fruit flies teeming about the tank that merely opening the lid for a few seconds allowed a small cloud of them to escape, a fact to which Dr. Okina seemed oblivious. Amanda, Derek, Evelyn and Sanjay all exchanged a silent look, wondering if the professor noticed the fruit flies now buzzing around above his curly grey hair like a halo. Apparently he did not. Instead, he squinted through his thick glasses into the net and, with a pair of tweezers, extracted a single fruit fly. Then he opened the lid of the tank once again and emptied the contents of the butterfly net back into it. In the process, he released even more flies into the classroom, another accident of which he seemed to be completely unaware. After a long and rather ponderous discussion of the merits of fruit flies, Dr. Okina concluded his lecture.

"That's all for today," he said. "I look forward to unlocking this puzzle with you. Now, your next teacher, Professor Thorne, is waiting for you in Room 4D. Good luck."

Dr. Okina smiled at them and waved, oblivious to a couple of fruit flies that were settling on the upper rim of his glasses.

☆

"That was weird," said Derek as they left the room. "I mean, he seems a nice enough bloke, but . . ."

"I wonder if he's some kind of savant?" mused Amanda.

"Don't you have to be smart about at least one thing to be considered a savant?" asked Sanjay.

"I'm just glad he's only keeping flies, and not poisonous snakes," said Evelyn. "His containment techniques definitely leave something to be desired."

"I hope Snootman's not off his nut when it comes to finding expert help," said Derek.

Amanda nodded as she considered the implications. She couldn't afford for any of them, including Snootman, to make mistakes.

"Well, here we are," said Evelyn, pointing out the "4D" marker affixed above the doorway of what had been a test laboratory when Oppenheimer was headmistress.

Amanda, Evelyn, Derek and Sanjay filed in with the other students. Standing at the far end of the room, next to a video blackboard, was a tall, gaunt man. His back was ramrod straight, but his head hung forward between his shoulders. His hair was grey, slicked back and had an oily sheen. His skin was a similar hue, but had a waxy rather than oily appearance. The greyness of his hair and skin was intensified by his crisp white lab coat. The overall effect was of someone embalmed—an impression made even more disturbing by his penetrating blue eyes, which moved alertly in their sockets behind his sallow eyelids, as if he were a skeletal robot lurking beneath the skin of a cadaver.

In front of him were tanks containing various parts of different creatures growing in yellowish nutrient solutions. Tiny bubbles made wet gurgling sounds as they broke the surface. The way the man narrowed his eyes, appraising his students as they filed into the classroom, gave Amanda the creeps. She wouldn't have been completely surprised to learn that he had recently emerged from the depths of one of these tanks himself. There was something so unsettling about him that Amanda didn't even dare whisper her thoughts to Evelyn, who walked silently up the aisle just behind her. The nervous students headed wordlessly to their workstations with none of their usual lively between-class chatter. Even Derek didn't utter a single word, let alone make one of his trademark wisecracks. Amanda guessed that he had already formulated a wry witticism about this strange apparition at the head of the class, but perhaps he thought it advisable to wait for a more private moment before daring to open his mouth.

The kids took their seats. The man in the lab coat folded his arms and walked back and forth, staring at his students as though they were specimens. Finally, he took his place behind a tank full of what appeared to be large white slugs.

"My name," he began, "is Professor Thorne. And for the duration of your time here, I will be your mentor in all things to do with gene modification and splicing. Now, before we begin, there's one fundamental concept I want you to understand: nature is a crapshoot—a fact that all but those who are themselves genetically predisposed to extinction should be able to plainly see."

He paused, evidently waiting for a laugh. But the students were too nervous to respond.

Thorne twisted his mouth sourly, then continued, "There are winners, and there are losers. But the odds are against most random mutations. It's a safe bet that at some point in the history of Earth, most species in existence will lose by becoming extinct. Even among those 'winning' species that don't fade away, most individual members are losers. Either through disease, competition or by becoming lunch for something else, they never get a chance to pass on their DNA. It doesn't matter how you cut the cards. Even with the fittest creatures transmitting their DNA to subsequent generations, there will be many failures and dead ends. The evolutionary roll of the dice, so to speak, will create more losers than winners."

He took a pair of dice out of his pocket and rattled them together. Then he looked around at the faces of the students, most of whom were staring down at their desks to avoid Thorne's prickly gaze. His eyes came to rest on Derek.

"You, young man. Pick a number between two and twelve."

"Seven," responded Derek without hesitation.

"Seven," said Thorne, rolling the word around in his mouth. "Did you choose it out of superstition—perhaps believing it to be a lucky number?"

"No," replied Derek. "I chose it because it has the greatest odds of coming up on the roll of two dice, since it can be created from the greatest number of combinations: 1 + 6, 2 + 5, 3 + 4, 4 + 3, 5 + 2, 6 + 1. That gives me a one in six chance of guessing correctly."

Thorne placed the dice in Derek's hand.

"How very clever of you, young man. Now roll them."

Derek shook the dice, then dropped them on the surface of his lab station.

Thorne examined them. Each die had a single dot facing up.

"Oh, snake eyes! Too bad! Not even close to seven, even though you gave yourself the best odds possible—because they were still stacked six to one against you," said Thorne. "Evolutionarily speaking, you're a squirrel with an OCA1A gene mutation—better known as an albino. Instead of dull grey or black fur, you have beautiful white fur. Just imagine how wonderfully that nice white fur will stand out to predators in the green and grey of the forest. You might as well be wearing a big red sign saying 'Eat me!' So you do not pass Go. You do not collect two hundred dollars. And you certainly do not live long enough to pass on your DNA. You'll be lucky to make it to the end of the week without being devoured by your enemies."

Thorne picked up the dice and began to pace up and down the aisles, clicking them together. His manner was so intimidating that all the students averted their gaze as he passed by.

"Of course, even a creature that is perfectly adapted to flourish in one environment may utterly lack the correct attributes for survival in another," said Thorne. "Take the polar bear, for example. His white fur works very well for him in the Arctic. He's the top predator, a voracious force of nature feared by every creature there. But place that same polar bear atop the Great Barrier Reef, without an ice floe to take refuge on, and by high tide he's nothing more than shark food, as helpless as a kitten in a rain barrel. So genetically defined abilities that help you in one set of circumstances may not assist you in others. To demonstrate, I need someone to help me. Someone highly intelligent. Well, I suppose that's any of you—that is, if intelligence tests devised by aliens are to be believed. So, let's see . . . Miss Forsythe, your reputation precedes you. Might you be so kind as to offer me your assistance?"

"Certainly," replied Amanda, trying not to sound nervous.

"Please approach the in vitro tank in front of me," said Thorne.

Amanda stood up and walked to the front of the classroom.

"Very good," he said. "Now, I understand that some people say you're the smartest person in the world. What an incredible stroke of genetic luck! You must be extremely proud of yourself."

Amanda considered his statement for a moment, then said, "If it's just genetic luck, there's not much to be proud of."

"Yet everyone acknowledges your genius. Building transmitters to send power through the air, designing photon-sail spaceships, adapting language-translation software to speak to an alien—your success at defeating the interplanetary invaders and your precocious scientific achievements have been trumpeted in countless newspapers and on television and the Internet. In laughably dumbed-down language for the lunkheaded masses, granted. But nonetheless, we all heard about it. How very impressive."

"Thank you," said Amanda quietly, suspecting that behind Thorne's compliment was a pendulum about to swing in the opposite direction.

Thorne looked at the class. "Now, I want the rest of you to watch closely." He returned his gaze to Amanda. "Do you know what a blastema is?" he asked gruffly.

"No, I don't," she replied.

Thorne put on a rubber glove, rolled up the sleeve of his lab coat and reached into a tank of liquid. He pulled out a gelatinous white object the size of small trout.

"Would you be so kind as to hold out your hands with the palms facing up," said Thorne.

Amanda did as she was told. Without warning, he dropped the wet, viscous object into her hands. Kids in the front row recoiled as drops of fluid splashed onto them. Amanda flinched at the feeling of this slimy, squishy object in her hands. Thorne looked at her with an intense gaze. She sensed that he was waiting for her to gag or show some sign of weakness. But she refused to give him the satisfaction, and instead held her hands steady, as if the sloppy white blob were nothing stranger than a pocket calculator.

"That, Miss Forsythe, is a blastema. It could potentially develop into anything: a jellyfish, a cat or a *photon-sail scientist*. But it lacks the correct cellular instructions, so it will remain what it is—just a blob. Do you think you have what it takes to turn this into a sentient creature?"

"I can try."

"Yes, you *can* try," said Thorne tartly. "But it won't get you anywhere—because this is *not* a blastema. This is a cellulose substance produced by an acetic bacterial colony. Otherwise known as mother of vinegar, it can be found in half the kitchens in this country. But you didn't know that, did you?"

"No, I didn't," confessed Amanda.

Some of the former members of Eugenia's entourage and Team Alhacen found their old habits hard to give up and snickered at Amanda.

"Some super-genius," muttered Henbane, who was seated behind Joules, Arsinée and Ethyl.

"Put a beaker in it, you prang," whispered Derek icily.

"And the reason you didn't know that, Miss Forsythe," said Thorne, "is because this is not your area of study. Even your big mind has not equipped you to deal with this problem. You're as helpless as a polar bear standing knee-deep in fifteen centimetres of water on a coral reef with the tide coming in and the sharks circling." He snatched the mother of vinegar from her hands. "Be seated."

As she turned and walked back toward her workstation, Amanda could feel her face getting hot. She hated that sensation, because she knew it meant that her cheeks were turning red and betraying her emotions.

"Don't mind him, he's just a prat," Derek whispered to her as she took her seat.

Thorne stepped on the pedal of a waste bin so the lid clattered open. Then he made a show of dismissively dropping the blob into the pail.

"There. It's just rubbish. No use to anyone whatever, except to make a point." He stared harshly at his students. "To summarize, nature in her supposedly infinite wisdom creates life willy-nilly, and most of it is doomed to failure. It's all a spin of the cosmic roulette wheel. But science is not. It's the role of genetic engineering to stack the odds so we win every time. While you are in my class, this is something you will all remember. With gene manipulation, we can create plants and animals that grow faster and are resistant to pests and disease. We can create humans who are stronger and smarter, impervious to illness, who can even hibernate in such a deep state of torpor as to create the outward appearance of death, if circumstances require it, until more advantageous living conditions exist for them. Meanwhile, you children will be pushed to achieve to the best of your genetically inherited abilities. Because Mr. Snootman has gambled on you and your talents by reopening this very expensive school and paying for all of you to come here to study. It's my job to make certain that his bet pays off. Dismissed."

The room was immediately filled with the sounds of chairs scraping and feet hurrying as the students, eager to escape Thorne's abrasive presence, quickly stood up and made for the door. This was in marked contrast to previous times, when Professor Leitspied's spellbinding lectures had kept the students lingering, hoping that she might have just a little more to say, just a little more wisdom to impart.

Amanda was almost at the exit when Thorne called after her.

"Miss Forsythe," he said brusquely, not bothering to look up from a tank of organs, "would you be so kind as to wait behind."

"Yes, Professor," Amanda answered.

She reluctantly headed back toward the front of the classroom. Derek, Evelyn and Sanjay hovered in the doorway, waiting for her.

"I require only Miss Forsythe's presence," said Thorne. "You three can leave. And close the door behind you."

"We'll wait for you in the cafeteria," said Evelyn.

"I've got a feeling that this is another of those times when it's preferable to be one of those 'three other kids,'" whispered Sanjay.

Derek was the last one out. He caught Amanda's eye, then shoved his shoulders up stiffly in imitation of Thorne, sticking his neck out and making a face that gave him the appearance of a constipated giraffe. Amanda had to bite her lip to keep from laughing. Derek winked and closed the door behind him.

Thorne removed his rubber gloves with a loud snap, then turned to Amanda. "Miss Forsythe, I'll be frank with you. I believe your talents are highly overrated. I don't see evidence of any special abilities that would make you a potential authority on DNA and gene splicing."

"I never claimed to have any special expertise," replied Amanda. "It's not my area of study. But—"

"And that is abundantly clear to me," huffed Thorne, cutting her off. "I know your kind. I've seen them gloating over their so-called accomplishments in every institute of technology from here to Tokyo. Your science is all about machinery; it comes down to levers, pulleys, wheels and screws. Any monkey can manipulate machinery given enough time. But manipulating the building blocks of life itself—that's *real* science."

Amanda felt the same sense of searing humiliation that she had felt when Principal Murkly and Mrs. Wheedlbum had mocked her science fair project on photon-sail spacecraft the year before. Only this time, she wasn't going to take it.

"I'd like to see you try to manipulate those building blocks of life while you are freezing in the dark, without light bulbs or heat or electron microscopes or precision instruments," she replied without missing a beat.

Thorne's nostrils flared and his eyes narrowed as he gave her a furious look. "I don't know what Snootman thinks he's up to with this program, but the odds are that you and your little friends will achieve nothing except to separate him from his fortune." He spat out the words as if they were sour milk. "If it weren't for the generous endowment he gave the university to which I am attached, they would never have agreed to release me. And if it weren't for the fact that he's paying me five times my usual salary, I would never have agreed to tutor the likes of you!"

"Well, how lucky for us, then, that Mr. Snootman was able to find the one thing in the world that would persuade you to lower yourself to our level," Amanda shot back.

Thorne's face looked like a big red balloon that was about to burst. Then he regained control of his emotions, though barely enough to speak. His voice became a raspy, caustic whisper.

"I'll have my eye on you, Forsythe. And if I think that you're not giving me 100 percent, or that you're not *capable* of giving me 100 percent, I will not hesitate to tell Bill Snootman to put you on his next private jet back to Dumbview, or whatever you call that backwater you come from. That's all. You can go."

Amanda's face stung as if it were being pricked with hot pins. She knew that Thorne wanted to see her cry, but she refused to give him the satisfaction.

He turned away from her and stomped off to the front corner of the room, to a workstation that was angled so only he could see the screen of his computer. There, he put on headphones and gazed intently at something on the monitor. He began to click furiously on his mouse. Amanda could hear a series of strange beeps coming from his computer. Normally, it would have aroused her curiosity, but right now, she just wanted to get out of there and away from Thorne as quickly as she could. She was never happier to close a door behind her than when she exited the classroom that day.

Amanda sat in her armchair, absent-mindedly twisting a lock of her long, wavy hair.

"No one has been so dismissive of me since Wheedlbum and Murkly back at Downview Public School," she said. "Thorne as much as said I'm an idiot."

"Forget it," said Derek. "He's just an old geezer."

"Exactly," agreed Evelyn. "He's precisely the kind of geneticist Snootman was talking about. Too set in his ways to appreciate new ways of thinking."

"Yeah, at home we would call him a *khoosat*," added Sanjay.

The others looked at him questioningly.

"An old fart," he explained. "Plus he's probably jealous of you too. I bet the film offers aren't exactly rolling in for him."

"Except maybe as an extra in a zombie flick," said Derek. "You see how grey his skin is? I'm afraid to get too close to him in case it's feeding time for the undead."

"Yes, maybe all those body parts he's growing in the nutrient tanks are actually his lunch," said Evelyn.

Derek jerked his arms stiffly like a zombie, made an angry giraffe face and chanted in a low zombie voice, "Mmmm, must have blastema! Must have blastema!"

Amanda laughed, finally, from the combined effect of their jokes about Thorne. Sitting in her favourite armchair, in the coziness of her dorm room, surrounded by her best friends, she felt her mood lighten at last. A couple of logs crackled in the fireplace, taking the chill off the night air and filling the room with a warm orange glow. Sanjay had made a pot of Indian masala chai tea. He poured out four steaming cups of it, took one for himself and handed the other three round to his friends. Amanda sipped the hot, sweet tea and felt better as soon as the spicy combination of cardamom, cinnamon, ginger, pepper and anise tickled her tongue. The sting of the incident with Thorne was at last beginning to fade—though not entirely.

"The thing is, Thorne has a point," said Amanda. "Even if he was a jerk about it and even if he looks like he just climbed out of a grave, it's still true: I don't know much about genetics.

And after what he said, I don't know how I'm going to live up to this deal with Snootman."

"Don't sweat it," said Evelyn reassuringly. "Snootman knows that most of us have studied areas other than genetics. That's why he hired these professors. To teach us about it. It's part of his deal."

"That's right," added Derek. "And I have a suggestion. It's not a very exciting one, mind you, but it's kind of my fault that we didn't do this last night. I'm thinking maybe we *should* watch some of those boring-sounding films that Snootman gave us."

The other three made unenthusiastic faces, as though they'd just been offered an egg salad sandwich made with rotten rattlesnake eggs. But then Amanda nodded agreement.

"So what's it going to be?" Derek examined the menu. "*The Genie in the Genes*, *The Beguiling Benefits of Blastemata* or *News about Nucleotides*?"

"After being reamed out by Thorne, I vote for all of them," said Amanda.

"Well, you're the boss," said Derek. "And also the one with the $100-million lawsuit hanging over your head—so all of them it is!" He queued up the first film, then paused it. "Something tells me we're going to need popcorn."

Amanda smiled. "Agreed!"

A few minutes and a few large bowls of popcorn later, the four of them sat watching the first of what would become an evening full of films about DNA and how it combines in every human to create a being who retains aspects of both her mother and their father, but in a way that forms a totally new person. To everyone's surprise, they found the subject matter fascinating, so when the ten o'clock bell chimed, calling them to bed, they were startled to realize how quickly the evening had gone. Now better acquainted with the details of genetics, Amanda, Derek, Evelyn and Sanjay all shared the same two thoughts: they were facing an unbelievable challenge—and they just might be able to pull it off.

CHAPTER 9

THE NEXT DAY, Amanda apprehensively entered Thorne's classroom along with all the other kids. He seemed distracted. Sitting at his computer in the far corner, he hid all but his long, pallid face behind the darkly tinted glass partition. Amanda was actually relieved that he seemed preoccupied by whatever he was doing on his computer.

"Be seated. I'll be with you in a moment," said Thorne without looking up.

There was a strange bleeping sound from his monitor, and a flash of green light illuminated Thorne's face, giving him, for just a moment, the appearance of a computer-literate Frankenstein's monster.

"Damn!" he said under his breath, staring at his screen.

"Looks like one of Thorne's computer models just hit an evolutionary dead end," whispered Derek.

"Shhhh!" cautioned Amanda.

Thorne then took his place at the front of the classroom.

He scanned the faces of the students with a deliberate, penetrating air.

"Let's pick up where we left off yesterday. Which was . . . let me see . . . oh, yes! Miss Forsythe, I believe we had just determined that contrary to what you believed, the by-products of improperly stored white vinegar cannot be encouraged to evolve into a rocket scientist, or even a lowly jellyfish. Do you have anything to add to your scintillating body of knowledge?"

"Yes, I do," replied Amanda. "A *blastema* is a mass of undifferentiated cells capable of growth and regeneration into organs or body parts. *Blastemata* are usually found only in the early stages of an organism's development such as in embryos, and in the regeneration of tissues, organs and bone. Though they behave like stem cells, they are not derived from them."

"Go on," said Thorne. "Let's see what else you know beyond fighting aliens and building photon-sail interstellar spaceships that will no doubt travel millions of light years across space and land you right back to where you were, fighting aliens."

Amanda refused to let him rattle her. "Well," she continued, "some amphibians and certain species of fish can produce blastema as adults. For example, salamanders can regenerate many of their body parts after amputation, including their limbs, tails, retinas and intestines."

"If only we could do the same thing as easily with our bank accounts," said Thorne.

The kids from Eugenia's former clique smiled sycophantically at Professor Thorne's joke and tittered appreciatively, making sure that he could see them. Thorne then pulled his pair of dice out of a pocket of his lab coat and rattled them together.

"So it seems that the salamander has won this particular evolutionary crapshoot. Can anyone explain the mechanism by which it achieves this?"

Joules thrust his hand up in the air so eagerly that his big bottom rocked in his seat, causing it to squeak. Thorne walked toward him, stopping in front of his workstation.

"I'm sure you can, Joules. But since Miss Forsythe appears to be on a roll, let's see if she can make it three for three." He gestured at Amanda to continue.

"When a salamander's limb is cut off, a layer of epidermis—in other words, skin cells—migrates to cover the surface of the amputation site. This epidermis transforms into signalling cells called the apical epithelial cap. These cells interact with tissues known as fibroblasts, which in turn interact with a protein. That kick-starts the blastema growth. The genetic coding in the blastema contains a positional memory about the location and type of missing body part. That data is stored in the Hox genes in the fibroblast cells, so they know which limb to replicate. Then—"

"Please, Miss Forsythe, leave something for the rest of the class to learn over the coming semester," said Thorne wearily. "I merely wanted a simple answer, not a long-winded speech." He turned away from Amanda to face the class. "We may not have figured out how to regenerate limbs," he said, with more than a hint of sarcasm in his voice, "but at least we've determined how to regenerate intelligent thought."

There was no way to win with Thorne, thought Amanda. So she was relieved that his next action was to roll out a giant video screen then dim the lights and show a documentary detailing the earliest genetic-modification experiments. Thorne watched for a while as the narrator explained the gene insertions taking place on screen. Then he looked distracted and went to his computer behind the tinted window. He put on some headphones so the computer was silent and began rapidly clicking his mouse as he stared intently at the screen. The light from the computer shone up at him, casting long shadows across his pale, toothy face, giving him the look of something that would leap out at you from a crypt, if you were unwise or unfortunate enough to find yourself in a graveyard on a night so stormy that no one could hear you scream.

"Do you think he's doing some kind of computer modelling?" whispered Amanda.

"More likely checking out this week's issue of *Illustrated Zombie News*," answered Derek under his breath.

"Please pay attention to the documentary," said Thorne without even looking up from his computer screen.

Amanda had no idea how he knew they were talking, but she didn't want to provoke his wrath. So she spent the rest of the class learning why it was potentially advantageous to have a fish gene inserted into a tomato or pig DNA added to that of a human.

When the documentary was over, Thorne turned up the lights and emerged from behind his workstation.

"Now, before tomorrow's class," he began, "I would like all of you to read a research paper published in the April 25, 1953, edition of the British scientific journal *Nature*. You'll find copies of it by the door on your way out. It's a little something called 'A Structure for Deoxyribose Nucleic Acid,' and it was written by J.D. Watson and F.H.C. Crick. For those of you unfamiliar with the names, they're the gentlemen commonly credited with discovering the precise mechanism that has made you what you are today—such as that is—and has ensured that you are not at this very moment sprouting fins on your derrières or planning a date with a chimpanzee. At least I hope you are not. Dismissed."

As she left Thorne's classroom, Amanda felt tremendously relieved that she had redeemed herself at least somewhat. She still had a strong sense that Thorne was out to get her, however. If she didn't know the material, he criticized her. And if she *did* know the material cold, he criticized her for that too. But she sensed that with someone like Thorne, being criticized for knowing too much was a safer position to be in than being criticized for not knowing enough. So she felt sufficiently relaxed to take some time off to indulge in some of her own interests.

She turned to Evelyn, Derek and Sanjay as they walked down the hall.

"Any of you want to go with me for a float in the zero-g simulator?"

"Cool!" said Evelyn. "I'd love to! I bet it feels a bit like being underwater!"

"Minus the eels, I hope," said Sanjay. "I hate eels!"

"No eels," promised Amanda.

"And no Thorne," quipped Derek.

"Yes, it's a Thorne-free zone," said Amanda. "In fact, according to Snootman, only he, Dr. Kovalevsky and myself have access cards for it, so I think it will just be her and the four of us. And you'll like her. She really knows her way around a zero-g environment."

They entered the high-security space lab to find Dr. Kovalevsky modifying a partly disassembled rocket pack. She looked up and smiled.

"Ah, Amanda. I see you've brought some prospective astronauts with you."

"Actually, most of them are more interested in earth-bound pursuits. But who can resist a zero-g environment?" she replied.

Amanda introduced her friends to Dr. Kovalevsky.

"Very nice to meet you all," said the doctor. "You caught me in the middle of making some adjustments to a personal jet-pack device I've been developing."

"Fantastic!" exclaimed Amanda. "How does it work?"

"It's based on some experimental designs from the 1960s. It's for astronauts when they're outside their ship in space. The idea is to enable them to make repairs, or carry out any nearby scientific missions, without being dependent on a tether line, which is a very slow and not particularly safe process. With one of these jet packs, an astronaut will have complete freedom in controlling his or her own movements. Down here on Earth, with the gravity, the pack needs to have far more thrust than it would in space. So in order to safely test it, I need lots of room—as in, outside. The zero-g simulator is way too confined to safely test it. But this will be fun once I get it up and running."

"How do you operate it?" asked Amanda.

"Well, first you strap it on," said Dr. Kovalevsky, pointing out the harness. "Otherwise, the moment you twisted the accelerator, it would leave you standing in the dust while it sailed off on its merry way. So once you're well secured, you hit the On switch," she said, pointing to a button on the rails near the handgrips. "That powers up the rocket motor for flight. The handgrips are like the accelerators on a motorcycle. There are right- and left-hand grip controls that you twist to increase and decrease thrust. You can increase them together to gain altitude, or increase just one if you want to turn."

"I'd love to take it for a ride!" said Amanda.

"Me too!" added Derek.

"Well, you'll both have your chance once I get the bugs worked out. At the moment, it's a bit skittish. You have to be really careful applying the acceleration or you'll splatter yourself against the ceiling like jelly. But in the meantime, the zero-g simulator awaits. Who's up for a spin?"

"I am!" cried all four in unison.

"Good! Let's get suited up and I'll show you the ropes," said Dr. Kovalevsky.

☆

Once they were all in their jumpsuits and helmets, Dr. Kovalevsky led them inside the big white chamber and explained the controls.

"Normally, if there's just one person in here, you adjust the fans yourself with these buttons on the wrist panel of your suit. But since there are five of us, I'll be controlling them all from my suit. That means the four of you can just sit back and enjoy the ride. Everybody ready?"

The four of them nodded eagerly.

"All right, then—here we go!"

Amanda smiled knowingly at the look of amazement that flashed across her friends' faces when they saw that their feet were no longer touching the floor.

"We're all airborne now. So hang on to your helmets, because I'm going to increase the lift," said Dr. Kovalevsky, tapping the control mechanism.

Amanda and the others felt a powerful air column pushing them upward. Derek spread-eagled himself to catch the maximum lift.

"This is unbelievably brill-iant!" he shouted, his voice tailing off as he tumbled toward the ceiling.

Sanjay and Evelyn were more cautious, adjusting their postures so they rose more slowly. Even so, they laughed giddily at the unfamiliar sensation of flight.

Amanda, being more experienced than her three friends, showed them how to tumble, climb, dive and float at will. Then she demonstrated the isometric exercises and yoga poses they could use out in space to keep themselves in shape. She concluded the demonstration by showing her friends how to lie on their backs and relax by doing deep-breathing exercises. After a couple of minutes, Amanda heard someone snoring through her headphones. It was Sanjay.

"Many people find a zero-g space environment very relaxing," said Dr. Kovalevsky. "It's not uncommon for people to fall asleep when they first learn to float. But it's important to stay alert. So I think that snoring is our signal to end today's session."

Derek tapped Sanjay on the shoulder. "Wakey-wakey, mate. We're about to return to terra firma."

Sanjay jolted upright. "I wasn't aslee— Whoa!"

His sudden jerking motion had caused him to start spinning. Derek and Amanda caught him by the arms to steady him.

"The snoring was just some kind of zero-g experiment, I presume?" teased Evelyn.

"I wasn't really snoring—was I?" asked Sanjay, embarrassed.

"Sawing logs," said Evelyn. "But don't worry, the doctor says it happens all the time."

"Yes, and it wasn't much louder than your usual snoring at night," added Derek. "Although you don't usually talk in your sleep as much as you were doing just now."

"I wasn't!" said Sanjay. "Er, was I?"

Amanda smiled slyly. "We'll never tell."

"Now that we're all awake, let's begin our descent," said Dr. Kovalevsky.

She tapped the controls on her wrist panel, and they gently began to descend, making an extra-soft landing.

"That was amazing!" said Evelyn as she lifted the visor on her helmet. "It felt like scuba diving."

"Minus the eels!" added Sanjay. "I do *not* like eels."

"Well," said Amanda, "any time any of you want to come and practise with me, be my guests."

"What I'd really like to do is have a go on that jet pack," said Derek.

"I hope you'll all be able to do that in the not too distant future," said Dr. Kovalevsky. "But until I get the sensitivity settings sorted out on the controls, I'm afraid it's too dangerous to use indoors. There's no margin for error in a confined space like this. But don't worry—you'll all get your chance. I'm sure of it."

CHAPTER 10

OVER THE NEXT MONTH, Amanda and the other students hurled themselves at the problem of undoing Eugenia's trans-species fusion. There were several major challenges facing them. First, Eugenia's head was fully integrated with the alien body, which meant she relied on it for nutrients and oxygen. Some of the more audacious students suggested that they find a human "donor" body, someone approximating Eugenia's age and size, then sever her head and attach it to the donor. Arsinée and Ethyl were very much against this, whispering to each other that if it failed and Eugenia died, they would never get any of the million dollars she had promised them for being her friends. And it was unclear who exactly would willingly volunteer to dispense with her own head so the richest girl in the world could have a human body. Other students suggested cloning Eugenia's body, then severing the head of the clone. The obstacle here was that even the most famous surgeons in the world had never succeeded in achieving a head transplant. The odds against success were astronomical. Bill Snootman was not prepared to risk his daughter's life on such an unproven procedure.

Then there was the fact that any human body that replaced the alien body would have to be age-appropriate life-support system. The prospect of having Eugenia's head attached to the body of a baby was only slightly less disturbing to Bill Snootman than that of having it attached to an alien. Therefore, Amanda realized, they would have to find some means for any new human body to regenerate itself into an eleven-year-old form. This would be monumentally difficult.

Having studied the problem intensely, Amanda and her team discovered that amongst vertebrates—meaning animals with spines, a category that included all humans, at least in the physical sense of the word—none of them, with the notable exception of the salamander, are capable of regrowing missing body parts. Amanda therefore believed that the key to restoring Eugenia would be to find a way to get her human DNA to behave like that of a salamander. But for this to work, she would also have to continue to use the alien body as a life-support system, since it could provide what Eugenia needed more effectively than any conventional medical machines. The trick would be to get the alien DNA to relinquish dominance over its human counterpart, something that it was proving very resistant to doing. In all of Amanda's early experiments, any new human growth was immediately hijacked by the alien DNA and mutated into something that would support its crab-like form.

Amanda and her team hit a further obstacle when efforts to study the alien DNA and learn how to switch it off were proving impossible. This was because it had a unique characteristic that made it different from any other DNA on earth:

it disintegrated so quickly once it was removed from the living organism that it was impossible to examine it in any detail. So Amanda decided to concentrate on what was doable—or at least theoretically doable: getting Eugenia's human body to regenerate itself. Then they would have at least part of the mystery solved.

After many long days and nights of experimentation using Dr. Okina's fruit flies, Amanda and her team finally succeeded in cracking the secret of the salamander's ability to regenerate its limbs. From there, Amanda created a serum that she was able to treat the fruit flies with, so that they could regenerate their own missing legs and wings. After successfully repeating the experiment a number of times, Amanda felt that they were ready to try it on higher life forms. Now she just needed Professor Thorne to set up the lab for a clinical trial.

Amanda entered the classroom to find that Thorne was once again seated behind his computer, the screen angled so only he could see it. He looked frustrated. One hand was clicking a mouse. His other hand gripped the edge of the desk so tightly that his knuckles were white.

"Excuse me, Professor Thorne."

"What is it, Forsythe? I'm busy working on a complex problem involving several theories of probability."

"I'm sorry. I don't mean to disturb your work. But my team and I have succeeded in transferring salamander DNA into fruit flies and getting them to regrow body parts. We're ready to try the same technique on a higher life form."

"That's quite a claim," snorted Thorne. "The United States military has been working on that problem for some time in the hope that its soldiers can regenerate arms and legs lost in combat. So far, they have failed. Are you telling me that you have succeeded where they have not?"

"I believe so," replied Amanda.

"You're cocky. That's a dangerous trait. A premature claim can totally discredit you. The history of science is littered with the names of researchers who gambled and lost with claims of discoveries they said were true just because they wanted them to be true: cold fusion, the phlogiston theory, the Piltdown Man. It would be wise to repeat your tests scores of times before going public with your thesis."

"I appreciate your concern for my reputation, but I'm certain that this works," said Amanda. "And according to Mr. Snootman, Eugenia's very depressed. Seeing some kind of progress would really lift her spirits."

"I see," exclaimed Thorne sharply. "So now you're an expert in psychology, in addition to biology and rocket science?"

"I don't think you have to be a psychologist—or a rocket scientist—to imagine that seeing some signs of progress would make Eugenia—and her father—feel better."

Professor Thorne pondered that for a moment. Then one corner of his mouth lifted up into a smile resembling a fish hook. He suddenly brightened.

"You know, I bet you're right. Now that you mention it, I'm quite sure that seeing the results of your experiment would indeed have a powerful effect on the morale of both Snootmans." He paused. "Can you be ready to carry out your experiments the day after tomorrow?"

"Yes," replied Amanda. "I could even be ready later today."

"Now, now, no need to rush," said Thorne. "I shall have the lab facilities prepared and find a suitable specimen on which you can carry out your experiment."

"What kind of animal will it be?" asked Amanda.

"I'd prefer to save that for a surprise," said Thorne. "If your serum is truly effective, it should work on any kind of animal. It gives you and your experiment more credibility if you don't know in advance. Now if you'll excuse me, I have to run some more probability programs."

With that, Thorne returned to his computer and gazed intently at the screen, frowning slightly at whatever it was that he saw.

As had become her habit, Amanda was floating in the air, enjoying a mid-afternoon workout in the zero-g chamber. The plan had been for Dr. Kovalevsky to join Amanda there, to show her some new exercises she had devised. But Dr. Kovalevsky had been held up by a meeting with Professor Thorne, so she left a message to start without her. Amanda was becoming quite skilled in the zero-g environment, so she was happy enough to begin her exercises on her own. First, she did yoga stretches, positioning her legs behind her parallel to the floor, then arching her spine so she could look up at the ceiling. When she first began doing yoga under Dr. Kovalevsky's instruction, she had discovered that its precise combination of physical and mental focus helped reduce the stresses of daily life. Thorne and his criticism, Snootman's lawsuit and the seemingly impossible task of finding the "silver bullet" that would solve Eugenia's DNA riddle—all of it seemed far away now. Feeling refreshed, Amanda moved on to the isometric workout. When she had completed all the exercises in the regimen, her muscles tingled and she felt pleasantly limbered up. Amanda decided to take a break, so she did what she loved to do most in the zero-g chamber: lie on her back and float. Like many people, she had often had dreams where she could fly—not like a bird or a plane, but more like a hot air balloon hovering in a gentle sky. And now she was enjoying precisely this sensation. She was amazed at how similar to her dreams this zero-g experience was—to be gently floating, legs and arms outstretched. She closed her eyes, savouring the sensation, and fell into a state of pure meditative relaxation. She pictured herself in the spaceship she would build, gazing out the window, admiring the beauty of the cosmos as her photon-sail ship hurtled silently toward new worlds.

Amanda didn't know how long she had been daydreaming when she was drawn out of that state by a minor but sudden change in the equilibrium of the room. At first, it felt quite pleasant, like being gently carried upward by a wave on the surface of the ocean. Amanda opened her eyes and saw that she was moving toward the ceiling. This, she realized, should not be happening without a command from her wrist-mounted control device. But she had given no such command. She hit a button to correct it. Nothing happened. She tapped the control again, but still there was no response. Amanda wasn't overly concerned yet. Since the zero-g effect was created by fans blowing air columns that played off against one another, she would simply have to change her shape—and thus her aerodynamics—to lose altitude and make her way to the hatch at the bottom of the chamber. But as she rolled over to face the floor, she saw to her horror that the screws on the bottom fan's protective cover had sheared off because of the excess air pressure. The cover itself was now levitating in the air, exposing the giant blades whirring beneath it. Finally, it blew clear away, coming to rest against a wall. There was nothing stopping her from falling into the blades now except the upward pressure from the fan itself. Amanda could make it to the door, which was just a couple of metres above the fan, but she'd have to be extremely careful. She shifted her position to create as little surface area as possible relative to the air column, so she could descend on an angle toward the door. But just as she put her hands together like a diver, getting ready to make her move, the air pressure from the fan above her increased and she was thrust toward the whirling blade. No matter what position she adopted, Amanda found herself being pushed down, centimetre by centimetre, toward the giant fan. She spotted a handhold on the wall, halfway between her and the doorway. To get to it, she would need to fly directly over the exposed blades. It was a risky manoeuvre. But if she stayed where she was, she would eventually be drawn into them anyway. So Amanda carefully calculated the angle of descent she would need to reach the handhold, factoring in the speed of the downward thrust and the additional acceleration that would be provided by the force of gravity. This meant having to make the angle a little less acute. The blast from the upper fan was increasing every second. She would have to make her move soon. Steadying her nerves, Amanda emptied her mind of all unnecessary thoughts, the way Dr. Kovalevsky had taught her. She dove. The downdraft drove her toward the twirling blades, but she kept herself focused, adjusting the angle of her body to stay in a line that would take her to a point just above the handhold. She felt herself rushing toward it now. She reached out with one gloved hand and grabbed tight to it. Her body hit the wall and bounced off, but Amanda didn't let go of the handhold. Fighting against the downdraft, she reached up with her other hand so both were now gripping it. The downward blast increased, making it harder to hang on. She was buffeted against the wall, and beneath her textured astronaut gloves, her knuckles were turning white from the pressure of supporting her entire body. She felt her arms growing weaker. Just as she thought she could hold on no longer, Derek appeared in the window below.

With the visor covering her face, she couldn't alert him to her distress, and she dared not remove either of her hands from the grip. Derek gazed at her quizzically, then put on one of Dr. Kovalevsky's headsets. A moment later, Amanda heard his voice inside her helmet.

"Hey there, you anorak, what're you doing? You look like a guano bat hanging upside down in a cavern."

Amanda screamed a response. "Derek, help! There's something wrong with the chamber. The fans are out of control, and the cover's blown off the bottom blades."

Derek looked through the heavy window at the giant fan blades swirling beneath her. He threw open the door to the chamber, which relieved the air pressure somewhat and bought Amanda a little more time. But it didn't solve the problem of how to get her out with those exposed blades slicing through the air just below her.

Derek threw every switch and pressed every button that looked like it might have anything to do with the power supply to the fans. But no matter what he did, the blades continued to whirl. Then he spotted Dr. Kovalevsky's prototype jet pack.

"Hang on!" he cried into his headset. "I've got an idea."

Seeing him run toward the jet pack, Amanda called out, "No! Dr. Kovalevsky said it's too dangerous to use that indoors. You might get yourself killed if you try it!"

"And you'll get yourself killed if we *don't* try it!" he answered.

Amanda watched as he strapped on the jet pack. She clung to the handhold, fighting against the wind, which was pushing her like a hurricane toward the whirling blades.

Derek checked the controls of the jet pack. He remembered Dr. Kovalesky's description of the functions. Everything seemed to make sense and be logically laid out. But what concerned him was that there was no way for him to know how much of a twist of the handgrips would be enough to get him off the ground—and how much would send him straight into the ceiling, where he'd be smashed to a pulp. Still, if he was going to save Amanda, he knew there was no alternative than to give it a try. He hit the On switch and heard the hiss of the rocket engine's pilot flame kicking in. He took a deep breath and twisted the accelerators. Instantly, he shot upward, the G-force snapping his head back and thrusting him against the harness. He felt himself blacking out as the ceiling approached far too rapidly. Fighting against it, he tilted the handgrips back and managed to do an inverted roll, coming so close to the ceiling that the toes of his Doc Martens scraped along the plaster as he looped back toward the ground. Derek had the sickening realization that if he had reacted a nanosecond later, or used slightly more thrust, he would at this moment be a corpse. But he forced the thought out of his mind, because there was no time for it.

Soon, he had determined the right degree of pressure to keep him aloft and learned how to control his movements. If not exactly graceful, he was at least now functional, able to maintain the desired altitude with reasonable accuracy. He leaned forward in his harness, took careful aim at the open doorway and flew through it. Derek was buffeted by the downward thrust of the fan as he entered the chamber, and for an agonizing moment, Amanda watched as he hovered dangerously close to the blades whirling just beneath his feet. Then he got the measure of the downdraft and opened up the throttle enough to compensate for it. He roared up toward Amanda. But he couldn't take his hands off the grips.

"Grab onto the harness!" Derek shouted over the din of the rockets and the huge fans.

Amanda let go of the handgrip and was immediately blown downward. But Derek had anticipated this, and he'd reduced his thrust so he sank a few metres. Amanda fell straight onto him. She grabbed the jet-pack straps, facing him.

"Hold on tightly to me. You ready?" he shouted.

He could feel her head nodding against his chest. "Yes!" she cried.

"Right, then. Here we go!" he said.

Derek gunned the throttle so they arced up toward the ceiling, no longer hovering but flying with their legs trailing out behind them. He cleverly kept himself on the outside as they circled, so the centrifugal force would push Amanda against him and make it easier for her to hang on. He made a series of descending circuits of the chamber, then prepared for the last burst toward the door.

"No matter what, don't let go!" he shouted.

"I wasn't planning on it!" responded Amanda.

"All right, I'm going for the doorway!"

He squeezed the right accelerator and the rocket pack rolled, inverting him so he was flying upside down. He was making gravity work for them instead of against them, and by keeping Amanda on top of him, there was less chance of her losing her grip—even if it made flying quite a tricky affair. With one last burst of speed, they shot through the doorway, out of the zero-g chamber and into the safety of the laboratory.

Derek manoeuvred the jets so that he and Amanda were now upright, hovering just a few metres in the air. With remarkable dexterity for someone with so little experience, he backed off the thrusters so that they sank gently till their feet rested on the solid floor. Then he cut the power to the rockets.

Amanda flipped up her visor. "Thank gawd for you!" she said, so rattled by her brush with death that she clung to him even after they were completely safe. With the weight of the jet pack pulling on him from behind and Amanda leaning against him from the front, Derek lost his balance and toppled over. Amanda fell on top of him. For just a moment, as they struggled to get up, their faces were only centimetres apart. That just happened to be the same moment when the laboratory doors opened with a hydraulic swoosh.

Dr. Kovalevsky coughed politely to announce herself. "Ahem. Um, I hope I'm not disturbing anything."

Amanda blushed. "Oh . . . um, n-no! We're, uh . . ." she stammered. Having recuperated somewhat from her more immediate concern of being chopped to bits, Amanda now felt embarrassed. She realized what the doctor must be thinking, seeing her like this with Derek.

Derek, however, didn't miss a beat. "No, Doctor, you're not disturbing anything at all. In fact, you missed all the excitement! I just saved this boffin from getting turned into the makings of a very large steak-and-kidney pie in your zero-g chamber."

"What do you mean?" asked Dr. Kovalevsky.

"I was practising the exercises you showed me," began Amanda, her voice still trembling. "Then the fans started increasing and decreasing power on their own. My wrist controls stopped working. I couldn't change the speeds. The bottom fan blew its cover off. Then the top fan started increasing in speed, forcing me toward the floor. If Derek hadn't come along when he did, I'd have been killed."

Dr. Kovalevsky gazed into the zero-g chamber. Her jaw dropped in horror at the sight of the massive exposed blades.

"I'm so sorry, Amanda!" she stammered. "I don't understand. I calculated the shear factors for all those fasteners over the fan's cover. And I personally designed the speed controls."

"That doesn't mean they couldn't have been tampered with," said Derek.

"Are you suggesting that somebody did this to me on purpose?" asked Amanda.

"I'm just saying it's within the realm of possibility."

Dr. Kovalevsky shook her head gravely. "I will launch an investigation immediately. But until I determine exactly why and how this happened, the zero-g chamber is closed."

CHAPTER 11

PROFESSOR THORNE STOOD at the head of the classroom, an inscrutable look on his waxy face as he gazed over the rows of students toward Amanda.

"So, Forsythe, you're ready to roll the dice on your limb-regeneration theory, are you?" he asked.

"Yes, I am," she replied calmly.

"Very bold of you. But are you quite certain you're ready? After that scare you had in the zero-g simulator, it would be understandable if you wanted to delay the clinical trials. After all, you could have been torn limb from limb. But speaking of losing limbs, I have located the perfect specimen for your experiment."

With a flourish, Thorne removed a cover that had been laid over a desk at the front of the classroom, revealing an aquarium with a small white mouse inside it.

"That's my aquarium!" shouted Evelyn. "And that's Lelie! What are you doing with him? You didn't ask my permission to go in my room, let alone to take Lelie!"

Thorne's lips curled into that little fish-hook grin again.

"Mr. Snootman told me that I had full use of all resources within the Academy. It never occurred to me, Miss Chiu, that you would wish to stand in the way of this very important project to which we have all committed ourselves."

Sanjay leapt from his seat. "Of course Evelyn's committed to the project! But Lelie's her pet, and he doesn't belong to Snootman—or you!"

Thorne dismissively wagged a rubber-gloved finger at the children. "My, my, what a display of sentimental irrationality. And coming from such supposedly intelligent children! Now, Miss Forsythe has insisted that she wants to go ahead with the experiment, and so we are going ahead. I am merely trying to move the project forward in the most efficient manner possible. So without further ado . . ."

Thorne reached into the aquarium and scooped up Lelie. The little white mouse squeaked with fright as he was exposed to the unfamiliar air of the classroom. Thorne held him by his tail, dangling him in the air so everyone could see him.

"A white mouse," Thorne began. "This is absolutely the perfect specimen for this experiment. Except for one detail. Or should I say, four details."

Still holding Lelie aloft, Thorne reached into his desk and pulled out something shiny. He held it aloft beside the squirming mouse. A small gasp went through the room as the students saw what the shiny object was. It was a surgical scalpel.

"Stop!" shouted Evelyn.

"Now, now," chuckled Thorne. "We will use proper medical procedures to remove your rodent's legs. I will administer a local anesthetic. Besides, if your friend Miss Forsythe is so certain that she's right, what reason do you have to be concerned? I thought you'd be eager to have your little mouse become part of medical history."

"That's cruel and unnecessary," said Amanda. "We weren't supposed to amputate the limbs of an animal. We were supposed to find one that had already lost its limbs."

"Dear me, what kind of scientist are you if you're going to get all sappy about something as utterly insignificant as a mouse?" said Thorne condescendingly.

"It's not just any mouse—it's Lelie," said Amanda. "It's Evelyn's pet."

"Fine, fine," said Thorne wearily. "If you're so squeamish about it, I'll just cut off *one* of its legs. And perhaps the tail. That should be enough to tell us whether this regrowth serum of yours works."

Amanda stood up and took a step toward Thorne.

"No. There's no reason to choose this particular animal, and I'm not doing it."

"Hmmm. Evidently we're not quite so sure about ourselves and our serum, are we?" taunted Thorne. "Very well, then. I shall have to find Mr. Snootman and inform him that an experiment of such vital interest to his daughter must be postponed while we try to locate specimens that meet the requirements of your delicate sensibilities."

"No need to look for me. I'm right here," said a voice from behind them.

Amanda and the others turned to see Bill Snootman entering the classroom. He walked over to where Amanda was seated and leaned in toward her.

"You do remember our agreement, don't you?" he asked. "And the consequences if you fail to uphold your end of the contract?"

Amanda steeled herself. "Yes, I do. But there's no need to use this particular animal."

Snootman paused for a long moment before turning to Thorne. "If Amanda doesn't feel comfortable amputating the legs of her friend's pet, that's perfectly understandable. There must be lots of other unlucky animals that have already lost their limbs and would be grateful to receive the benefits of this procedure."

As Snootman spoke, he removed a small device from his pocket and, thumbs flying, rapidly typed out a text message.

"As you wish, Mr. Snootman," said Professor Thorne, bowing his head slightly, his face expressionless. "Although I should point out that this will of course delay finding a cure for your daughter's condition."

"Be that as it may, I don't want to traumatize our researchers," replied Snootman. "Besides, I have just contacted my senior aides, and they are all at this moment searching for animals that would be suitable for the experiment."

"That's all well and good," said Thorne, "but we must bear in mind that for all we know, the longer Eugenia is exposed to the alien DNA, the more it will take root in her. By delaying, we may even pass a point of no return."

Amanda wondered why Thorne, who had tried to persuade her to postpone her experiment, was now so eager to carry out the procedure without delay.

Snootman's communicator chimed.

"Excuse me," he said as he put the device to his ear. "Yes. Where? How many? How soon can you get them here? Very good."

Snootman clicked the communicator off.

"Excellent news," he announced. "My people have located some unfortunate creatures that fit the bill for the regrowth experiment. Seems there is to be a big party to celebrate a deal between Samsara Electronics and some rapper named Emcee Squared to make a video game based on his life. They are marking the occasion with a champagne-and-lobster feast. The lobsters had to be flown in from Nova Scotia, and by happy coincidence—for us, if not the lobsters—some of the more aggressive ones worked themselves free of the elastics binding their claws. As you may be aware, lobsters are cannibals. So it wasn't long before the unbound lobsters in the shipping tank set about attacking each other. The result is that there are now about half a dozen lobsters missing a claw or two. Evidently this makes them unsuitable for celebrating an event as auspicious as the creation of a video game glorifying the life of a convicted carjacker turned rap singer. The caterer preparing the food for the party just happens to do a lot of work for Snootman Global Enterprises, and he was able to put the amputees aside for me. They will be arriving here tomorrow. Not such a huge delay after all. So, Professor, if you would, please have the lab ready for the experiments in the afternoon."

"Yes, Mr. Snootman," replied Thorne. "It shall be my great pleasure."

But Amanda noted that nothing in Thorne's expression suggested he was experiencing any pleasure whatsoever.

The next day, Amanda returned to Thorne's classroom, ready once again to carry out the experiment. Thorne scanned the faces of the other students, then looked at her sourly.

"So, Miss Forsythe, I hope you're not going to get squeamish on me again."

Amanda gazed into the tank that held the clawless lobsters rejected from the Emcee Squared party. Then she looked up at Thorne and gazed straight into his eyes.

"These are perfect," she replied.

She opened a small black carrying case and laid out a hypodermic needle and a few bottles of serum. Then she gingerly reached into the tank and withdrew the first lobster.

Thorne looked annoyed. "Miss Forsythe, if you don't mind . . ." He grabbed the lobster away from her before she could inject the serum. "You lack the skill to administer needles. It's bad enough that these poor creatures have already suffered loss of limb. I don't want you inflicting any more torture on them than what they've already endured."

"But I'm perfectly capable of giving the injections," Amanda protested.

"Nonsense," replied Thorne. "This requires an experienced hand."

He placed the lobster on his desk, then snatched the serum and the hypodermic needle from Amanda. He opened his desk drawer and set the serum and needle down in it while he searched for something.

"*I* will administer the serum. I just need to put my rubber gloves on first."

Thorne retrieved them from the drawer and, with a loud snap, stretched them over his hands. He reached back into his desk and took out the hypodermic needle, which had rolled beneath a stack of papers, then stabbed the needle into a bottle of Amanda's serum. Holding the squirming lobster in his other hand, he carefully injected the serum into the animal's soft abdominal tissue. Then he did the same for all the remaining lobsters, which were missing various combinations of claws and legs.

"There," said Thorne as he finished with the last one and placed it back into the saltwater tank. "Now we'll see if there's anything to this so-called regrowth serum of yours. If it doesn't kill the lobsters outright, there's still the matter of whether it actually works. But only time will tell. We shall check back in twenty-four hours and see if any of them are once again suitable for being served up at a fancy cocktail party. Meanwhile, let's give them some privacy to simulate their natural environment."

He draped a cover over the tank, cloaking the lobsters in darkness.

"If you're right about this, Miss Forsythe, you will no doubt become a hero—at least in the eyes of grateful fishmongers around the world. In the meantime, would you all please turn to page 479 in your copies of *Advanced Gene Splicing*."

That night, Amanda, Derek, Evelyn and Sanjay were too nervous to celebrate. They didn't want to jinx the outcome, even though they realized that the very notion of jinxing was completely unscientific.

The next day, when they returned to the classroom, Thorne was looking uncharacteristically cheerful. The cover was still draped over the lobster tank, so Amanda couldn't see what had happened. When the class was seated, Thorne pressed the intercom button on the wall.

"Mr. Snootman? Professor Thorne. Sorry to disturb you, but we are about to unveil the results of Miss Forsythe's work. It promises to be a historic moment. I thought you might like to be on hand to witness it."

"Thank you, Professor Thorne. I'll be right down."

Thorne strolled to his desk, opened a drawer and took out his rubber gloves. Humming a happy little melody, he rolled up the sleeves of his white lab coat and once again stretched his rubber gloves over his hands. He had barely finished this when Bill Snootman entered the classroom, walking briskly and looking anxious.

"Please proceed, Professor."

"Very good, Mr. Snootman," responded Thorne. He turned to Amanda. "Miss Forsythe, since this experiment is your brainchild, perhaps you'd like to step up to the front of the class to unveil the results."

Amanda had tested her regrowth serum many times over the past month, but there was something about Thorne's jaunty air that made her nervous. Derek, Evelyn and Sanjay felt it too. They all shifted nervously as she climbed out of her seat. Derek gave her the thumbs-up sign, but she noticed that his smile seemed a little forced. She approached the tank.

"Now, Miss Forsythe, let's see how your spin of the wheel turned out," said Thorne.

He partially removed the cover over the tank, just enough for Amanda to retrieve a lobster. She peered into the dark waters, detected a shadowy movement on the bottom and reached in. Something scuttled about in response to her touch. She felt for its tail, made sure her hands were well behind the claws and lifted one of the lobsters out.

For a moment, Amanda wasn't certain what she was seeing. But the horrified gasp that went up all over the room told her that her eyes did not deceive her. The lobster had a claw growing directly out of its mouth. It had another claw growing off the end of its tail. Amanda gagged as she looked at the writhing, hideously deformed creature in her hand.

"Well, Miss Forsythe, you have succeeded in regrowing its claws all right, but the lobster now has no means of taking in food. It will starve to death," said Thorne. "We will have to destroy that animal and put it out of its misery. But no matter, there are still five lobsters left. Perhaps the odds will be with you on the others."

Thorne gestured toward the water, inviting Amanda to reach in again. As she began searching around in the nutrient tank, he sat at his desk, running a chemical analysis on the serum, Amanda's syringe and her Petri dishes. She pulled out the remaining lobsters one by one, but they were all as grotesquely deformed as the first. Some had legs growing off their claws. Others had so many claws growing off their backs that they couldn't support their own weight.

"My, my, this doesn't look good," said Thorne. "Not good at all. I'd say that Lady Luck was definitely not smiling on you, Miss Forsythe. But that comes as no surprise, given what I have just discovered about your work. My analysis shows that your Petri dishes were contaminated. The serum was contaminated too. Even the needles had pathogens in them. That's why the regrowth serum had such an unexpected effect."

"But it was produced in a sterile environment," Amanda protested. "This isn't possible."

"Evidently it's more possible than you realize—which is exactly the problem," retorted Thorne. "Once again, it's shoddy work from someone more accustomed to widgetry than the intricacies and mysteries of life!"

With a bony finger, Thorne tapped his computer keyboard, and reams of paper began spewing out of his printer. He examined the printout, then turned to Bill Snootman.

"Mr. Snootman, it is my opinion that until this girl is far better educated on the subject, she should not be allowed to go anywhere near a living creature."

"Please go on, Professor," said Snootman. "I'd like to hear your explanation for that opinion."

"I have here in my hand a list of 205 pathogens found in Miss Forsythe's so-called serum," replied Thorne. "Some of them are particularly lethal for humans."

To emphasize the point, he waved the computer printout. It was too far away for Amanda to read any details, but she could see that it was black with numbers.

"My analysis reveals substances in the serum that, while posing no threat to lobsters, are toxic to humans. If the serum had been injected into Eugenia, the result would have been catastrophic. For all we know, given Miss Forsythe's past animosity toward Eugenia, that may well have been her intent."

"That's a lie!" shouted Amanda.

"And what you're saying doesn't make any sense!" added Derek, glaring at Thorne. "If Amanda had wanted to harm Eugenia, she wouldn't have introduced pathogens into the serum at this stage and given away her plan."

"Spare me, Mr. Murphy. This is not a debating club," hissed Thorne. He turned back to Bill Snootman. "From the outset, I have had serious doubts about Miss Forsythe's aptitude. She always seemed to me at best a dark horse. This incident confirms the worst of my fears. I suggest that you send her home immediately, and that she be barred from ever entering the Academy again."

Bill Snootman stood in silence, rubbing his chin. Amanda felt her stomach twisting in knots. She had fought so hard to get the Academy reopened and to create the unique conditions that would allow her, Evelyn, Sanjay and Derek to get together. If she was kicked out, that would put an end once and for all to her dreams of working with her three best friends. And then there was that matter of the $100-million lawsuit. Amanda felt the knots in her stomach twisting tighter.

Finally, Bill Snootman spoke. "I'm sorry, Amanda, but this incident *has* cast doubt on your abilities. It also casts doubt on my judgment, since it was my belief that you had the intellectual flexibility to lead this project, even though it was outside your area of expertise. My thesis may have been faulty."

"But, Mr. Snootman, I'm sure I did everything correctly!"

Thorne smirked slightly, the edge of his lip curling into that fish-hook grin of his.

"Please, Amanda, don't make this any more difficult for me than it already is," said Snootman.

She felt as though she would faint. It seemed that Snootman was about to expel her.

"Now, Professor Thorne," he continued, "it seems that Miss Forsythe made an honest mistake based perhaps on a lack of experience in lab hygiene. And who knows, there may be something to her regrowth theory yet. At least let's hope so. In any case, there is no indication that this was a wilful act. Therefore I see no need to expel her from the Academy."

Thorne's fish-hook smirk disappeared. His face went rigid, and he bit his lip.

Then Snootman turned back to Amanda. "You will continue your studies and be allowed to use the facilities, independently, as per our original agreement. However, any work you do on the project to rehabilitate Eugenia will be closely supervised by Professor Thorne. Your contributions, if any, will be determined by the new student team leader."

"N-new student team leader?" stammered Amanda.

"Yes. I'm afraid that a change in leadership is called for," said Snootman. "I will leave the task of choosing that leader, and the core group around that person, to Professor Thorne, who is far more knowledgeable in such matters than I am. Professor?"

"Why, thank you, Mr. Snootman," replied Thorne. "I'm honoured to have your confidence. As to a new leader . . . well, from all accounts, Eugenia herself was the student most skilled in manipulating DNA. So it makes sense that the four friends who were closest to Eugenia and her work would have an unusually high aptitude in that area too." With a flick of his hand, as if he were rolling his dice, Thorne pointed to a small group of students clustered near the front. "Joules, Arsinée, Henbane and Ethyl."

The members of Eugenia's former Alhacen entourage smiled smugly. All except Joules, who had the same concerned, faraway expression that Amanda had seen on Bill Snootman's face whenever the subject of his daughter's condition was raised.

"From this moment on, these students, headed by Joules, shall determine the direction of the program. I have absolute confidence in their abilities."

"Very well," said Bill Snootman. "I look forward to hearing their ideas."

Amanda felt like she was going to throw up. Under Eugenia's influence, Joules, Arsinée, Henbane and Ethyl had had it in for her since her first day at the Academy. And now they would be in a position of authority over her. She felt horribly betrayed, although she couldn't put her finger on who had betrayed her and why."

But right now, it felt like the entire universe was against her.

CHAPTER 12

AMANDA ROLLED OVER in her bed for what seemed like the hundredth time that night and found herself still maddeningly awake. She hadn't slept so much as a nanosecond since climbing under the covers. From the sound of Evelyn's slow, regular breathing on the other side of the room, she knew that her friend was deep in slumber. Lying on her side, Amanda opened one eye just enough to see that Lelie too was peacefully snoozing under his ceramic pirate ship in the aquarium. Frustrated, Amanda turned onto her back and glared up at the ceiling. She recoiled in fright at what she saw there—the shadows of what appeared to be long, skeletal arms reaching out across the room. The arms had smaller arms growing off them; these were covered in warts and had curled claws at the end of their spindly fingertips. Amanda's heart pounded. Her pulse raced. She turned and looked out the window, quickly realizing that it was just the effect of the moonlight filtering through the old maple trees outside her window.

She relaxed and settled into her bed once more, closed her eyes and lay flat on her back, hands outstretched by her sides, palms facing up. She began slowly inhaling and exhaling to a count of six. It was a form of yogic breathing that Dr. Kovalevsky had taught her as a means of clearing her mind and relaxing her body in the zero-g simulator. "Focus on the breath," she imagined Dr. Kovalevsky's calm, self-assured voice telling her, as she had done so many times before. But despite her best efforts, she kept reliving the humiliation she had suffered earlier that day. The scenes played out in her mind over and over again: the fishhook smirk on Thorne's face as he suggested expelling Amanda from the Academy; the way he belittled her mercilessly; Bill Snootman's doubting her; the writhing, hideously deformed lobsters, and her inability to explain how they had ended up that way. How could she have been so careless with the preparation of the serum? Or was it a slip-up from someone on her team? Derek, perhaps? He was always so cocky, so sure of himself. Maybe he had taken careless risks. Or Evelyn? She always seemed so serious and dedicated, but Amanda knew that her heart was in oceanography. Maybe Sanjay. From the night he arrived back at the Academy, he had resisted learning about DNA. She remembered his comment about this whole exercise being a "necessary evil" to allow him to pursue his real interest in nanobots. But instantly, Amanda felt guilty for having such angry thoughts about her friends. She had no evidence that any of them had made an error, but her mind was roiling with negative thoughts she couldn't control. Unpleasant memories intruded: Eugenia threatening her with the hissing, repugnant Tinkerbell; Oppenheimer and Leitspied in their exoskeletal alien forms, chasing Amanda and Evelyn through the hallways, trying to sweet-talk them into surrendering so the aliens could lobotomize them; the escape through the sewer, with her and Evelyn bobbing through the waist-deep water, buoyed by their waterproof outfits; the banging on the door growing fainter, fading to nothingness as they drifted within the quiet, womb-like tunnel. The image was strangely soothing, and Amanda at last experienced the delicious sensation of drifting off into slumber without even realizing it was happening.

She didn't know how long she had been sleeping—it felt like no more than a few minutes—when she gradually became aware that her eyes were open and staring into the blackness of the ceiling. Amanda noticed the shadows on the walls again, only this time, they looked even more menacing. The wind must have come up, she thought, because the claw-like shadows were sweeping across the walls crazily now, as if probing or searching for something to dig their talons into. She heard a tapping and scratching at her window; it sounded as if an animal was trying to get in. She imagined the repugnant Tinkerbell slithering into her chambers to attack her in her sleep and decided to see what was making the sound. But Amanda found that her body felt strangely heavy. It took all of her willpower to push her feet out of bed, pull herself upright and lumber over to the window. There, she was relieved to see that the suspicious sound was caused by dead leaves, uncollected the previous fall after the aliens' hasty departure, being pelted against the glass by the wind. Looking down into the cemetery, Amanda saw that the layer of leaves was so thick between the gravestones that the swirling gusts of air made it appear as if something underneath was pushing them aside. She calmed herself with the thought that this was just the result of atmospheric conditions, air flowing from high-pressure to low-pressure zones and carrying anything light along with it. But then she felt an icy shockwave shooting through her as she saw bony hands reaching up out of the leaves. It was no illusion. Amanda reflexively ducked behind the curtains. Her heart pounded. She was breathless with terror. Then, feeling foolish, she decided that what she had seen could not possibly be real, that it must have been fatigue and a trick of the light. There was always a scientific explanation for everything. So she peeked round from behind the curtain—only to see now that the bony hands were attached to corpses that were climbing out of their graves. Standing ankle-deep in the dead leaves, they stared straight up at her, somehow knowing exactly where she was. The sallow-faced cadavers and mouldering skeletons all pointed their fingers at her accusingly. As if that wasn't horrifying enough, Amanda could see now that each of the corpses had too many arms, and that these were growing in places where they shouldn't be growing—from backs, stomachs and hips. Then the undead began to sing a terrifying song, their unearthly, discordant voices carried on the yowling winds straight to Amanda's window. She was even more startled to discover that she was the target of their mocking ditty, which went:

Amanda Forsythe, she thought she was a so-special girl
Amanda Forsythe even thought she once saved the world
But she's a space case, in so deep right over her head.
Amanda Forsythe—all in all, she's better off dead.

In a gruesome pantomime, one of the undead, a girl wearing a frilly Victorian gown that was hanging in rotten greyish-white tatters, began to rebury herself with a shovel. The others now started shuffling slowly toward the doors of the Academy, shrieking and laughing. Amanda didn't know what wicked science had reanimated the corpses, or who was responsible for it, but she knew that she couldn't handle a crisis on this scale. The students and staff would have to make a break for it to escape from these zombie mutants, and she would alert the authorities, no matter what Bill Snootman said. She tried to call out a warning to Evelyn, but for some unknown reason, all she could squeeze from her lungs was a tiny, almost inaudible whimper. She felt pathetic and weak, like a helpless little animal so frightened that it's unable to utter a peep, even to save its own life. So she went to shake Evelyn awake instead. However, after slowly and laboriously dragging her heavy feet over to the bed, Amanda discovered that her roommate wasn't there anymore.

"Evelyn!" she attempted to shout. But again, all that came out of her mouth was the tiniest sound, a little chirp. A moment later, she heard something squeaking in response. It was Lelie; he was scratching at the side of his tank, looking up at Amanda. With a start, she noticed that he now had an extra pair of legs growing off the back of his head. "Squeak!" he chirped at her angrily, waving his extra legs at her accusingly. Amanda went for the door. But her progress was so slow, it felt like she was running through wet concrete. She fumbled for the door handle but was unable to find it in the dark. It was as though someone had removed it. In her desperation, she gave the door the biggest shove she could muster. It swung out on its hinges so suddenly that Amanda lost her balance and fell forward through the doorway. But instead of finding herself in the hall, Amanda discovered she was in some kind of small, windowless chamber resembling a tomb. A dim ceiling lamp faded up, its weak, flickering light revealing Eugenia in the centre of the chamber, her head atop the alien body. She looked at Amanda pleadingly and opened her mouth to speak. But instead of words, she emitted a tortured, deafening shriek: "Screeeeeeeeee-ok!" Then everything went black.

The next thing Amanda knew, she was jerking upright in her bed. She gasped. She may have cried out, but she wasn't sure. Then she realized to her immense relief that she was waking up, and that the corpses climbing out of their graves, the mutant Lelie in her aquarium and Eugenia in a burial tomb outside her bedroom had all just been a horribly vivid nightmare. She caught her breath and looked over to see Evelyn and Lelie deep in slumber. Lelie, she noted gratefully, had his usual four legs. But her relief was quickly replaced with the depressing realization that the incident with the lobsters, Thorne's attack on her and Bill Snootman's decision to relieve her of her duties were all very real.

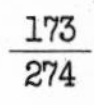

Instead of torturing herself by trying to fall asleep again, Amanda decided to get up and use her wakefulness to shake off her anxiety. She considered going into her soundproof lab in the dorm. George had created these scaled-down workspaces so that if inspiration struck in the middle of the night, a student could carry out experiments without disturbing her roommate. But the small lab in the corner of the bedroom felt too claustrophobic, given the anxious mood Amanda was in. She may have been disgraced in front of the other students, but she still had the run of the Academy. Thorne hadn't convinced Snootman to take that away from her. So she slid quietly out of bed, put on her slippers and robe, then padded out into the hallway, leaving Evelyn and Lelie behind, sleeping peacefully.

The corridors were dimly lit and shrouded in shadows. But having spent the better part of the night staring into the blackness, Amanda's eyes had already adjusted to the dark, so she had no trouble finding her way. With the staff and other students asleep behind closed doors, the Academy felt strangely lifeless. Amanda's soft slippers made no sound, and in the silence of the midnight halls, she felt as if she weren't even really here and that this could be yet another dream.

Amanda reached the staircase and descended. On the main floor, she passed the Constellation Hall, the various labs and finally her old homeroom class. She had intended to continue downstairs to her space lab. But seeing her classroom at a time when she had been bumped back to square one, she felt compelled to enter. It had been such a place of wonder that she still felt a special bond, even though the space was now occupied by Dr. Okina and his breeding tanks of fruit flies and rotting mangoes. Amanda felt a powerful need to reconnect with the happier times of the Academy, when it was a magical world of opportunity, rather than a prison filled with failure and humiliation.

She slipped her pass card in the slot. Nothing happened for a moment. Amanda wondered if she had now been shut out of this part of her past too. Then a tiny green light flicked on and the door slid open. Snootman was as good as his word. Despite his disappointment with Amanda's performance, he had maintained her special access to the Academy's facilities. She entered, quietly closing the door behind her.

The room was lit only by moonlight filtering through the large windows that rose all the way to the ceiling. Amanda walked to the lab station that Evelyn had so shyly but eagerly led her to that first day the previous September. She gazed at the desk where she had first seen Sanjay, utterly engrossed in his brilliant nanobot creations. And she looked at the now-empty spot where Derek's amazing holographic Earth projection globe had sat, mesmerizing her when she walked into the classroom as a newbie.

It occurred to Amanda that the Academy that previous autumn had been a high-tech palace of smoke and mirrors, one equally well suited to good and evil. As if to confirm her thoughts, the moonlight reflected off the empty glass wall panels that had once held George's incredible assortment of living holograms. The creatures that George had programmed into the system were mostly on the endangered list, and all of them were utterly exquisite and fascinating to watch. He had placed them there in full view, in the everyday classroom environment, so that the students would be exposed to the beauty and mystery of nature. That way, George hoped, they would think of science as not just about technology, but about the living world too, and then they would come to love it and want to protect it. Amanda desperately wished at that dark moment that she could recreate that sense of wonder to inspire her and the other students. But now it all seemed hopeless. She hung her head, feeling despondent. Then her gaze fell upon a faint glow leaking out from a crack in one of George's hologram panels, where the wall met the floor. It was so dim that Amanda had never noticed it before in the daylight. Evidently no one else had either.

Curious, Amanda unscrewed the panel, revealing a computer power module. She became excited when she spotted some of the same alien symbols that she had seen on the coded star map George gave her just before he returned to his home planet.

"This must be one of George's systems," she whispered to herself in amazement.

Amanda climbed inside the wall and traced some cables until she located the master console. The controls were unfamiliar, but after studying the layout for a few minutes, she was able to reboot the computer that generated the holograms. The complex system, which George had probably never intended anyone else to operate, was daunting, and Amanda cycled through the computer files, trying to figure out how to open them. But even the file names identifying the animals were in some code that represented George's mother tongue on whatever planet he was from. With painstaking care, however, she was eventually able to determine their meaning. She tapped in a code, and a tiny pinprick of light appeared inside the case. It gradually grew in size, morphing into the image of a Madagascar jewel beetle. Another exotic insect appeared, then another. Amanda tapped in more code, and a leafy tropical tree took shape within another case. In its branches, a ring-tailed lemur materialized, then a second one. Soon both of them were leaping about as if imbued with life force. Next, a lorikeet faded up into three vivid dimensions, standing on the branch of a eucalyptus tree, its feathers brilliant shades of green, yellow, orange and blue. A Sumatran striped rabbit loped through some underbrush that had grown as if by magic. Then, deep in the holographic woods, Amanda spotted the Malabar civet that she used to observe stalking about when she sat at her workstation in Leitspied's class. She smiled to see the tropical environment restored to this verdant state, teeming with life and full of happy squawks, snuffles and shrieks. The lorikeet flapped down to a branch right in front of Amanda.

"Look at you. You're so beautiful!" she said to the bird. She immediately felt embarrassed. "Silly me! Of course you can't hear what I'm saying. But you just look so gorgeous, so real, that I couldn't resist speaking to you!"

To Amanda's surprise, the bird cocked its head as if listening to her. Was it just a coincidence? She slowly moved her finger in a zigzag pattern in front of the lorikeet, and could see its eyes tracking the movement.

"Can you hear me?" Amanda asked incredulously.

The bird ambled down the branch toward her, an inquisitive expression on its face. Reaching the end of the branch, it looked directly at her.

"Brawwk!" it croaked, staring into her eyes.

"Unbelievable!" said Amanda. "You *can* sense me! I guess we were all too busy before to notice that you were more than just a pretty picture."

At this point, Amanda realized that there was still one unopened hologram file. She was certain that the plants and animals she saw before her now were the only ones that had ever been there before. Curious about this last file, she typed in a series of commands. She saw that this file was bigger and contained much more data than those of the other animals. So she presumed it belonged to a larger, more complicated creature. Her assumption was soon proven correct. As soon as she hit the Enter key, tiny pixels of light began shimmering on the other side of the glass, then crystallized into the form of a thin, unusual-looking man. He appeared to be in his early thirties. He had a narrow face, a long nose and large, childlike eyes full of curiosity; he took in everything around him with a sense of wonderment, as if he was seeing it for the first time. He was wearing a lab coat over an outfit that looked about sixty years out of date. His hair was neatly trimmed in a style of the late 1940s. Amanda was so taken aback that she couldn't even speak for a moment. Not quite believing her own eyes, she leaned in for a closer look, pressing her nose up against the glass like a child gazing into a shop window. She felt a flood of emotions. There was no mistaking the figure on the other side.

"George!" shouted Amanda. "It's so good to see you!"

"Thank you," responded George, smiling sweetly. "It's good to see you too. Very lovely, indeed." Then he hesitated. "Um, by the way . . . who are you?"

"Who am I? Why, I'm Amanda, of course."

"Amanda of Course," replied George. "What an unusual surname. Sounds medieval, like Catherine of Aragon. Are you a European princess too?"

Amanda smiled, but it was a rather bemused smile. "No, silly. I'm definitely not a princess. You know that my surname is Forsythe and I'm from Downview. But what are you doing here? I thought you'd returned to your home planet."

"Ah," replied the man on the other side of the glass. "Your question provides an explanation for both our states of confusion. You see, I'm not George, exactly. Rather, I am a hologram that I—meaning George—made of myself. I—or *he*—wanted to make absolutely certain that the three-dimensional visual technology, as well as the voice and movement-recognition systems, worked. And so I—or *he*—thought, Who better to use as a sample than me?"

"This is incredible," said Amanda. "You look exactly like him!"

"I should," answered the image. "George took the most advanced motion-capture technologies available and refined them until they could record even the subtlest details of the way he moved while in human form. He compared video recordings of his actual self to the holographic version of him doing the same motions, adjusting the sensors until the two images were identical. Once he had perfected it on himself, he was able to create all the amazingly lifelike animals you see around me—I mean *him*—as well."

Amanda was overjoyed at seeing the lifelike image of her good friend, but she felt a little wistful too. George had been so unfailingly kind to her. He had been her mentor and confidant during her time at the Academy the previous autumn, and ultimately a critically important ally. His sense of decency and unwavering devotion to Amanda and the other students set him on a moral collision course with Oppenheimer and Leitspied and their plans for world domination.

So it was with pangs of both hope and melancholy that Amanda now asked, "Are you actually George, then? Do you have his mind—his intellect and his emotions—or do you just look like him?"

The image gazed at Amanda thoughtfully. "I don't know. That remains for you to decide, really. I have all of George's memories up to a couple of weeks before the Academy first opened. He, Oppenheimer and Leitspied were supposed to be the only ones to know that I exist."

"But you do call yourself George," countered Amanda, "and you say 'I' when referring to him."

"Yes," responded the hologram. "George thought it would be too confusing to analyze a hologram that referred to itself in the third person, so he programmed me so that I would answer all questions—with a few exceptions, such as the type you're asking me now—in the first person, as though I were him. But he was the only one who ever asked me questions before. So you can see my dilemma. Now that you are asking me about both George and myself, I'm not sure whether to say 'he' or 'I,' or even if I should refer to myself as 'George' or something else. Perhaps, 'the hologram with the characteristics of George.' That would technically be correct."

"Hmm," replied Amanda. "'The hologram with the characteristics of George'?" She thought for a moment. "I guess it would be technically correct, but it's rather long. And it doesn't seem very personal, either. If it's all right with you, I think I'd prefer it if you called yourself George."

"Very well," said the three-dimensional moving image. "From this point onward, George it shall be."

He smiled, then looked at Amanda with an intensely curious gaze.

"How did you come to know the George who created me? Were you one of the Earthling children selected to come to the Academy to become goodwill ambassadors?"

"Yes, I was," replied Amanda. "George helped me with my experiments and a lot else. He and I became close friends."

"I'm glad to hear it. But from the way you greeted me, I get the impression that you haven't seen him in some time," said the hologram.

"That's right," replied Amanda. "Long story, but the short answer is that Oppenheimer and Leitspied went off mission. Instead of teaching us what they knew, they tried to fool us into making inventions to help them take over planet Earth. They came very close to succeeding."

"What a horrible thing. How dreadful of them!" said

George, his face adopting an expression of such deep concern that Amanda almost laughed. "I would never have guessed that they were capable of such skulduggery!"

"Neither did the George who created you," replied Amanda. "nor any of us kids. Oppenheimer and Leitspied fooled everybody. Fortunately, you—or rather, the George who created you—remained true to the mission. He refused to go along with their plan to send out synapse-blocking signals to every human on Earth so they could take over the planet. With George's help, we stopped them from taking control."

"And a good thing! The cads!" exclaimed George, his nostrils flaring in a rare show of temper. "What happened to them all?"

"George put them in the disembodiment chamber and loaded them into the spaceship so they could face justice on his planet," said Amanda. "I helped hold off the Earthly authorities until he had enough time to get away."

"That was very good of you," said George. "He loved his home, and his friends and family there. As for Oppenheimer and Leitspied, you can be certain that they will face justice. I expect they'll be sentenced to community service of some sort. Probably picking shreeblgloppers off the sidewalk. Oh, sorry, you don't know what those are."

"Actually, I do," said Amanda. "George told me. I believe it translates roughly as 'snot,' does it not?"

"Indeed," said George, smiling. "Although it's much stickier. After a few months of scraping it off the sidewalks, they'll regret the day they ever thought about galactic conquest. Anyway, that was very decent of you to help George like that," said his image.

"Well, the George who created you was very decent too," said Amanda. "In fact, he could have taught a course in decency.

He was more ethical than not only Oppenheimer and Leitspied, but also all the government authorities from Earth who came to debrief us. They just wanted to find out if our inventions could be used as weapons, to give them a military advantage over other countries."

"Yes, we've observed that your species is reasonably intelligent but also quite warlike," said George, "at least judging by the television signals that reached our home planet."

"That reminds me," said Amanda, "what *is* the name of your planet? George never got a chance to tell me."

"I don't know," responded George. "Its name and location are the only pieces of information that were omitted from my memory bank of George's life. This was done as a security measure, to keep these details secret in the unlikely event that someone was able to hack into the program that created me. It was always George's intention to reveal everything in person, once he was certain that no harm would come to his home planet. Other than that, I retain all of his memories—except his early attempts at spinning plates on sticks, which I gather were an embarrassment to him. He had hoped to perfect that skill so he could appear on something called *The Ed Sullivan Show* when we arrived here. He also wanted to be on *You Bet Your Life*."

"Yes, he mentioned that," said Amanda, smiling. "And he would have been a great contestant too—if the show hadn't been cancelled fifty years ago."

"Indeed he would," said George. "It's quite astounding how much he knows about so many things."

"Oh, believe me, I know. Whether the subject was astronomy or yogurt cultures, he always seemed to know a lot about it."

"Well," said George, "I'm glad to hear that after all that commotion, everything at the Academy is back to the way it was, and nobody's the worse for wear."

"Unfortunately, that's not quite true. One of the students, Eugenia Snootman, somehow implanted Headmistress Oppenheimer's DNA into herself."

"Oh my," said the George hologram. "Then I'm afraid she's in a bit of a pickle."

"You can say that again," replied Amanda. "A whole barrel of pickles. That's why we're all here. Her father is the richest man on Earth, and he reopened the Academy and has us working on a way to change her back to human form."

"That will be a difficult task. The DNA of my species is extremely dominant. It was designed to be so."

"*Designed* to be so?"

"Yes. Several of your Earth centuries ago, in the time of my great-grandfather and great-grandmother, my planet began to undergo certain atmospheric changes as a result of our activities. The temperature began to increase, the seas began to evaporate, deserts began to spread and the planet's oxygen levels began to drop. A lot of people denied it at first. But then it became obvious to even the most stubborn contrarians that our planet's atmosphere would soon be unable to sustain us. We stopped doing the thing that was hurting our planet—which in our case was using scented room freshener to make the outdoors smell as pleasant as the indoors—but it was too late. The damage had been done, and our beautiful planet was no longer able to support us. We realized that we would die out as a species.

"Efforts were made to locate other planets to inhabit. But nothing suitable was found—luckily for Earthlings, we didn't yet have the technology for long-distance space travel. So our greatest scientific minds produced all sorts of ideas for coping with the changes: putting reflectors in space to deflect the intense sunlight, moving our civilization underground, and building vast false skies above us and huge subterranean oceans around us. But our experts determined that these solutions would be far too expensive for all but a select few to afford. They knew that there would be tremendous struggle and bloodshed if most of our citizens were left to die. So they ultimately decided that it made more sense to change *ourselves*. Our re-engineered bodies became the apparatus by which we would sustain our civilization. They were designed to be incredibly tough and durable, to support our minds and to enable us to live on through the most harrowing conditions. That is the body that you saw in Oppenheimer and Leitspied, and the body to which Eugenia now finds herself attached."

"But if your bodies are so tough," asked Amanda, "how come the DNA breaks down so quickly? Every time we extract some to study it, we can't, because it immediately begins to decompose. Perhaps it's our atmosphere?"

"No," said George, "it's a safety mechanism built into the DNA itself. When our geneticists arrived at the perfect combination of attributes to help our species survive, they wanted to avoid further mutations that might introduce vulnerabilities into our bloodline. So they designed this DNA to immediately overwhelm anything unfamiliar. Its strength, as you on Earth would say, is a double-edged sword. Our leaders felt that there was a danger of it being used for other purposes—specifically, creating new and unauthorized species of animals. So while it is immensely dominant in the living organism, it was designed to deteriorate rapidly when removed."

"Then it's hopeless? There's no way to reverse Eugenia's condition by removing the alien DNA?"

"Not by removing it. But there *is* a way of switching it off."

"How?"

"Our geneticists built a tiny biological control centre into our bodies as a fail-safe mechanism, so we could reverse or remodify our genes yet again to deal with our planetary conditions, should it become necessary to do so. It functions rather like what you humans refer to as the Hox gene in Earth organisms—it carries a copy of our genes, yet at the same time, it's a master controller for all the other genes."

"Is there any way to make it reverse the modification?"

"In order to do that—for example, to return your acquaintance to human form—you must remove the bio-controller."

"Is that very difficult?" asked Amanda.

"Difficult? Yes," replied George, "quite difficult. But not unachievable. The bio-controller is extremely tiny. Yet with the correct surgical equipment, it would be possible to remove it without damaging any of the vital life-support systems around it."

"But can *we* do it? Her father says that if I don't succeed in helping her, he will sue my family for $100 million. It would ruin them completely."

George looked at her with a kindly expression. "Clearly you have a lot on your mind. But if you fetch a sheet of tracing paper, a pencil and some tape, I believe I can help you find a solution to your problem."

Amanda ran to her workstation, found the required items and raced back to where the George hologram waited.

"Excellent!" he exclaimed. "Now, tape the paper to the glass in front of your face."

Amanda did as he instructed.

"Good. Take your pencil, and when I move my finger against the glass on the other side of the paper, trace my precise motions."

George raised his index finger to the glass. Amanda placed the pencil so it was at the exact same point as George's fingertip.

"Ready?" he asked.

Amanda nodded. "Ready."

George then began carefully tracing a series of lines and curves, which Amanda followed with the pencil. Beside that, he traced a series of shapes that Amanda copied. She soon realized the shapes were numbers. George looked carefully through the glass at the mirror image on Amanda's paper.

"Good," he said. "You now have a picture of what the bio-controller looks like, so you can recognize it when you see it. The number sequence represents its exact location, as measured from the extremities of the exoskeleton."

Amanda looked at George hopefully. "Do you mean that with this, I can begin planning an operation to remove it, so the alien DNA is no longer dominant?"

"Precisely," replied George. "Once the bio-controller is removed, our DNA can be switched off so the human organism will be allowed to regrow. But there's one catch."

"What's that?"

"The bio-controller in this picture is one hundred thousand times larger than the real one. And the real one is located among some rather vital bundles of nerve endings. So you want to be very careful when you go in and try to snip it out. You mustn't shut off any of the body's vital functions until Eugenia has regrown her human body."

Amanda looked perplexed for a moment. Then she smiled. "Sanjay's nanobots!"

"Nanobots, perfect!" replied George. "That would be just the ticket."

"But even assuming that I'm able to remove the bio-controller and regrow Eugenia's human body, how do I get the alien body to disengage from her?"

"The Death Gene," replied George. "When our scientists re-engineered my species' DNA to allow us to survive in the increasingly harsh conditions of our planet, they discovered a way to modify our genes to permanently put an end to natural death. But we realized that programming ourselves to live forever would be unwise. Our world was already crowded. If we lived forever, there would be no room for anyone else to ever be born. It was such a momentous decision that my ancestors held a planet-wide vote. In the end, they decided that it would be selfish not to give future generations a chance to have lives of their own. So they voted against modifying the genetic feature that brings about our death with old age. To this day, like all other species, we carry the seeds of our own destruction. Death is normally a process of decay, as it is for other organisms. But it can also be triggered through chemical conditions that simulate the cellular changes that come with advancing years. Put your pencil up to your paper again."

Amanda did as he asked, following his finger with her pencil as he traced out a complicated diagram showing a strand of alien DNA. Beside it, he wrote out a formula.

"Once the bio-controller is removed and her human body has been regrown," said George, "introduce this chemical into any remaining part of the alien body. Once you do this, it will trigger a termination reaction within the cells. The body will gradually shut down, just as it does naturally with my species on my home planet."

Amanda finished tracing the information. "Thank you," she said. "You have no idea how much you've helped me."

Then she stifled a big yawn. George looked at her with a kindly expression.

"You're most welcome. Now, I deduce from the angle of the moonlight in the room that it must be fairly late at night in your Earth time zone. And if I may say so, you look rather tired. I suggest that you get some sleep. You will need all your energy and mental resources for this project. It will be extremely challenging."

"But there's so much I want to know about you," said Amanda.

"All in good time," replied George. "All in good time. You can visit me here whenever you want—after you have had some sleep and are refreshed."

"That would be wonderful!" said Amanda. "I've really missed our conversations . . . well, you know, the ones with the real George. No offence."

"None taken," offered the holographic George. "I do have one request, however."

"What is it?" asked Amanda.

"Please keep my existence a secret, even from your closest friends. I don't think there are any flaws in my programming that would allow anyone to find out about my home planet, but you never know. Even George is capable of mistakes."

Amanda thought back to the hair-raising drive with George to the Academy the previous autumn and nodded her head in agreement.

"Good idea," she replied politely.

"Additionally," continued the George hologram, "I'm certain that the sight of a man standing inside this box, alongside all the other animals, would be an unnecessary distraction. Besides," he added, waving aside a large emerald leaf that hung down near his nose, "I just don't fit into a Madagascar setting. I'd really look quite out of place in among the civets and the lemurs, don't you think? Unless I grew a tail."

"I think a tail might suit you very nicely," teased Amanda.

George laughed quietly, then looked serious. "I wonder how much reprogramming that would involve?" For a moment, he actually seemed to be considering the technical challenges involved in giving himself a tail.

"One thing's for sure," said Amanda. "You really do sound like George."

The holographic George looked pleased by that.

"And you're right about it being late," she continued. "So I'll say goodbye for now. I'll come back when we can chat in private."

George grinned at her affectionately. "I shall look forward to it, Amanda Forsythe. Good night and sweet dreams."

Amanda went to the keyboard and tapped in a complex command. A moment later, the forest and the animals disintegrated and disappeared. Then George, his image frozen in mid-wave, began to pixelate and slowly vanish too. Amanda could have sworn that she caught a glimpse of his grin hovering faintly in the air for just a moment after the rest of him had gone. Then she was staring once again at an opaque glass panel.

She yawned and turned toward the door. Having renewed the acquaintance of a trusted friend—or at least an entity that had his knowledge, as well as his warmth and mannerisms—her mood lightened. She felt as if a great weight had been lifted off her. And with the instructions he had given her on how to remove the bio-controller, Amanda felt hopeful again. Of course, Snootman wouldn't have confidence in her to carry out the operation. Not yet. But eventually she would regain his trust. She wasn't sure how, but she was determined to find a way. Until then, she would work in secret on the problem of how to extract the bio-controller.

Amanda padded through the darkened hallways, back to the dorm. At the door to her room, she swiped her pass card and silently turned the door handle. She slipped inside and climbed into her bed, taking care not to disturb Evelyn. The shadows on the walls no longer resembled claws reaching out from the cemetery. Instead, they looked like just what they were: branches from a majestic old maple tree silhouetted on a beautiful moonlit night. Amanda realized too that what she had thought were warts on long, spidery claws were actually tiny buds growing on the tree's branches. Soon they would open into new leaves, beginning the cycle of life again. Amanda pulled on the eyeshades that she always wore to bed and soon fell into a deep, luxuriant sleep.

CHAPTER 13

"WAKE UP, sleepyhead."

Amanda heard Evelyn's voice as if she was calling to her from the bottom of a well. Then she felt her shoulder being gently tapped.

"I've already let you sleep in an extra half hour. Time to get up, lazybones."

"Please don't say the word 'bones,'" groaned Amanda.

"Why not?" asked Evelyn.

Amanda removed her eyeshades.

"Long story," she replied, sitting up in bed.

Amanda saw that it was almost eight o'clock. Golden morning light poured in through their window. She paused, enjoying its warmth on her face for a moment, and noted that the sun was higher in the sky than it had been only the previous week. Then she remembered her encounter with George the night before. It felt like a dream. But Amanda knew it was not, and smiled.

However, Amanda's buoyant mood quickly turned to apprehension when she arrived at Thorne's classroom that morning and saw him having a whispered conversation with Joules, Arsinée, Henbane and Ethyl. Arsinée spotted Amanda and smirked slightly, then nodded at Henbane and Ethyl, who turned to watch her with expressions of self-satisfied superiority on their faces. The only one of the group who didn't look smug was Joules, whose brow was furrowed in concern as he jotted down some notes.

Thorne looked up at the rest of the arriving students. "Come in, class. Come in," he said in an uncharacteristically jovial tone, his waxy face creasing into something resembling an actual smile.

"Wonder what Mr. Happy is so chuffed about?" whispered Derek.

"I don't know," replied Amanda under her breath. "But I've got a bad feeling we're about to find out."

Thorne took a pair of dice from the pocket of his lab coat, rattled them as if he was going to roll them, then put them away again. "I have some exciting news for all of you."

Amanda and the rest of the students took their seats. Thorne cleared his throat.

"I realize that the complete failure of Miss Forsythe's regrowth experiment was a big disappointment to everyone. We all want to return Eugenia to her human form as soon as possible. But when the racehorse of life bucks us off onto our behinds, it's important to get back on that beast and gallop to the finish line just the same. We have learned lessons from that setback. And one of those lessons, I believe, is to allow the most talented people to step forward and contribute in the most effective manner. It is no secret that Eugenia had the greatest skills at manipulating DNA of anyone in the Academy. This is evidenced by her monumental achievement in creating *this*!"

Thorne pointed to an object concealed beneath a dark cloth shroud on his desk. With a flourish, he whipped away the covering, revealing a cage. Behind its bars was the repugnant Tinkerbell, the animal that Eugenia had concocted with her gene-splicing experiments, before becoming an even more impressive experiment herself. It was about the size of a ferret and had short legs sprouting from a long, hairy body that undulated like a belly dancer's. Its head was pointed and reptilian, and it had a mouth full of needle-like teeth. At the tip of its snake-like tail was a rattle, which it now shook ominously. The hideous little animal narrowed its eyes and looked menacingly at Thorne, whose gloved fingers were wrapped around the handle of the cage. It hissed angrily and struck at his hand. The students nearest Tinkerbell reared back in their chairs.

"Aghhh!" shrieked Joules in a high-pitched voice.

Joules had always been terrified of Tinkerbell, but he'd carefully hidden this fear because of his even greater fear that he might offend Eugenia and lose her friendship.

Thorne, meanwhile, merely smiled, despite the fearful reactions of the students and Tinkerbell's continued efforts to bite him. A protective plate beneath the handle of the cage prevented Tinkerbell from sinking his fangs into Thorne's flesh, something the animal clearly wished to do as deeply and painfully as possible.

"Figures that Thorne would admire something that's part crocodile, part weasel and part rattlesnake," whispered Derek.

"I heard that, Mr. Murphy. And you're absolutely correct. Just look at this marvellous creature. It takes the most aggressive behavioural traits of several predatory species and combines them in one body. It is a stunning achievement in genetic modification. Let us cast our eyes on it admiringly as an inspiration to us all."

As Thorne set the cage back down on the table at the front of the classroom, Tinkerbell hissed and struck out one last time, his little fangs projecting through the bars in one final attempt to inflict injury.

"There, there," said Thorne to Tinkerbell, then he turned to the class. "But enough of me flapping my gums. I'll let your new project leader tell you all about the exciting research strategy." He patted Joules affectionately on the back. "Please give this brilliant young man a big round of applause."

The students clapped, but only politely. Even the former members of Eugenia's intramural house, Alhacen, couldn't rouse themselves to enthusiasm at the thought of once again working under the domination of her inner circle. After hearing Joules's plan, they would be even less enthusiastic.

"Thank you, Professor Thorne. As you all know, Eugenia is not just a wonderful person"—he paused, taking a gulp of air—"but also a genius of the highest order." He clasped his hands together over his heart and swooned slightly. Amanda heard Derek groan involuntarily. Joules regained his breath and his balance and continued. "As Professor Thorne has pointed out, her great achievement, Tinkerbell, is a testament to that fact."

Amanda noted that despite Joules's professed admiration for Eugenia's "pet" project, he cast a wary eye on Tinkerbell as the creature slithered about its cage.

"So I think it's appropriate that in our efforts to return our beloved Eugenia to her human form, we use her own groundbreaking research to assist us. Having successfully combined the

DNA of several land-based animals to create Tinkerbell, Eugenia was eager to move on to altering aquatic life. Just before Oppenheimer, Leitspied and George were exposed as aliens, she had been in the planning stages of an experiment to combine the DNA of a lamprey eel and a squid to create a superior marine predator. Eugenia had planned to call it a quidprey."

The lamprey eel, as many people who live around the Great Lakes of Canada and the United States will know, is a singularly unpleasant parasite. Growing up to a metre long, it feeds by attaching its suction-cup mouth to its victim—usually a fish but occasionally an unwary human swimmer. It then bores its prey with grinding disc-like teeth, literally sucking the life out of them by draining their blood and bodily fluids. As if this did not qualify the lamprey as objectionable enough, Eugenia evidently had envisioned making it even more revolting.

"This is a really bad idea," whispered Evelyn. "Squids are one of the most aggressive creatures in the ocean, and providing the lamprey with tentacles will give it a huge advantage over its prey. It will completely upset the balance of nature."

As unpleasant as the concept sounded, what Joules said next was even more disturbing.

"And so, I now intend to revive Project Quidprey. That in itself would be a worthy homage to Eugenia. But to make the experiment relevant to our research, we shall take it a step further. As you all know, it is one thing to insert DNA into a still-developing embryo. It is something else again to coax a fully formed organism into absorbing DNA from another creature and taking on some of its physical characteristics. Until now, that is. I have developed a special receptor gene that will make it possible for the quidprey to integrate additional genetic information even after it has progressed beyond the embryonic stage. This will allow it to mutate into a new form."

"I'm sure you can all see the importance of Joules's brilliant plan," said Professor Thorne, looking pleased. "If you are able to perfect this technique, you could successfully reintroduce human DNA into Eugenia, thus enabling her to regenerate the human components that have been replaced by the alien counterparts. Of course, you will still need to devise a means of deactivating the alien DNA and triggering this growth. But I believe that Joules's experiment, if successful, will be a major step toward reconstituting Eugenia. And so I have today arranged for the full resources of the department to be put behind this program. I want all of you to help Joules and his team in any way they ask."

Amanda put up her hand.

"What is it, Miss Forsythe?" asked Thorne with a note of exaggerated weariness, as though just the sound of her voice was like a lamprey draining the life out of him.

"I think this idea is potentially very dangerous," she replied. "The quidprey could absorb the DNA of an animal that we hadn't planned for it to absorb. It could evolve unpredictably into a really dangerous creature that could then pass its mutated genes on to its offspring."

Thorne snorted derisively. "Do you think me such an idiot that I don't know how to contain a potential biohazard situation? I've worked in military labs on the most virulent forms of biological weapons, without incident. There are protocols for such things. Compared to aerial bombs designed to spread lethal viruses over entire cities, a Petri dish of eels hardly gives us much to worry about."

He mugged to the class. Only Arsinée, Joules, Henbane and Ethyl laughed. The rest looked very concerned.

"Could we at least use animals less dangerous than a lamprey eel and a squid?" asked Amanda. "Something that isn't a vicious predator, perhaps?"

Thorne scowled. "Miss Forsythe, this discussion was tiresome thirty seconds ago. Nothing you have said is making it any less so. This classroom is a secure area. Once the door is closed, nothing can enter or exit. So if I were you, I would quit seeking to discourage your rivals and try emulating their hard work and ingenuity instead. If you're capable of it, that is."

Thorne turned to Joules and smiled.

"Joules, you may commence Project Quidprey now. As for you, Miss Forsythe, I'd like you to stay away from the class until further notice. I don't want your bad attitude and lack of enthusiasm to undermine the project. Now if you'll excuse me, I have urgent probability experiments to attend to."

Thorne strode behind the tinted glass panel of his workstation, put on a pair of earphones and began intently clicking his mouse. Flashing coloured light from his monitor reflected off his grey skin, giving it a hint of life. As Amanda exited the classroom, she caught a glimpse of his lips moving. Thorne didn't utter a sound, but he seemed to be blowing on the mouse for some inexplicable reason. Amanda closed the door behind her and shook her head. He was impossible.

CHAPTER 14

HAVING BEEN BANISHED from the classroom, Amanda had more time than ever to work on her space projects. She surprised her friends by focusing her efforts on a modest undertaking: a small, slender rocket, a high-altitude, suborbital craft devoted to collecting weather data. She also built a manual ground-control station, from which, as she explained to Evelyn, Derek and Sanjay, she could control the rocket's re-entry path.

"Once it's ready," she told her friends one afternoon in the lab, "you can make the rocket land anywhere in the world simply by pointing to a spot on the map on this computer screen."

"But why would you want to do that?" asked Derek.

"Say you can't land because there's a severe storm at the original site," explained Amanda. "With this device, you can simply redirect the rocket to an alternate landing site. You don't have to know anything about flying. You just point to a location on this touch screen, and the software will recalculate everything automatically."

"Good idea," said Derek. "But I thought your ambition was to travel to other galaxies. What about the photon-sail ships you used to talk about building?"

"Well," replied Amanda with a hint of sadness in her eyes, "as I've found out the hard way, you have to learn to walk before you can run. I'm not sure if I'll ever be able to tackle a project like that. But this is a start."

Evelyn, Derek and Sanjay pretended to be impressed, but they were more than a little concerned by Amanda's sudden lack of confidence. So one evening, while she was in the lab working on the rocket, they had a discreet conversation in the dorm.

"I'm worried about Amanda," said Derek. "Her ambition has always been to achieve interstellar travel. Weather rockets are beneath her. People have been building them for more than fifty years. There are amateur clubs devoted to making them. A bunch of geeks in a garage might accomplish the same thing in a few weekends."

"That's true," said Sanjay. "It certainly isn't something that would push her creativity to its limits. Do you think this thing with the lobsters has affected her mental health?"

Evelyn was more philosophical. "Amanda suffered a big shock when she was taken down like that in Thorne's class. Perhaps this is her way of doing something that she can master, something that she knows for sure will work."

"But it's so far beneath her capabilities," said Derek.

"I know," replied Evelyn. "But she may need an easily attainable goal to rebuild her self-confidence. I think we should just support her in it."

"Makes sense to me," agreed Sanjay, somewhat reluctantly. "Maybe this will help her get her mojo back. Then she can progress to once again doing her photon-sail research, or at least building something more advanced than a weather rocket."

"I hope you're right," said Derek. "And that our least favourite zombie hasn't finally got to her."

Meanwhile, away from Thorne's prying eyes, Amanda set about solving the problem of removing the bio-controller from Eugenia. First, she built a computer model based on the diagram that George had given her. But after reading a number of medical journals detailing the latest breakthroughs in microsurgery, Amanda felt that even the most advanced techniques available to science were too risky. So that evening, as she and her three friends sat in her dorm, she broached the subject with Sanjay.

"Could you develop a nanobot that was so small it could enter a living organism, travel six centimetres or so and remove a particular object?"

"How big would this particular object be?" asked Sanjay.

"About one hundred microns in diameter," she replied.

"One hundred microns?" asked Sanjay, astonished. "About the size of a grain of sand?"

"That's correct," Amanda confirmed.

Sanjay whistled through his teeth. "Whoa, that's a very tall order. Or should I say, an extraordinarily tiny order."

"There's more," said Amanda.

"Such as?" he asked.

"It would have to navigate through an area densely wired with nerves controlling vital biological functions. If these were damaged, it could cause critical injury or death."

"What are we talking about here, Amanda?" asked Sanjay.

"I'm afraid I can't tell you," she replied.

Derek sat up. "Can't tell us? Oooooooh, a woman of mystery now, are we?" he teased.

"I'm serious," Amanda repeated. "I really can't tell you."

"Is this some weird thing that Snootman put you up to?" Derek asked.

"I can't tell you that either. Let's just say that I made a promise and I can't break it."

"But, Amanda, we're your best friends. We'd never betray a secret," said Evelyn.

"Then you'll understand that I wouldn't either."

"Wow, I really thought I knew you better than this," said Derek. "To think that there's somebody else in this school you're more loyal to than us."

"It's got nothing to do with being more loyal to someone," said Amanda. "It's to do with being loyal to a promise."

She felt a gnawing sensation in her stomach as she saw Derek's upset expression. But the problem was not just that she had given George's holographic double her word that she wouldn't reveal his secret. Amanda also knew that if Derek, Evelyn or Sanjay found out about him, and accidentally revealed his existence to anyone else at the Academy, she might be prevented from speaking with George ever again, and that could doom the project to failure.

"You know, you're acting very strangely," snapped Derek. "All this secrecy, even with us. And that kindergarten rocket project. It's ridiculous."

"*Derek*!" said Evelyn under her breath. "Shut up."

"It's true," Derek continued. "You could do it in your sleep. I worry about you, Amanda."

"Well don't!" Amanda replied sharply, becoming annoyed by his dismissive tone.

"Fine, then," snapped Derek. "Whatever your big secret project is, have fun with it. I've got my own things to do."

Amanda regained her composure. "Derek, please wait," she called.

But Derek stalked out of the room and closed the door heavily behind him. The other three remained there in uncomfortable silence, then Sanjay moved toward the door.

"Sanjay, please don't go," said Amanda. "I really need you. And I need you to trust me about why I can't tell you."

Sanjay frowned. "The four of us have never hidden anything from each other. Frankly, it bugs me a little that you don't believe I can keep a secret. You didn't believe me about the aliens either."

"This is totally different. I made a promise," said Amanda.

"How do I know that this experiment isn't part of some big corporate or political conspiracy to do something wicked?"

"Because you know I wouldn't do that," replied Amanda.

"Not intentionally," said Sanjay. "But perhaps whoever has put you up to this is a shill for some conspirators trying to develop a technology for something evil, just as Oppenheimer and Leitspied were."

"Please trust me," said Amanda. "It's nothing like that."

"Derek will be upset with me over this." Sanjay sighed. "But if you *really* think this is so important . . ."

"I do, and it is."

Sanjay hesitated, then nodded.

"All right, I'll do it."

"Thank you, Sanjay," replied Amanda. "And I promise that when the time comes, this will all make sense."

"I hope so," said Sanjay. "I really, really hope so."

They needed a live subject on which to test Sanjay's nanobots. And they knew that there would be a lot of failures. But none of them had the heart to sacrifice any living creatures.

So Amanda sneaked out to Dr. Okina's classroom that night and, after a pleasant conversation with the computer-generated version of George, came away with the recipe for the in vitro meat he had served in the cafeteria the previous autumn. That meat, of course, had no nerve endings—the whole point was to make meat that wasn't attached to a being with feelings and intelligence. But the holographic George was able to suggest a slight modification to generate a primitive nervous system. The meat would feel no pain, since it did not have a brain, but it would nonetheless react as any living creature would to Amanda's experiments. Now she could begin her tests.

The dorm became their centre of operations, a place where they could work on the project away from the prying eyes of Professor Thorne, who would surely put a stop to her experiments if he discovered them. Derek had been avoiding Amanda, but in case he found out, she made up a cover story about trying to create in vitro meat that would produce its own barbecue sauce, as a way of raising money to pay off Snootman's lawsuit if that became necessary.

Several weeks and many failed experiments later, Sanjay, Amanda and Evelyn were in the dorm, breathlessly awaiting the results of their latest effort. Today, Sanjay had for the first time been able to manipulate the nanobot so it was able to reach the target zone without damaging any of the meat's nerve networks. The three of them watched a large video monitor that tracked the nanobot's movements as it made its return journey. *If* the nanobot had succeeded in removing the tiny test object that Amanda had placed there, and *if* it succeeded in returning without injuring any of the meat's nerves, then maybe—just maybe—they had some chance of removing the bio-controller from Eugenia. But she couldn't reveal that to her friends yet. For now, she waited tensely for the nanobot to complete its journey.

Meanwhile, momentous events were about to unfold elsewhere in the Academy. Had Amanda not been banished by Thorne and forced to carry out her experiments in secret in the dorm, she might have chanced to see Joules sauntering toward Thorne's classroom from the direction of the cafeteria. She might have seen him carrying a gooey, sugary fruit custard tart in each hand. And she might have noticed that while he was shovelling one of the tarts into his mouth, the second tart was attracting the attention of some fruit flies that had just escaped from Dr. Okina's lab. Amanda might also have caught a last glimpse of Joules raising the second tart to his lips, unaware of the tiny halo of fruit flies scattering off it as he closed the classroom door behind him. But of course, neither Amanda nor anyone else was there to witness those events. So it was not until some time later that the results of the fateful attraction of the fruit flies to Joules's custard tart were discovered.

CHAPTER 15

LATER THAT AFTERNOON, Amanda, Evelyn and Sanjay were huddled around the workstation in the dorm, anxiously watching as Sanjay's tiny nanobot finally emerged from the in vitro meat.

Sanjay gazed into a powerful magnifying eyepiece. "It's holding something in its retrieval mechanism," he said. "But I can't tell what. Can you take a look, Amanda, and tell me if that's the target object?"

She squinted into the eyepiece. Then she burst into a smile. "That's the object I placed in there, all right! You've done it, Sanjay! This is wonderful."

Amanda felt a moment of absolute relief and joy. Finally, it would be possible to remove the alien gene controller, and there was a chance—however slim—that Eugenia could be returned to normal, freeing Amanda of Snootman's $100-million lawsuit. Now she would just have to confirm that she really knew how to regenerate organs and limbs. That task would be tougher.

Because of Thorne's relentless hostility toward her, he would put a stop to her experiments if he found out about them. She would have to get hold of everything she needed and do her work outside of his lab, in secret.

Amanda gazed into the middle distance, as she often did when pondering a dilemma. She found that this helped clear her mind and allowed her to see fresh possibilities. But this time, instead of seeing a fresh possibility, she saw something inching its way in from the hallway, under the door. The "something" was tubular, no longer than her baby fingernail, and used some kind of grasping device to pull itself toward an air vent. Being so used to Sanjay's nanobots wandering about her room, Amanda thought nothing of it. That is, until the object opened up a tiny set of wings and flitted from the wall to a nearby floor lamp.

"Sanjay, since when did you create nanobots with wings?"

"Um . . . since never," he replied. "Why do you ask?"

"Because something that looks not unlike one of your nanobots just crawled in under the door, went up the wall and flew across to the floor lamp."

"If it's a nanobot, it's not one of mine," replied Sanjay. He furrowed his brow. "But that could mean it's been sent to spy on us!" he suddenly remarked with alarm. "I wouldn't put it past Joules and his crew—although I don't know how all of them combined would have the brains to figure out the technology. That means it would have to be spying on us for some rogue corporation or government, or perhaps a criminal organization!"

The three of them approached the lamp and examined the tiny object, which was crawling up the edge of the shade. Sanjay looked through his eyepiece.

"But I guess not, because this isn't a nanobot at all," he said. "Nobody's nanobots are this supple. It appears to be an organic life form."

Amanda held a magnifying glass over it so they could all see the tiny creature.

"Whatever it is, it's revolting," she said. "Looks like a worm or something."

Evelyn leaned in to get a better look. "The mouthparts appear to be the sort you would find on a parasite. Perhaps a lamprey eel."

"Ugh, I hate eels," said Sanjay.

"But it appears to have tentacles," added Evelyn. "I would say from a Pacific squid, judging by the shape. I think we all know what this means."

Amanda looked gravely at the others. "Squids and lampreys don't have wings. So Joules's receptivity gene must have enabled this quidprey to absorb DNA from some other life form—something that flies."

"If that's true," said Evelyn, "it will be able to pass those genes on as it reproduces. A predator parasite that functions in the air, under water and on the ground. God help us."

Just then, the tiny mutant reared up, waving its head back and forth rhythmically like a cobra.

"Gross. What's it doing?" asked Sanjay.

"If it *is* partly a lamprey eel, it may be trying to detect the presence of flesh using its sense of smell," said Evelyn. "That's how they locate their prey."

"Gawd, I hate eels!" said Sanjay.

Then the creature pointed its tiny nose straight at them.

Sanjay screwed up his face. "If you're right about that, I don't like the way it's looking at m—"

Before he could finish his sentence, the little mutant shot through the air, wings buzzing, and headed straight for his throat. Amanda swung the magnifying glass like a tennis racket, catching the creature in midair and slamming it to the floor, where it lay crumpled.

"Do you think it's dead?" asked Sanjay.

Amanda brought her heel down hard on it. "I hope so," she said.

"I thought you were against hurting animals," said Evelyn.

"I make an exception for things that want to eat me," replied Amanda, grinding her heel a few more times for good measure.

Just then, they heard a spine-chilling scream from downstairs.

The three of them raced down the stairwell toward the sound of the commotion, arriving just in time to see Joules stumbling out of Professor Thorne's classroom.

"Agh! It's after me!" he shrieked.

A metre-long eel-like creature was diving after Joules, wings flapping like a seagull, teeth whirring, trying to attach itself to his neck with its sucking mouthparts and squid tentacles. Amanda pulled out her cellphone and dialled 9-1-1. But instead of an emergency operator, a different voice answered.

"Bill Snootman here. What seems to be the problem, Amanda?"

"I don't know why I got you on the line instead of the 9-1-1 operator," Amanda replied, "but we have an emergency situation. Something has gone horribly wrong with Joules's experiment. The hybrid he made absorbed DNA from fruit flies. So there are now blood-sucking eels that can fly and breathe air hatching in the lab. We need to call the authorities."

As she spoke, Amanda could see Joules running down the

hall toward the cafeteria, trying to escape the quidprey. He was screeching like a macaque, flailing blindly at the mutant with a copy of Darwin's *On the Origin of Species* as it tried to fasten itself to the back of his neck. Worse, Amanda could see a cloud of tiny hatchlings winging their way out of Professor Thorne's classroom. Evelyn noticed them at the same moment and slammed the door shut, preventing any more of them from escaping.

"There are hundreds of hatchlings now," said Amanda to Bill Snootman. "They're small, but judging from the size of the adult that is chasing Joules, they grow very, very quickly. We've got to evacuate the Academy and get an emergency response team in here before they get too big."

"I'm afraid I can't do that," said Bill Snootman.

"What? Why not?"

"If the authorities come in, someone might take a picture of Eugenia and release it to the press. I can't risk that. The effect on her would be devastating."

"But the effect on *all of us* will be devastating once these things grow to full size and start feeding on everyone," Amanda replied. She saw that the escaped parasitic eels were now flying toward the cafeteria.

"They're probably following some chemical signal sent out by the larger mutant," said Evelyn. "A lot of species communicate with pheromones."

"Or maybe they just smell blood!" said Sanjay.

"Unfortunately," replied Evelyn, "that's quite possible too. And once they all know there is prey nearby . . ."

"Mr. Snootman, you've got to evacuate the Academy!" Amanda shouted into the phone. "We have very little time."

There was silence at the other end of the line.

"Did you hear me?" she screamed. "I said we have very little time!"

Finally Snootman answered. "Yes, Amanda. I heard you. But I'm afraid this goes beyond having pictures of my daughter circulating in the trash press. If the exact nature of the dangerous genetic experiments we are carrying out here ever became known beyond these walls, the public outrage would be such that no amount of money would keep the authorities from closing us down. That would doom my daughter to a life as a freak. And that is something I can't permit, no matter what the cost."

Amanda heard a metallic clanging. She turned in time to see metal shutters sliding down over the windows and doors sealing off any means of escape to the outside world.

"I have just locked down the Academy," said Bill Snootman. "I had those isolation systems built the week before you came, just in case. And the barriers were installed in the sewer system too, so don't think of trying that trick again. From this point on, nothing enters or exits this building without my permission. We will defeat these creatures or die here together."

"You're insane!" shouted Amanda.

"That may well be," replied Snootman, "given everything I've been through. But I am in control. Now, do you have a plan?"

Amanda thought fast. "Yes. Get all the students and staff into the Constellation Hall—everyone but me, Evelyn, Sanjay and Derek. We need to find him, now!"

Just then, Derek appeared in the stairwell.

"Why do you need me? And what's all the commotion?" he asked.

"There's been an accident with Joules's experiment," said Sanjay.

"What sort of an accident?" Derek asked skeptically. "Or is that another secret?"

"This is no joke," said Evelyn. "The quidpreys have grown wings and escaped! They're taking over the Academy!"

Derek looked uncertain for a moment. Then he heard a cry of terror echoing down the hall. He turned to see Joules in the distance, shrieking as he desperately flapped his arms trying to fend off the quidprey, which had been joined by a second, slightly smaller one. The two quidpreys seemed to be acting as a team, with one distracting Joules by swirling around his head while the other attempted to fasten its whirling teeth onto his ample buttocks.

"Ooooo! Ow-ooo!" howled Joules. "Youch!"

Derek turned to Amanda without hesitation. "Right, then. What do you need me to do?"

"Come with us to the space lab right away," she replied. "And I need you to alert Dr. Kovalevsky," she shouted into the phone to Snootman. "Tell her to meet us by the zero-g simulator. Once everyone else is in the Constellation Hall, seal it off, including the air vents."

"I hope you know what you're doing," replied Snootman.

"I hope so too. Because you've left me very few options." Amanda hung up.

A chorus of terrified voices was reverberating through distant halls, as other students saw the hordes of quidpreys swirling in the air.

A moment later, Bill Snootman's voice came over the intercom.

"Attention, all students and staff. We have a biohazard emergency. Please make your way immediately to the Constellation

Hall for protective isolation. This is not a drill. We have a biohazard emergency situation. All students and staff are to make their way to the Constellation Hall immediately for protective isolation! I repeat—this is *not* a drill!" he shouted, his voice rising in pitch.

Snootman needn't have repeated it. The panicky tone of his voice made it clear that something had gone terribly wrong. In moments, the halls were choked with students and staff, jostling and frightened out of their wits.

"Come on," shouted Amanda. "Let's get to the rocket lab!"

Amanda, Derek, Evelyn and Sanjay raced for the lab as quickly as they could—no easy feat, given that they were running against a human tide that surged desperately toward the Constellation Hall. Some of the greatest minds on Earth, thought Amanda, but all of them now reacting by instinct, looking no more intelligent than a bait ball of sardines being pursued by sharks.

☆

In less than a minute, Amanda, Derek, Evelyn and Sanjay had sprinted through the stampede and made their way down to the rocket lab. Dr. Kovalevsky was already waiting for them at her workshop table.

"I was down here modifying the rocket packs when Snootman called me," she said. "Something about an experiment gone wrong?"

"Gone wrong is an understatement," said Amanda. "Not even Dr. Frankenstein made anything this dangerous. We're talking flying lamprey eels with squid tentacles to help them latch on to their victims."

"Gawd, I hate eels," said Sanjay.

"If it's that serious, we should evacuate the Academy and bring in the military," said Dr. Kovalevsky.

Amanda shook her head. "Can't. Snootman has locked the building down. When I tried to phone 9-1-1 for help, he had my call redirected to him. He refuses to contact the authorities in case they shut the Academy down and the media find out about Eugenia's condition. He says we've got to handle this on our own."

"Or die trying," said Derek, though he needn't have added that information.

"These mutants are like lamprey eels in water. They're drawn to the smell of blood," said Evelyn. "Unless they're destroyed, they'll find us no matter where we go in the Academy."

"And they've crossbred with fruit flies," said Amanda.

"Which have a keen sense of smell, as well as a rapid reproductive cycle," said Dr. Kovalevsky gravely.

"So if the ones that are already in the Academy get a chance to reproduce . . ." mused Amanda.

"We're in deep, deep doo-doo," concluded Derek.

"Gawd, I hate eels," said Sanjay.

"We've got to keep them from getting that chance," said Amanda. "I've got a plan. We'll need to fire up a couple of jet packs and turn on the zero-g chamber."

"But the safety covers are still off the fans," Dr. Kovalevsky pointed out. "The blades are exposed. It's very dangerous."

"That's exactly the way we need it," Amanda said. "What about the speed control?"

"I was just about to discuss that with Mr. Snootman. I have examined the system closely. Someone tampered with it, although I have no idea why. But I have corrected the problem, and it's working properly again now."

"Good, then we just need to sort out our timing," said Amanda. "Derek and I will each need a jet pack. And you, Evelyn and Sanjay will need to put on containment suits."

"What do you have in mind?" asked Dr. Kovalevsky.

"Wearing the jet packs, Derek and I will lure the quidprey into the anti-gravity room. You will control the fans in the chamber, putting the bottom fan on high reverse once we're in there. We will use the thrust of the jet packs to counteract the suction of the fan so we can get away. The quidpreys, on the other hand, will lack sufficient lift to escape."

"We hope," said Derek.

"Got any better ideas?" asked Amanda.

"Nope," he replied.

"I should be the one to go," said Dr. Kovalevsky. "I have far more flight time with the jet packs than either one of you."

"There's no question that you're the more experienced flyer," replied Amanda, "but the hallways are very narrow. Derek and I are smaller and can fit in the tight spaces better. And because we're lighter, we'll use less fuel and will have more flight time. Besides, you're the only one who can safely operate the fan controls in the chamber."

Dr. Kovalevsky nodded her head grudgingly. Amanda's logic was grimly flawless.

"Evelyn, you will wear a full spacesuit and man the lower door to the chamber. The suit is designed to be worn in deep space. It is completely sealed, so the eels won't be able to detect any pheromones or blood."

"As long as you don't tear it and start bleeding," said Derek.

"Thanks for that," said Evelyn.

"We, on the other hand, will leave some skin exposed so the eels will be attracted to us."

"You mean we're going to be the bait?" asked Derek.

"Precisely," said Amanda. "It's risky, but I think that with these jet packs, we can outfly them. When we come back, we will zoom through that hatch into the chamber. The eels should be right behind us. Once we're certain that we've got all the eels in the chamber, Evelyn will close the bottom hatch. Dr. Kovalevsky, you will then turn the bottom suction fans on high, preventing the eels from getting to Derek and me. Sanjay, you'll man the top hatch. Once the bottom hatch is sealed and the fans are keeping the eels from reaching us, you'll open the top hatch to let Derek and me out. Then we seal both hatches and put the induction fans on high. End of eels. We hope."

"That all makes sense, but why do you need two jet packs?" asked Dr. Kovalevsky.

"These things breed so fast," said Amanda, "we won't get a second chance. Having two of us is a fail-safe measure. If something happens to one of us, there will hopefully still be a survivor to lure the eels into the zero-g chamber."

Nobody argued. It was a grave point, but a graver situation.

"I've adjusted the sensitivity on the handgrips," said Dr. Kovalevsky. "There is a greater range of thrust settings now, so you'll have more control. You won't have to worry as much now about blowing yourselves through the ceiling. And it will have just as much acceleration and lift as ever, but not until you open it up all the way."

"Got it," said Amanda.

"Brill," added Derek, whose Doc Martens still bore the scars of his previous flight.

Amanda and Derek slipped hurriedly into their flight suits.

"I've added some new safety equipment to go with the personal jet pack," continued Dr. Kovalevsky. "It was supposed to be a surprise, but . . ." She opened a cabinet and took out something that looked like a two-piece human exoskeleton with a chest protector, bulletproof plastic joints built into the elbows and shoulders, and plates to protect their legs.

"Looks like motorcycle body armour!" said Derek.

"It is," said Dr. Kovalevsky, "with some modifications. Eventually, I will develop more specialized equipment, but for now, this should do the trick. It's light, gives you full mobility, and you should be able to glance off a wall at up to eighty kilometres an hour without doing any serious damage to yourself."

"Cool," he replied.

"But I don't recommend that you test that claim."

Dr. Kovalevsky strapped the body armour to Amanda and Derek as they got their helmets on. Amanda removed her visor.

"Derek, take yours off too. We've got to be able to maintain eye contact," she said. "And besides, for this to work, the quid-preys have to be able to smell us."

"My mission success depends on my ability to be smelled by eels," mused Derek. "You just never know where life's going to take you, do you?" He removed his visor.

"Are we all set?" asked Amanda.

"Ready for flight," Dr. Kovalevsky confirmed.

"Okay, Derek, let's get some lift happening, get used to these jet packs, then roll."

"Roger that!" he shouted.

They hit the ignition switches on their packs, and the rockets hissed to life. Then they increased the thrust. Their feet lifted off the floor, by just a few centimetres at first, but within seconds, they were both feeling confident enough to hover several metres off the ground. They each made a few circuits of the hangar-like space, to get a feel for the new controls. Then they were ready.

Dr. Kovalevsky gave them one last caution. "Depending how hard you push these packs, they have enough fuel for about fifteen minutes of flight. That means fourteen minutes are left after the testing you just did. You'll hear a warning buzzer when you're down to your last minute."

Amanda nodded.

"Okay. We're ready. We'll take the doors at a fly in case any of those things are down here. If you'll do the honours, Doctor?"

"I've got you covered," said Dr. Kovalevsky, her hand on the switch controlling the security doors into the lab.

"Good luck!" shouted Evelyn.

"Yes!" chimed in Sanjay. "And don't worry, we've got your backs."

Derek and Amanda nodded to each other and twisted on the accelerators. In an instant, they were streaking headfirst across the lab, straight toward the heavy vault doors. Dr. Kovalevsky counted down silently to herself, then hit the controls. Just when Amanda thought they were about to get their heads relocated to between their heels, the doors opened with a swoosh and they zoomed out into the hall. Their feet were barely clear when the doors slammed shut behind them again.

"Looks clear," whispered Amanda.

"Agreed," replied Derek.

They hovered at the bottom of the stairwell for a moment.

"Let's start at the top," said Amanda. "If they're up there, there's less chance of alerting them and getting cut off from our route back to the zero-g chamber."

"Makes sense to me," said Derek.

Amanda and Derek twisted their accelerator handgrips, and a moment later, they were corkscrewing up the stairwell. They used the thrust controls to weave like fighter planes in combat, flying from side to side instead of in a straight line to make themselves more difficult targets in case they were ambushed by any quidpreys lurking in the doorways. They passed floor after floor until they had zoomed all the way up to the upper-level dormitories. There, they hovered in the stairwell for a moment, looking down the hall.

"You see anything?" said Amanda.

"No," replied Derek. "Doesn't look like there's anything here."

"Only one way to find out," said Amanda. "Let's go!"

"I'm with you!" he answered.

They hit the accelerators and were soon flying down the hall of the boys' dormitory. They slowed as they reached a tight bend in the corridor where the next wing began. They braced themselves as they rounded the corner, but they saw nothing. Then they flew the length of the hall and rounded the next bend, which led to the girls' dorms. Again, there was no movement. Amanda and Derek didn't speak. The entire floor was eerily silent, except for the hiss of the pilot light in their rocket packs.

They took off again, weaving down the corridor till they reached the final corner.

"If the quidpreys are here . . ." Amanda's voice tailed off.

"This'll be the place," concluded Derek.

She nodded. They flew around the corner, but it too was devoid of life.

"Should we try the attic?" asked Derek.

"No point," said Amanda. "Snootman gave me the tour the first day back. The only thing there now is Eugenia's living quarters. It's hermetically sealed. You'd have an easier time breaking into the Tower of London."

"Right, then down it is."

As they jetted back down the staircase, Derek looked warily down the corridors.

"Second floor—ladies wear, children's laboratories and hopefully no flying eels."

But these hallways too were quiet and empty. They set off once again, flying past the labs reserved for the kids' personal experiments. Each one had a large, explosion-proof window in it. They checked them all, but again, there were no signs of life.

"If my deductive reasoning is correct," said Derek, "this can mean only one thing."

"Yes," replied Amanda.

She drew a deep breath, slowly, to a count of six.

"Centre, centre," Amanda whispered to herself as she lowered her eyelids for a moment and focused her thoughts.

"I haven't the faintest clue what you're doing," said Derek. "But if you're doing it, it must work."

He closed his eyes lightly, stared into the blackness of his own mind, and felt the cool breath through his nose focusing his energy and thoughts.

"Okay," said Amanda, "this is it."

"Just remember, we're too young to die," said Derek.

"We're also too young to be fiddling about with spaceships and alien DNA," replied Amanda, "but that hasn't stopped it from happening. Dying, on the other hand, is very low on my to-do list, so . . ."

They bumped their fists together, smiled slightly, then hit the accelerators. As soon as they had corkscrewed through the air, down to the main floor, they knew that this was where the action was. Scattered across the floor were notepads, textbooks and handheld computers that students had flung away in their frenzy to escape.

"Check the cafeteria first?" asked Derek. "Deductive reasoning: if it's an easy meal that the quidpreys are looking for, that would be the place to find it."

"Makes sense," said Amanda. "Let's do it."

They shot off down the hall, then entered the cafeteria through the wide main doors. There they saw tables overturned. Untouched and unfinished food was everywhere—left behind as the panicked students had raced for their lives.

"Interesting," said Amanda, looking at a large roast of medium rare beef still warm, sitting unmolested at one of the hot tables. Beside it was an equally undisturbed tray of steaming tandoori chicken that Derek and Amanda would have thought smelled like a delicious meal, had they not been preoccupied with ensuring that they didn't become a delicious meal themselves.

"The eels have been here, but they haven't touched any of the meat," she said. "What does your deductive reasoning tell you about that?

Derek gulped. "That they're interested only in live flesh."

"My thoughts exactly," replied Amanda. "In which case, we'd better get to the Constellation Hall right away."

"Right," said Derek, taking a deep breath. "More than two hundred people locked up there—all of them living, breathing . . . and made entirely of meat."

"The quidpreys will be looking for a way in," said Amanda. "And if they've inherited the intelligence and aggression of the squid, they'll find it."

They twisted the handgrip accelerators and took to the air, flying out of the cafeteria and down the main corridor of the Academy. Amanda remembered her first day here, when she walked with Evelyn through these halls on the way to Professor Leitspied's class. She would never have guessed then that less than a year later, she would be airborne in this same corridor, preparing to do battle with a genetic mutant.

Within moments, they had reached the end of the hall. Amanda gestured to Derek to set down on solid ground, then she put a finger to her lips to signal him to be quiet. She turned her jet pack down to its lowest setting, just enough to keep the pilot light burning.

"Do you hear that?" she whispered.

Derek nodded grimly. They could hear dull thuds echoing from around the next corner.

"It's like birds striking a window, only heavier," whispered Derek.

"I hear something else too."

Derek cocked his head, then he noticed it too—a rhythmic clicking.

"Sounds like hundreds of rats gnawing on wood," he replied.

"It's the quidpreys," said Amanda. "They smell everyone in the Constellation Hall, and they're trying to bore through the wood with their lamprey teeth to get to them."

They also became aware of the whimpers of some of the terrified students on the other side of the door. One voice stood out above the others.

"Sounds like Joules," said Derek. "Tough as a burned marshmallow, that one."

"Maybe," Amanda answered. "Or maybe it's just that he created these things and knows what they can do."

Derek considered her comment. "Then we'd better get at it. Once more unto the breach."

They fired up their jet packs, ready to do battle. Or so they hoped. But nothing prepared them for what they saw when they flew around the corner and gazed down the hall.

"Whoa, look at that. They're as big as a grown man's arm!" shouted Derek. "There must be at least sixty or seventy of them!"

Some of the quidpreys were hurling themselves against the door in a frantic attempt to get at all the untapped flesh and blood huddling in terror on the other side. The more intelligent ones, meanwhile, had already progressed to the next logical stage. Realizing that they weren't strong enough to batter down the door, they instead were hovering like nightmarish hummingbirds, using their wings and tentacles to stay in position while they bored through it with their lamprey teeth. By the amount of sawdust on the floor, Amanda and Derek could see that the quidpreys were making good progress.

Amanda leaned over and whispered to Derek. "Once we see the eels—or rather, once they see us—let's separate and do a climbing loop in opposite directions, meeting in the centre of the ceiling. That will spread our scent through the air and make sure they've all had a good whiff."

"And to think I showered this morning for nothing," he replied.

"I think we can outfly them, so once they've chased us up to the ceiling, let's head straight for the staircase to the zero-g chamber. Sound good?" asked Amanda.

"Any plan that involves not hanging around here is okay by me," answered Derek. "So let's go attract some flying eels, shall we?"

"Affirmative," responded Amanda.

She hit the accelerator. Derek was right behind her. They quickly flew down the main corridor to the two-storey rotunda, which had more room to manoeuvre than anywhere else in the building. The Constellation Hall was not just a relatively safe place for the students and staff to wait it out. It was also the only part of the school where the hallway gave them sufficient room to dodge and weave, a factor that could be a lifesaver. Amanda and Derek flew to within ten metres of the eel mutants. But the creatures were so preoccupied with hurling themselves against the door or trying to drill through it to get at the cowering masses on the other side, that they were oblivious to the two perfectly edible humans hovering right behind them.

"They don't care about us," said Derek. "Cor, what am I, chopped liver?"

"Not yet," said Amanda. "And if I were you, I'd keep it that way. They just haven't noticed us. We have to draw their attention."

"I think I can manage that. Wait here," replied Derek. "I'll be right back."

He flew straight for the door and, at the last moment, whipped himself around so that he was able to give it a good, loud kick while using the force of the impact to spring away from it and back into the air.

"Suppertime! Come and get it!" he shouted.

The quidpreys paused momentarily, startled by the sudden sound. The smarter ones—those that had been grinding through the heavy wooden door—turned toward Derek and Amanda, nostrils flaring as they sniffed for the scent of living flesh. Then their circular teeth began to whirr. They immediately lost all interest in what was on the other side of the door, and their small black eyes fixed themselves on the two figures hovering in the air like a floating buffet.

"I reckon they've decided that we'll make a much handier snack," said Derek.

"Let's keep them thinking that as long as we can," said Amanda. "Come on!"

They flew off in opposite directions, tracing an arc from the bottom of the hallway to the top. That sent the eels into a frenzy. Racing after them toward the ceiling, the air filled with the thrumming of their wings, they closed in on Amanda and Derek.

"Okay. One, two, three—go!" shouted Amanda.

Each one did a banking turn away from the other, momentarily confusing the quidpreys, who couldn't decide which one to chase. Then Amanda and Derek met up on the far point of their turn and flew down the corridor with all the quidpreys in frantic, blood-driven pursuit. They banked sharply, hurtling headfirst down the staircase toward the basement, twisting and turning to throw their pursuers off course. Derek momentarily lost control as he went into a tight turn too quickly, sending up a shower of plaster dust and splinters as he scraped along the wall. But Dr. Kovalevsky's body armour held, and a moment later, he was back under control, no worse for wear despite the shards of wood embedded in his chest plate.

"Hang on, Derek. Keep it together. Just one more set of stairs," shouted Amanda as she executed a barrel roll to curve around the last twist in the staircase.

Finally, they were in the corridor leading to the zero-g chamber—and flying straight toward the stainless-steel vault doors.

"All right, Dr. Kovalevsky," said Amanda into her helmet microphone, "we're approaching the doors. Get ready to open up."

Amanda and Derek were relieved to hear Dr. Kovalevsky's calm voice in their earphones. "Roger, I've got you on the video monitor. Ready to open on your command."

"Right. On my count," said Amanda. "Three . . . two . . . one . . . open!"

The heavy steel doors parted, and Amanda and Derek zoomed through the gap, the swarm of quidpreys following just metres behind them. Amanda could see Evelyn in her full containment suit, waiting behind the open hatch to the chamber. Amanda and Derek darted inside. The quidpreys funnelled themselves through the small opening in ravenous pursuit. As the last of the creatures flew in, Evelyn slammed the door shut.

"Now!" called Amanda into her microphone. "Bottom fan on high reverse!"

Amanda and Derek could see Dr. Kovalevsky through the blast-proof glass at the floor level of the chamber. Using a remote control, she revved the bottom fan, creating a powerful downward suction. The slowest, least fit quidpreys were immediately sucked shrieking into the whirling blades, which Amanda noted with irony were not unlike the quidpreys' own circular teeth.

But the stronger and faster of the mutants persisted, fighting against the air current like salmon swimming upstream, desperate to latch on to Amanda and Derek, who were now hovering up near the ceiling.

Then they heard an unwelcome sound: the buzzer warning them that they had one minute of fuel remaining in their jet packs.

"The suction from the fan must be making our packs use fuel faster," shouted Derek. "We'd better get out of here quickly."

"Not yet," called Amanda. "The quidpreys will escape out the hatch along with us."

It was true. Some of the mutants were more persistent than they had expected, and despite the downward suction, they were near the top of the chamber, literally nipping at Amanda's and Derek's heels.

"We need more downward force on them, Dr. Kovalevsky!" called Amanda.

"Okay! Increasing power to the top fans," replied the doctor. "Brace yourselves!"

A moment later, Amanda and Derek felt a rush of air around them. The chamber vibrated as the fans roared to full power. The jet-pack alarms began to chime more stridently.

"Thirty seconds of fuel remaining!" warned Dr. Kovalevsky.

"Get ready to open the ceiling hatch, Sanjay," called Amanda.

"Ready!" Sanjay's voice betrayed a slight tremble.

Amanda and Derek used maximum thrust to get as close to the ceiling hatch as possible. Bobbing in the turbulence, they looked down and saw quidpreys being sucked into the fan by the score. Only the strongest few persisted, but these hovered midway up the chamber.

"Natural selection, see?" Amanda noted. "Only the fittest ones are still alive."

"That's fascinating from an evolutionary point of view," shouted Derek. "But I for one do not want to create a superstrain of anything based on one of Eugenia's designs! Nor would I like to face personal extinction from them. We've got to get them all."

Amanda and Derek sighed with relief as they saw the last few quidpreys get sucked into the fan. The fifteen-second warning now chimed on Derek's jet pack.

"Sanjay, get ready!" shouted Amanda. "Cut the power to the fans, Doctor. Derek, you go first. You're almost out of fue— Aaghhh!"

Amanda felt something seize her ankle. One of the creatures, more diabolically clever than the others, had used its tentacles to hang on to a handgrip and stay out of sight. Now that the fan was slowing down, it had hurtled itself through the air toward Amanda and wrapped its tentacles around her foot. She could feel its whirring teeth already trying to grind through the heel of her boot.

Despite the low-fuel warning, Derek was instantly by her side. He kicked at the quidprey. "Back off, you!" he shouted.

"Derek, you've got to get out!" warned Amanda, trying unsuccessfully to shake the quidprey loose.

"No way! I'm not leaving you in here with that thing!" he shouted. "Now hold still!"

He paused a split second, carefully calculated the angle that would maximize his striking force, then let loose with a ferocious karate snap kick. The impact sent the quidprey tumbling end over end. It bounced off the wall, then spiralled toward the floor, its cold black eyes staring at them all the while. It continued whirring its teeth in a circular motion, ready to reattach itself to either of them given half a chance.

Dr. Kovalevsky gave the fan a last burst of power, sucking the eel toward it. The creature yowled with rage, struggling to get at Amanda—wings flapping, tentacles grasping, teeth clicking—right up to the moment when it was finally sucked into the swirling fan blades and shredded.

"Now, Sanjay! Open the hatch! Dr. Kovalevsky, kill the power to the fans," shouted Amanda.

A moment later, the hatch clanked open, revealing Sanjay's concerned face. The alarm on Derek's jet pack was a shrill, constant tone now.

"Hurry!" shouted Dr. Kovalevsky. "You've got less than ten seconds of fuel!"

Derek was about half a metre from the hatch when his jet pack sputtered. He began to sink. He opened the throttle all the way, using the last vapours of fuel to stay aloft. Then his engine shuddered and died.

Amanda zoomed beneath him. "Stand on my shoulders!" she shouted. She pushed Derek toward the hatch, using extra thrust—and extra fuel—to boost his weight. He grabbed the edges of the hatchway and, with Sanjay's help, pulled himself onto the roof of the chamber. Then Amanda's own ten-second warning siren began to wail.

"Come on, Amanda!" shouted Sanjay.

Her jet pack sputtered and she dipped slightly. The uneven thrust from its two jets pitched her forward, and she could see the fan blades, still whirling lethally below. She experienced a sinking sensation in her stomach and knew that she would be dead in seconds if her pack didn't regain thrust. But an instant later, she felt four hands firmly gripping her shoulders and looked up to see Derek and Sanjay in the hatchway. Their faces were intense with effort as they pulled her through the narrow opening, out of the zero-g chamber and at last to safety.

CHAPTER 16

THE DOOR TO Thorne's classroom was closed. Holding an improvised high-voltage stun gun at the ready, Dr. Kovalevsky turned to Amanda, Derek, Sanjay and Evelyn.

"Don't make a sound," she whispered.

Then she slowly turned the handle and gently pushed on the door. As it swung open, they saw to their relief that there were no signs of any quidpreys flying about.

"Professor Thorne?" called Dr. Kovalevsky quietly. "Professor Thorne?"

There was no response. As they crept warily into the room, a pungent chemical odour wafted into their nostrils.

"Ugh, smells like bleach," said Amanda, crinkling her nose.

Dr. Kovalevsky sniffed the air. "It's coming from that tank."

"That's where the quidpreys were grown," said Derek.

Evelyn, the aquatic-life expert, borrowed one of Sanjay's eyepieces and carefully inspected the vat. Holding her nose to ward off the smell of the bleach, she saw that it was full of lifeless quidprey eggs and hatchlings, the latter no bigger than a baby finger.

"They're all dead," she declared. "It looks like they've been poisoned."

Derek spotted an industrial-size bleach container. The cap was off, and the bottle was empty. "I reckon this is what did it."

Evelyn studied it a moment and agreed. "That would have made a very toxic soup when mixed into the nutrient solution."

Then their attention was drawn to a faint chiming coming from the direction of Thorne's computer. As they approached the tinted panel that shielded his workstation from view, they saw the bodies of a number of large quidpreys. Their rasp-like teeth were projecting out of their sucker-shaped mouths, as if in preparation for attack. But they were motionless and appeared to have been beaten to death.

Dr. Kovalevsky pointed her stun gun in front of her, put her finger on the trigger and crept into Thorne's sanctuary behind his tinted workstation panel. Amanda and the others followed. There, they saw several more dead quidpreys. The chiming noise was louder now. Amanda followed the sound to a set of headphones lying on the floor; their cable led to Thorne's computer. She held them to her ear.

"You're not going to believe this," she said.

She yanked the cable, unplugging the headphones so the sound came through the computer's speakers instead. The room was immediately filled with the bleeps and bells of a slot machine, along with a cheesy computer-generated instrumental version of "Happy Days Are Here Again."

As they gazed toward the source of the electronic racket, they noticed a hand sticking out from under the desk. Amanda crouched down to get a better look and saw the motionless body of Professor Thorne. His face was contorted into a scream, and his arms were in front of him in a defensive pose, palms facing out, as if he was trying to ward off an attack. His skin was no longer grey, but white as a freshly hewn headstone, except for the red circular marks where the quidpreys had drilled into him to feast on his flesh and blood.

"Crikey, looks like he's been sucked dry!" said Derek.

The sight of Thorne's bloodless corpse was terrifying, though given his nasty temperament, it was a sight only slightly more terrifying than if they had found him alive and well. On Thorne's computer monitor, a flashing graphic with big yellow letters proclaimed, "Congratulations! You're a winner!" Below those words was the image of an ace, king, queen, jack and ten of hearts against a green background.

Sanjay looked at the screen, mystified. "Playing cards?"

Just then, Bill Snootman appeared in the doorway, looking furious.

"Has anyone seen Professor Thorne?" he snapped. "He never responded to my message to come to the Constellation Hall, and he's not answering any of his pages. I don't know how he let this happen, but when I find him, I'm going to give him a piece of my mind."

"I'm afraid you're too late for that," replied Dr. Kovalevsky.

"Unbelievable," Bill Snootman said as he took in the sight of Professor Thorne lying on the floor in front of his colourfully lit monitor.

"What do those cards on the screen represent?" asked Derek.

"In the game of poker," Snootman replied, "it's what's called a royal flush. A winning hand. Big time. Not that I'm much of a gambler, but Snootman Global Enterprises does own a few casinos in Europe and Asia."

He sat down and tapped out some commands on the keyboard. Amanda and the others crowded around, watching. With his mastery of software, it took Snootman just minutes to open the locked files on Thorne's computer. All the pages were for online gambling.

"Clearly a full investigation is in order," he said. "In the meantime, Dr. Kovalevsky, can you check on the students and make sure they're all safe?"

"Certainly, Mr. Snootman," she replied.

"Also, I know genetics isn't your specialty, Doctor, but after this incident with Thorne, I think the students need the influence of someone they can look up to and trust. Would you be willing to take over his class?"

"I would be delighted to do so," she replied.

"Excellent," said Snootman. "Now, I would like you four to join the other students. I will be conducting an immediate investigation and will announce my findings the moment it is completed."

☆

The large bodyguard outside Bill Snootman's office nodded as a voice crackled in his earpiece. He turned to face Amanda, Derek, Evelyn and Sanjay.

"Mr. Snootman would like to see you now," he said, gesturing toward the office door, which opened automatically for them.

They found Bill Snootman gazing at a report and shaking his head. Then he turned to them.

"Please sit down. Let me get straight to the point: my security officers have completed an exhaustive inquiry, and they discovered that Professor Thorne was a gambling addict. He owed more than two hundred thousand dollars for bets that went wrong. I don't think there was a horse, dog or hamster race between here and Las Vegas that he hadn't lost money betting on."

"But other than perhaps throwing off his concentration, how could his gambling habits have affected his work at the Academy?" asked Amanda.

"By making him want to keep his job here as long as possible," replied Snootman. "You see, I paid him five times his usual university salary."

"Right, I remember him telling me that," said Amanda. "So you think he hoped to stay here long enough to pay off his gambling debts?"

"Precisely," replied Snootman. "But he was a spectacularly unsuccessful gambler, and even while he was here collecting a huge salary, he kept racking up more debt."

"How ironic that the last hand of poker he ever played was a royal flush," Amanda pointed out. "Perhaps he was finally on a winning streak."

"Yes, and that's probably what distracted him so much that he didn't notice the embryonic quidpreys growing around him until it was too late," said Snootman. "By the time he poured that bottle of bleach into the hatching tank, there were enough fully grown quidpreys in his classroom to take him down. He managed to destroy them, but he was so weakened from their sustained attacks, the effort killed him."

"So his last gamble was his biggest. And he ultimately lost," said Derek.

"That's right," replied Bill Snootman. "And his risk-taking behaviour seriously jeopardized our work on the project to rehabilitate my daughter. I had my technicians go through his desk. He switched your hypodermic needle and serum, Amanda, with an identical one to which he had added a toxin and other impurities."

Derek scowled. "Thorne must have known you were on to something with your experiments. That's why he didn't let you give the serum to the lobsters."

"Correct," said Snootman. He turned to Amanda. "He hoped to get you expelled, thus delaying our work by months, or even years, and buying himself time to pay off his gambling debts. He knew the quidprey experiment was doomed to failure, which is why he encouraged it."

Derek shook his head. "And the quidpreys turned out to be his undoing. To borrow one of his pet phrases, what are the odds?"

"Thorne also sabotaged the anti-gravity chamber," said Snootman, "in an effort to get rid of you to keep you from finding a solution."

"It's incredible that anyone would try to kill someone just to pay a gambling debt," said Evelyn, shaking her head in disbelief.

"Truly as low as you can go," Snootman replied. "But in the end, he was the one who died over his gambling debts."

"What are you going to tell his family?" asked Amanda.

"Nothing," replied Bill Snootman, "because he didn't have any family. At least, no one who wanted anything to do with him.

His wife left him and took the kids years ago, after he pawned their furniture and even their wedding rings to get more gambling money. Evidently he had borrowed so much money from other family members to pay off his debts that none of them would speak to him anymore. The only people who cared whether he lived or died were the owners of the casinos he owed money to. I paid them all off earlier today so they wouldn't come snooping around the Academy looking for him. Meanwhile, I'm keeping him in cold storage in the basement until Eugenia is returned to human form. I can't afford to have the authorities coming here and asking a lot of questions while she's stuck to that alien body. And on that note . . . Amanda, I owe you an apology. I'm sorry I didn't believe you. I should have been more suspicious of Thorne when someone as intelligent as you failed so spectacularly."

"Thanks. I accept your apology," said Amanda. She paused thoughtfully, then spoke again. "Thorne probably had a genetic disorder with his D2 receptors. Those are the ones that make people take risks, because it stimulates the part of their brain that senses pleasure. Too bad he never came forward and admitted his problem. With the gene therapies we've been working on, we could have replaced the faulty genetic code that made him want to gamble."

"Well, it's too late for Thorne," said Snootman. "But I know someone who is in great need of innovative gene-replacement techniques. There's no time to lose, if you kids are up for the challenge."

Amanda, Derek, Evelyn and Sanjay glanced at one another for just a moment.

"Yes, we're up for it all right," replied Amanda.

CHAPTER 17

OVER THE NEXT few days, Amanda and her team created several batches of serum, painstakingly testing each one on a variety of creatures that, through misadventure, had lost one or more limbs. The animals ranged from an over-eager bomb-sniffing dog to a circus monkey that had escaped its handler and been foolish enough to tease a tiger by poking a stick between the bars of its cage. In every case, Amanda's regrowth stimulant caused the animals' limbs to regenerate perfectly within several weeks, and they regained full mobility (though the monkey was none the wiser for its experience, and tried to jab the bomb-sniffing dog with a laser pointer, almost losing its new arm in the process). Finally, the friends were ready to try the serum on Eugenia—or as ready as they'd ever be.

☆

Amanda's footsteps echoed down the otherwise silent corridor as she approached the vault-like entrance to Eugenia's suite. Two guards flanked the doorway, their steely gazes tracking Amanda as she approached. She tried not to look too nervous.

"Hello, Miss Forsythe," said the one in charge. "Please place your right index finger on the scanner."

She did so. The scanner began to glow with bright green light. Then a computer-generated voice declared, "Identity confirmed: Amanda Forsythe."

"Very good," said the guard politely. "You're free to enter." Then he leaned down and whispered, "Brace yourself. Eugenia's mental state has declined since you last saw her."

Amanda nodded. "Thanks."

The vault door slid open, and Amanda found herself in something that looked like a luxury penthouse. To her surprise, instead of it being dark, as she imagined the windowless container to be, sunlight streamed in through floor-to-ceiling windows. She could hear birds twittering and the distant sounds of traffic outside. Gazing out the window, she saw not the graveyard and cow pastures that surrounded the Academy, but a wide boulevard filled with fashionably dressed people. Some sat in cafés, reading newspapers, talking or people watching, while others strolled beneath the trees that lined the sidewalks. On the opposite side of the boulevard, Amanda saw a beautiful five-storey building made of finely hewn stone. Behind its windows, people went about their business. Just then, she became aware of someone standing nearby. She turned to see Bill Snootman.

"This looks like Paris," said Amanda. She had no idea how this was possible.

"It *is* Paris," replied Snootman. "The Boulevard Saint Michel, in the Latin Quarter, to be precise. This scene is composed of images and sounds recorded by numerous cameras and microphones that I had installed in our Paris apartment. Every detail is exactly what Eugenia would see if she were there—which, of course, she can't be. But the illusion makes her feel at home and keeps her from getting too severely depressed. She's in her bedroom, watching a tennis match on television. The irony is, with her eight arms, she could beat both players combined. Anyway, I'll take you in."

As they reached the bedroom, Bill Snootman lowered his head and paused a moment, then gently rapped on the door.

"Eugenia, honey. Amanda's here to explain the procedure to you. Can we come in?"

"Brrr-twee-awk!" came the high-pitched response.

"She still can't speak," whispered Bill Snootman. "But she understands everything."

Amanda tried not to gasp at the sight of Eugenia hanging upside down from the ceiling. She was ignoring the tennis match and was instead using three of her spindly arms to hold and turn the pages of a fashion magazine dedicated to clothing for girls with only two arms and two legs. Amanda took it as a hopeful sign.

"Hello, Eugenia," she said.

Eugenia swivelled her head on her spidery body to look directly at Amanda. "Kree-whup-whup!" came her response.

"Well, I'll leave you two girls to . . . um, chat," said Bill Snootman, trying to sound optimistic as he exited the room.

"How do you communicate these days?" asked Amanda.

Eugenia pointed to a marker fastened to the end of one exoskeletal leg.

"So you have to write out everything you want to say?"

Eugenia nodded her head to indicate yes.

"That seems so time-consuming," said Amanda. "Have you thought about using a voice synthesizer that you trigger with eye or cheek movements, like the one Stephen Hawking uses?"

Eugenia clambered down and began writing a message on a big sheet of paper, holding it so Amanda could see.

"People think Stephen Hawking can speak in real time because of the way they've seen him on television," read Eugenia's message. "But those are prepared speeches. It can take him up to seven minutes to answer a spontaneous question."

"Really? I didn't know that," replied Amanda.

"Finally I know something that Amanda Forsythe, great saviour of the world, doesn't know," wrote Eugenia, smiling wryly. "Writing is slow, but not *that* slow. Still, I wish there was another way."

Amanda thought for a moment.

"Do you know what prison tap code is?" she asked finally.

Eugenia shook her head no.

"It's a grid system of letters that prisoners use to tap out messages to each other—using a bar of soap on a radiator, for example—without getting in trouble for talking. I'll show you."

Amanda picked up a sheet of paper and drew out a grid, then filled it with five letters across and five letters down, running from left to right in alphabetical order.

"If you want to indicate the letter A, you tap once to show it's on the top line, then pause and tap once more to indicate it's in the first position on the vertical line. B is the next one over, so you would tap once, pause, then tap twice. If you wanted to make the letter S, you would find that on the fourth line down,

TAPS	1	2	3	4	5
1	A	B	C	D	E
2	F	G	H	I	J
3	L	M	N	O	P
4	Q	R	S	T	U
5	V	W	X	Y	Z

three letters from the left. So you would tap four times, pause, then tap three times. With all your limbs, you could probably tap messages really quickly. Why don't you give it a try?"

Eugenia stared at the grid, taking it in. She may not have been pleasant or even decent, thought Amanda, but she *was* highly intelligent. So it was no surprise to her that within minutes, Eugenia was tapping out words as quickly as if she were text messaging.

"I bet you could hook that up to a synthesizer so you could actually speak with a human voice triggered with your taps," said Amanda.

Eugenia looked at her, then began tapping rapidly with five of her legs.

"I'm sure you are correct," came her coded reply. "But I don't intend to stay in this condition long enough to make use of it."

"Fair enough," replied Amanda. "I'll give your father a copy of the tap code so he can understand what you're saying."

"Thanks, that would be great. In the meantime, he tells me that you and your team have made a breakthrough."

"Yes, we have," said Amanda. "But like all experimental medical procedures, this method carries an element of risk. I want you to understand exactly what you're getting into."

Eugenia nodded, so Amanda began explaining her research and the procedure.

"We have now successfully regrown limbs in everything from lizards to dogs. We haven't tried it on a human yet because of the media attention it would bring—which of course is something your father wants to avoid. However, a human body should respond the way another animal's does. Hypothetically, at least."

"But I don't have a human body anymore," replied Eugenia. "This alien DNA doesn't allow human DNA to grow."

"I know," said Amanda. "But I have found a way to block the influence of the alien DNA. That will allow the human DNA to reassert itself."

Eugenia smiled hopefully. "Really? That's wonderful news!" she tapped.

"Yes, it is hopeful, for sure. But there's a catch," replied Amanda. "To do so, I must enter an area that is dead centre in the middle of the most densely wired part of the alien body. It is full of nerves that do things like regulate temperature and keep your heart beating. Once my procedure is complete, your body can regrow its own human limbs and organs. Until then, you remain dependent on the alien body as your life-support system. So if there's any damage to its nervous system during the removal operation . . ." Amanda hesitated, looking for the right words.

Eugenia tapped it out for her. "I will die. Is that what you are trying to say?"

Amanda nodded. "It's a possibility. I don't know exactly how the alien body works. The only way to find out would be to dissect one."

"And I'd have to be dead for you to do that," replied Eugenia. "In which case, the whole issue becomes academic."

Eugenia gazed into the distance, as though looking at something very, very far away. Then she looked back at Amanda.

"I know we've had our differences," she tapped, in a massive understatement from someone so accustomed to tormenting Amanda, "but if anyone can do this—other than me, of course—it's you. As long as you're in charge, I'm willing to take a chance."

"In that case," responded Amanda, "I will make the arrangements."

Just then, there was a knock on the door. Amanda checked the video monitor to the hallway and saw that Bill Snootman was standing out there, looking anxious.

"Come on in," she said.

She pressed a button, and the steel doors parted. Bill Snootman entered the inner chamber.

"Sorry to interrupt," he said. "Just checking in."

"No problem," replied Amanda. "I have explained the procedure. But there's something else I need to know. Eugenia, do you have your original DNA stored somewhere? Just in case the alien counterpart had some influence on your DNA that we don't know about, I think it's safest to start with something fresh."

Eugenia looked perplexed. She tapped out a response. "I saved all kinds of DNA from other animals, but I never thought to save my own. I guess if we need some fresh DNA, I'll just have to make do with somebody else's. Yours, perhaps, Amanda? I won't look like me anymore, but at least I'll still be a human . . . if not as beautiful."

Amanda bit her lip and handed Bill Snootman the tap code chart. He studied it for a minute, until he had deciphered his daughter's message.

"Wait," he said, "I think I can help."

He undid the top buttons of his shirt, reached in and produced a locket on a chain. On the front was a photo of a young Bill Snootman and his wife, Charleze, smiling and holding a baby Eugenia in their arms. He opened it and removed a lock of downy baby hair.

"I saved this from Eugenia's first haircut, when she was six months old."

Eugenia looked over at her father, astonished. She began to tap out a message. "You never told me that you kept a lock of my hair with you."

His expression was touched with melancholy. "I know," he replied. "I was afraid that if you found out I did things like that, it would make you weak and sentimental. I wanted you to be tough and strong, so you could make it on your own in this world. I didn't want anyone to think you got what you got just because of who your father is. But I guess I went too far."

A single tear welled up in Eugenia's eye and rolled down her cheek.

Bill Snootman reached over and wiped it away.

"I'm sorry, Eugenia. I wish I'd told you years ago how much you mean to me. So I'm telling you now."

Nobody spoke for a moment. Then Bill Snootman turned to Amanda.

"Do you need all the hair?"

Amanda smiled, deducing his meaning. "No, I think half should be enough to do the trick." She produced a sterile plastic pouch and placed half of Eugenia's baby hair in it. "You can keep the rest," she said gently.

"Thank you," he replied.

Eugenia watched as her father slipped the locket back around his neck. She smiled wistfully.

"All right," said Amanda, "it's time to get working on the regrowth serum."

Using the combined efforts of the kids at the Academy, Amanda and her team soon synthesized the regrowth stimulant using Eugenia's DNA and were ready to administer it. But first, they would have to remove the bio-controller. Apart from shutting down the alien body once Eugenia's human form had been regrown, this was the most hazardous part of the entire procedure.

CHAPTER 18

ON THE APPOINTED morning, Amanda, Evelyn, Sanjay and Derek gathered in the operating room that Bill Snootman had constructed in Eugenia's quarters. It was sealed like a spaceship and had its own oxygen supply and guards posted at the door. After the quidprey incident, Snootman didn't want to take a chance on letting any more rogue DNA escape into the world to run amok and attract the attention of the press. Amanda knew that it was actually the bio-controller and its master DNA, and not the regular alien DNA, that posed the threat. But she thought that the less any adults knew about the bio-controller, the better. If it fell into the wrong hands, it could be put to very dangerous use; someone could create, for example, a virtually unstoppable army of alien-based life forms with eight appendages, superhuman strength and a bullet-proof exoskeleton. No, the bio-controller was something that had to be put where nobody with the wrong sort of ideas could ever find it.

Eugenia was lying on a large operating table that had been created specifically for this event. Her eight limbs were restrained to keep her steady throughout the procedure. Derek still did not know precisely what the operation was all about. But he trusted Amanda enough not to ask any questions. He knew only what Sanjay and Evelyn knew: that there was some tiny object that had to be removed before they began Eugenia's regrowth phase. The three of them had their suspicions about what that object was, but they knew better than to ask. Instead, Derek just did what he could do to help, which was to create a special microscope to attach to the nanobot that would make its way deep inside the alien body. This would allow them to find and remove the bio-controller. He had also created a system of sensors to track the nanobot in three dimensions, so they would know precisely where it was.

As Eugenia waited on the operating table, Sanjay made some last-minute adjustments to the nanobot. Then he turned to Amanda. "It's ready."

She looked at her former tormentor. "Are *you* ready?"

Eugenia nodded.

"Okay, here we go," Amanda announced.

She administered a mild anesthetic, and soon Eugenia was peacefully sleeping. Because the nanobot was so tiny, Eugenia would feel no pain during the procedure, but Amanda thought it wise to have the subject relaxed—especially when that subject was attached to such a powerful body.

To reduce the distance the nanobot would have to travel, Amanda drilled a tiny hole through the chest plate of Eugenia's alien exoskeleton, not far below her chin. Using a long, thin tube as fine as a human hair, Sanjay slipped the nanobot inside.

Derek checked his monitor. "It's on its way."

To avoid damaging any sensitive nerve areas, Amanda confirmed the coordinates periodically to make sure that the nanobot's path was matching the course George had laid out for her. Meanwhile, Evelyn monitored Eugenia's vital functions. Everything was good. So far. The minutes ticked by slowly. Finally, after a tense hour, a light flashed on the nanobot monitor.

Derek checked his tracking equipment. "We've reached the target zone."

Sanjay turned to Amanda. "I can make out an object that's different from everything else. Is this the mysterious something that you're looking for?"

He passed an eyepiece to her.

"That's it!" she exclaimed. "Let's remove it and head home!"

"Okay, here goes," said Sanjay. He squinted into the eyepiece as he manipulated controls that moved tiny blades and mechanical grasping devices on the nanobot. "I am about to make contact. In three . . . two . . . one."

An alarm began to ring on the monitor checking Eugenia's vital signs.

"What's that?" asked Amanda.

"I don't know," replied Evelyn.

"I think I do," said Derek. "My sensors are picking up something unusual moving through the bloodstream toward the nanobot. My guess is that they're killer cells. In which case, Sanjay, you'd better step on it!"

"Okay, okay! No need to say that," shouted Sanjay. "I'm already going as fast as I can!"

Amanda had seen Sanjay look this nervous only once

before, when he had discovered that Oppenheimer and Leitspied were aliens.

"All right," said Amanda, "let's all stay calm so Sanjay can focus. Derek, can you set up a 3-D model of the nerve centre, showing the attacking cells?"

"Yes, I ought to be able to do that by tracking any unusual heat movement."

"Good, make it happen!"

Meanwhile, Sanjay manipulated the nanobot's tiny scalpel, his hands moving with incredible precision and just a hint of panic. A moment later, he pressed a button.

"I've removed the target! The nanobot has begun the return journey. It will be fully automated; it simply has to reverse through the same moves it used to get there."

Meanwhile, Derek's equipment had begun to reveal the drama taking place deep inside Eugenia's alien body. On the monitor, flashing green dots appeared like incoming attackers on a video game. The dots were moving toward the nanobot as it fled. And something unnerving was becoming clear: they were gaining on it.

"They're like hornets protecting the queen in a hive," said Evelyn. "They're trying to protect that thing, whatever it is."

"That means if they catch the nanobot, they might not just destroy it," added Derek, "but they'll put whatever it's carrying back wherever it's supposed to go."

"That's possible," agreed Amanda. "And if that happens, the operation will be a failure. Okay, Sanjay, you focus on controlling the nanobot using Derek's 3-D map. We're going to look for a shortcut to get you out of there. Evelyn, keep me updated on the vital signs."

"Roger that," replied Evelyn.

By recalibrating the sensors on the tracking equipment, Derek was able to focus on the nanobot and the killer cells, while eliminating distracting input from the rest of the body. "They're still gaining," he observed anxiously.

Amanda gazed at Derek's digital representation of the web-like network within the alien body. "Sanjay, I see a capillary you can use," she said. "If you can get in, you can get a jump on the defender cells. Off to your right, about ten seconds ahead of you at your current speed."

"Right, I've got a visual on it," Sanjay replied.

He manipulated the joystick to turn the nanobot toward the capillary. "I'm cutting through the walls right now." He held his breath a long moment. "I'm in!"

"The defender cells are changing direction!" cried Derek. "They seem to know what you've done. Any way you can cover your tracks?"

"Yes, I can seal the capillary wall behind me," he replied. "Then they'll have to find another way in."

Sanjay hurriedly worked the controls.

"Done!" he said, relieved. "I'm on my way."

They now watched as the nanobot rapidly navigated a course through the bloodstream to a point very close to Amanda's entry hole.

"Almost there, mate!" called Derek, watching the monitor.

Sanjay began boring through the capillary wall to make his escape.

"Gonna leave this one open," he said. "The hole is so tiny, there won't be any significant internal bleeding. I need the extra time to get out ahead of the killer cells."

The nanobot was almost at the entrance tube when the

monitor showed the defender cells regrouping for a final attack. Just as they were closing in, Sanjay literally began to see daylight through the optical sensor implanted in the nanobot.

"I'm going to tap in to the nanobot's reserve power to get some extra speed. I think I can make it."

Just as the attacking cells moved in for the kill, the nanobot suddenly gained speed. It wasn't putting any distance between itself and its pursuers, but at least they weren't gaining on it as quickly.

"They're still coming," said Derek.

With a final burst of tapping, Sanjay's nimble fingers manipulated the controller. He was so tense that he was standing up, hovering over his equipment. Switching to his eyepiece, he gazed into the entry tube, then shouted, "We're out!" as the miniscule nanobot emerged from the alien exoskeleton. The instant the target of their fury disappeared, the defender cells ceased moving and became dormant.

"Whoa, that was close. George, why didn't you tell me?" Amanda whispered absent-mindedly.

"What do you mean, 'George'?" asked Derek.

She was caught off guard. "Um, I meant, 'By George'—as in, 'By George, that frazzled my nerves!'"

Derek raised an eyebrow at her. He didn't buy her explanation for a moment. But he said nothing more.

Their attention was drawn to Evelyn as she gave her report. "All the vitals are looking good. Everything in the body has returned to normal function."

"Thank gawd," said Amanda under her breath. For all his brilliance, George did occasionally make mistakes . . . like the near-miss collision and not knowing about the defender cells.

"What just happened?" asked Derek.

"If I'm correct, we just removed the bio-controller that regulates the alien DNA," she replied. "Sanjay, can you give me the nanobot, please?"

Sanjay laid the tiny robot on a workbench beside the operating table. Using a miniscule set of remotely operated tweezers, Amanda removed the object from the nanobot's grasp. She placed it in a container she'd had specially constructed, a small stainless-steel cylinder about the same diameter as a pencil and one-quarter its length.

"If this has gone as I planned, the alien DNA will no longer halt the growth of human tissue. Eugenia can regenerate a human body, then disengage from the alien exoskeleton. At least I hope she can."

Amanda slipped the container inside a secret pocket of her lab coat.

"Now it's time to put it to the test with the regrowth serum."

Amanda injected the serum at the point where Eugenia's head joined the alien body. Then the team hooked a device that looked like a long umbilical cord to Eugenia and began feeding in a nutrient solution. A few seconds later, Eugenia began to stir. She sighed. Then her eyes opened. She gazed up nervously. With her legs still restrained, she was unable to communicate in tap code. But Amanda could read her expression.

"We believe that we have successfully completed the first stage of the treatment," she told Eugenia reassuringly. "Now comes the difficult part. You're going to be bored out of your mind for the next while. We've connected you to a nutrient solution that will provide you with everything your human body needs to regrow. But until all your parts are fully formed, you must move as little as possible."

Eugenia managed a weary smile, then winked.

Amanda turned to Evelyn. "How is everything looking?"

"Vitals are all still normal," replied Evelyn.

"Excellent. We're done for now, Eugenia. So I suggest you rest up. You're going to need strength for all that growth."

Eugenia looked up at Amanda and the others and silently mouthed the word "Thanks."

"Try to get some sleep," Amanda replied. She led her team out of the operating room and dimmed the lights.

As the four friends exited Eugenia's private quarters, the armed guards nodded politely. The heavy steel doors slid shut behind them.

Amanda paused and looked at the one in charge. "No one is to go in there without my knowledge," she said. "Not even Bill Snootman."

"Yes, Miss Forsythe. Understood," the guard replied.

When they were out of earshot, Derek looked at Amanda in amazement. "Whoa, now you're even giving orders to Bill Snootman?"

"Later," she replied.

Once they had stepped out of the private elevator and were back in the main hallway of the first floor, Amanda turned to Derek to answer his question.

"Sorry, but that's an ultra-high-security area. Everything anyone says or does is monitored. Here, we can talk freely because Snootman hasn't wired it. I don't want to worry him unnecessarily, but the regrowth procedure is physically and mentally taxing. It's very important that Eugenia not be disturbed. And I'm afraid the biggest problem is that we won't even know for certain if we removed the actual bio-controller, or just something that looks like it, until we see evidence of human regrowth.

"Meanwhile, it's vitally important that we not speak about the existence of the bio-controller with anyone. Understood?" The others nodded.

"Understood," replied Derek.

CHAPTER 19

WHILE THEY WAITED out the long days and weeks to see whether the regrowth process with Eugenia had been successful or not, Amanda, Evelyn, Derek and Sanjay focused on their pet projects. Dr. Kovalevsky had re-engineered the anti-gravity chamber so it was tamperproof, and Amanda never used it except under the doctor's watchful eye. Having been relieved, at least for the moment, of the responsibility of returning Eugenia to human form, Amanda was able to spend many long and happy afternoons within the chamber, trying out new zero-gravity exercises as she dreamt of voyages to distant worlds. She also worked on her suborbital weather rocket in the workshop she shared with Dr. Kovalevsky. In the cafeteria during the days and in the dorm in the evenings, Amanda told Derek, Evelyn and Sanjay how much progress she was making on it, how it would soon be ready for launch, and how close she was to perfecting the software so the rocket could be adjusted to land anywhere in the world. As she frequently reminded them, this rocket was so revolutionary that even someone with no experience could change its landing location just by putting a finger on a touch-screen map. Her friends still thought it was a bit peculiar that Amanda was so absorbed in such a modest project, but since she was doing so well overseeing Eugenia's regrowth, they chalked it up to eccentricity and stopped worrying about her mental state.

Evelyn, meanwhile, was working closely with Derek on her efforts to trace the sources of the trash accumulating in the North Pacific Gyre. Snootman had promised them that once they gave him all the relevant details, he would use his considerable political clout to bring pressure on the parties responsible. Sanjay continued his nanobot research; he was now set on designing ones that could be programmed to construct even smaller nanobots than themselves. And Amanda checked in on Eugenia regularly throughout the tedious process of what they all hoped was her human self regenerating within the alien body. Finally, the day came.

CHAPTER 20

AMANDA, DEREK, EVELYN AND Sanjay stood around the operating table. Amanda had administered an anesthetic to Eugenia according to the instructions George gave her. She was nervous, although she didn't want the others to know this. George could give her only his best guess about what the correct dosage was, since aliens and humans are so different. With too little sedation, Eugenia's human head would sleep, but her alien body's nervous system might go berserk, break free of the straps and thrash itself to pieces once the death gene was administered. With too much sedation, the alien body would stay nice and quiet—but so would Eugenia's brain. Forever.

"How are the vital signs?" Amanda asked Evelyn.

"In the sweet spot so far," she replied. "Eugenia's off in dreamland, and according to the signals I'm getting, that alien body isn't about to get up and start running around either."

"Good. Let's hope it stays that way. I'm about to deactivate it now," said Amanda. "This is where we succeed or fail."

She took a deep breath and began the process that, although utterly invisible to the naked eye, would activate the alien death gene. Soon, a message would be transmitted cell by cell within that body from a distant world, each one telling the next in turn that it was time to return to the inanimate compounds from whence it came. At least that was the hope. Amanda now looked for tell-tale signs of change. For a few minutes, everything was deceptively quiet. Then Eugenia's face began to twitch. Her eyes were moving rapidly beneath their lids.

"Is she waking up? Or is she in distress?" asked Amanda.

"It's just the involuntary nervous system. She can't be feeling any pain," replied Evelyn.

A moment later, they heard a faint clattering, like the sound of pebbles on a beach being jostled together by the outgoing tide.

"Her legs," exclaimed Derek. "They're beginning to bend!"

As the exoskeletal legs flexed, tiny cracks appeared and viscous yellow liquid oozed out. More of the gelatinous substance dripped from the joints, where the various sections of the leg were now separating from each other. Then the abdomen made sharp snapping noises, like dry twigs being broken. The monitoring equipment emitted a rapid series of beeps and tones, and one by one, the wave forms on the screen lost their peaks and valleys. The numbers on the digital readouts began fluctuating wildly.

"What's happening?" asked Amanda anxiously.

"I'm not sure," Evelyn responded. "The vital signs are changing. Every one of them." She paused, reading the monitors. The electronic waves were all flat green lines now. The machines were giving off one continuous high-pitched tone.

"Are we losing her?" Amanda shouted.

"All the vital functions of the alien body have ceased," replied Evelyn.

Amanda had a vision of her and her family huddled under a bridge—their new and future home—reading lawsuits by the light of giant blimps overhead bearing her image, shilling for artery-clogging snacks that someone else would no doubt sue her over at a later date. Back in the operating room, everyone stared tensely at the monitors. Suddenly, the flat lines flickered and took on the shape of waves once again, only in patterns and speeds that were different from before.

"The vitals have resumed, but they're changing," Evelyn confirmed. She smiled slightly. "They're becoming like those of a human being."

Large fractures opened up in the exoskeletal legs, releasing more of the thick yellow bodily fluids onto the floor.

"Ugh, this is so gross," groaned Sanjay. "I think I'm going to be sick."

"Just pretend they're the legs of a giant nanobot," said Derek. "A giant nanobot with— Whoa!"

A greenish-white liquid the consistency of gravy squirted out from between the leg joints, straight at him. Derek ducked just in time to avoid being sprayed in the face by Eugenia's alien bodily fluids. When the gusher had subsided, he stood up again. "As I was about to say, just pretend they're the legs of a giant nanobot with some really gross, disgusting stuff inside it."

"Thank you for that insightful analysis," said Sanjay. "I feel much less revolted now that you've expressed it in such articulate scientific terms."

They heard a loud, sharp crack; it was so sudden that all four of them flinched. Eugenia's abdominal exoskeleton was splitting.

One by one, the legs detached and fell to the floor, dripping more goo. Amanda tried not to gag as the abdomen began to fall away.

"It looks like a crab shucking its shell," said Evelyn. "I've seen them do this."

"Looks more like a snake shedding its skin to me," said Derek, "but maybe that's just my bias talking."

"Shh!" chided Amanda. "Even under anesthetic, patients can sometimes hear."

"Well, I didn't say a bad snake. I just meant, you know, a snake," he whispered. "Maybe one of those nice ones, like the . . . uh, I don't know, garter snake? They do that . . . um, don't they?"

"Not now, Derek," sighed Amanda.

Then they saw an incredible sight: as the shell slid away, there emerged something pink and white in its place. Beneath a gooey protective coating was a distinctly human form. Amanda was pleased—and hugely relieved—to see that the regrowth process had taken firm hold. Arms, legs, pelvis, belly, chest, shoulders and neck all emerged from under the receding exoskeleton, all in the right places and all age appropriate for an eleven-year-old. An eleven-year-old human, that is. Amanda laid a thermal sheet over Eugenia's emerging body, to protect her modesty—assuming she had any—and if not, to at least prevent her from catching a chill.

"How are the vital signs now?" asked Amanda.

"Good," replied Evelyn, smiling. "And getting better."

Then the monitors indicated an increase in mental activity. Eugenia was awakening. Her eyes slowly began to open. She looked at Amanda expectantly.

"Am I . . . ?" she croaked.

Eugenia was unable to finish her sentence because her mouth was so dry. But she had used her human voice—a voice that she had been unable to use since that fateful day with Oppenheimer and Leitspied so many months ago.

"Yes," replied Amanda. "The procedure was a success. But you'll have difficulty speaking for a while; you're dehydrated from the anesthetic, and your vocal cords will need to gain strength after regrowing."

Eugenia raised her hands and wiggled her fingers. An expression of delight came over her face.

"It's true!" she whispered hoarsely. "My hands and arms—they're back!"

She lifted up the sheet so she could see the rest of her body.

"And the rest of me too. Oh, this is wonderful! I'm as beautiful as ever!"

"Yep, she really *is* back to normal," whispered Derek to Sanjay.

Amanda could only smile. Eugenia *was* back to normal. Her mission was accomplished.

CHAPTER 21

THE CROWD FELL silent as Bill Snootman strode onto the stage of the Constellation Hall. He smiled at Amanda, Derek, Evelyn and Sanjay, who sat in a place of honour. Then he looked out over the faces of the other students assembled before him.

"Today is a momentous day for me," he began, "because this is the day that I got my daughter back."

There were murmurs of excitement throughout the hall.

"Yes, it's true. I am very pleased to confirm that the work all of you have dedicated yourselves to has been a total success. And here is the proof . . ."

A spotlight picked out a point to the right of Bill Snootman. Within the circle of light was Eugenia. She was in a wheelchair. Joules, his eyebrows knitted in an expression of concern, leapt from his seat in the front row.

"Eugenia, you're not . . . are you?" he whispered, wringing his hands nervously.

"Have no fear," said Bill Snootman. "Eugenia is in the wheelchair only because her new limbs are not yet capable of supporting her weight. However, Dr. Kovalevsky, who, as you know, is an expert on keeping muscles strong during long space flights, assures me that with her regimen of physiotherapy, Eugenia will return to full strength in a matter of weeks. I am grateful to each of you for being part of the process that has led her to this point. Please give yourselves a big round of applause."

When the clapping died down, Snootman continued his speech.

"Now, I had an agreement with each of you that if you returned to the Academy and dedicated yourself to finding a cure for Eugenia's condition, I would arrange for the finest facilities and fund your education. But because of changing circumstances, I intend to terminate that agreement with you."

Throughout the hall, there was stunned silence, then muted grumbling.

Snootman smiled. "Please don't be alarmed. What I mean is that I would like to offer you something else. Over these past months, I have been amazed by your abilities to adapt your intellectual powers to solving the problem of Eugenia's condition. I have also been impressed by your personal projects, from solar-powered airplanes and space travel to language decoders, medical breakthroughs, alternative energy, and on and on. In short, I have come to the conclusion that the world needs you kids—and all kids, for that matter. Our planet faces immense challenges. And yet there is no regular educational facility in the world capable of nurturing your talents. Therefore, here is my new offer: if you promise to continue your work with the kind of imagination and energy that I have seen from you these last few months, I will fund the

Academy permanently. I am prepared to give every one of you the opportunity to live here, study here and develop your projects, all expenses paid, for as long as you wish."

There was a moment of silence as the implications sank in. Then the crowd of kids broke out into cheers and thunderous applause.

Evelyn leapt from her seat and hugged Amanda. "You did it! Now we can all be together forever!"

"Or for as long as I can handle being around you anoraks," teased Derek with a lopsided grin. He bumped his fists on Amanda's, then he hugged her too. "You're brill!"

Sanjay clapped her on the shoulder. "Way to go, Amanda!"

Bill Snootman smiled, then raised his hand. The room quieted down.

"Now, I know that all of you have worked very hard. And you know what they say about all work and no play. So I believe a celebration is in order. There will be a party in the courtyard in exactly half an hour. That gives you just enough time to go to your rooms, change into your favourite clothes and get ready to have some fun. We have two of the best rock bands in the world waiting to perform for you, and our chef has outdone himself preparing a delicious feast. So what are you waiting for?" he joked. "Get out of here! See you in half an hour!"

Everyone began streaming out of the Constellation Hall, chattering excitedly. Amanda, Evelyn, Derek and Sanjay leapt from their seats and raced for their dorms, as eager as everyone else to get ready for the celebration.

CHAPTER 22

AMANDA AND EVELYN approached their dorm room. Amanda was exhausted, but she felt incredibly relieved that this nightmare of the $100-million lawsuit was over.

"I'm telling you," she said to Evelyn, "now that the threat of financial ruin has passed, all I want to do is lie down and sleep for a hundred years."

Evelyn gave her a disbelieving look.

"But not until *after* the party!" Amanda quickly added.

"Good," replied Evelyn, laughing. "I was worried about you there for a minute!"

Amanda swiped her pass card to open the door, but the moment she entered, she sensed that something was wrong. She scanned their room and saw that the top drawer of her dresser was ajar. She hadn't left it that way. She strode over to take a closer look. Sitting on the top edge of the drawer was a tiny origami skull, grinning up at her. Its placement seemed too deliberate for it to have been left behind accidentally. It looked like someone's sick idea of a calling card. Following a hunch, Amanda unfolded it and saw that on it was a note written in very small letters.

"Yes, someone has been in your room without authorization," it stated. "And if you want to save yourself from a world of pain, read on." But there were no more words in the note. How was she supposed to "read on"?

Just then, she was startled by Evelyn's cry.

"Oh gawd! Lelie!"

Amanda turned and saw Evelyn staring, horrified, into Lelie's aquarium. Amanda raced across the room and peered into the aquarium. She saw that Lelie was cowering behind the pirate ship in the bottom of the tank. Just a few centimetres away, a piranha lunged repeatedly at the terrified mouse, trying to sink its needle-like fangs into Lelie's flesh. Leaning in closer, Amanda saw that the piranha was restrained inside a small, transparent enclosure—something like a hamster ball—that someone had placed inside the aquarium. Only its thin walls prevented the voracious fish from feasting on Lelie.

Evelyn reached in and removed the container holding the piranha.

"Who would do such a horrible thing?" she asked, tears welling up in her eyes.

"I don't know," responded Amanda, "but I've got a really bad feeling we're about to find out."

Looking back at the origami note, she noticed that the period at the end of the last sentence was larger than the period at the end of the sentence before it. It was also perfectly circular, too precise to have been made by hand. She suspected that it was a microdot—a tiny disc often used by secret agents that attaches to paper and contains words written so small that they cannot be read by the naked eye. This allows them to send hidden messages to each other, undetected by police or counter-spies because they are concealed within otherwise tedious accounts of visits to one's spinster aunties in Saskatoon, or a particularly enjoyable walk in the park with a favourite pet labradoodle. So Amanda took the origami skull to her desk and placed it under her microscope. She aligned the dot and peered through the eyepiece. Sure enough, the magnifying lens revealed a previously hidden message.

"Glad you solved this latest mystery," it read. "Now on to the business at hand. The piranha that you have no doubt by now noticed in Lelie's tank is just my way of showing that I can get to you any time I want. There's nothing Snootman or anyone else can do to stop me. Even your dorm room isn't safe from me. But if you do as I say, you have nothing to fear. Because I now know for certain that you have something I want: the bio-controller for the alien DNA. Give it to me tonight, and you'll never hear from me again. Well, at least until my army of alien mutant soldiers is unleashed, and I become ruler of the entire planet. But have no fear, there will always be a role for a clever person like you in my inner circle. So tonight, I want you to leave the bio-controller on the Tesla coil sconce on the right side of the entranceway to the Academy. Do not fail me, or the consequences will be dire."

Amanda turned to Evelyn. "Get Derek and Sanjay and tell them to meet us up on the roof immediately. I'm going down to the lab to get the control station for the weather rocket. Ten minutes to launch."

"Are you going to tell me what this is all about?" asked Evelyn.

"Sorry, there's no time," said Amanda.

CHAPTER 23

THE EVENING WAS settling in around the Academy, and from Amanda's vantage point on the rooftop deck, the headstones below were casting long shadows over the graveyard. Meanwhile, in the inner courtyard, workers were hanging brightly coloured patio lanterns and making last-minute preparations for the party. Amanda heard footsteps rushing up the stairs, and a few seconds later, Derek appeared on the deck, hair still damp from the shower. Sanjay and Evelyn followed a moment later, panting and breathless.

"I still don't know why this weather rocket is so important to you," Derek said, tucking in his shirt, "or why you have to launch it now, right before the party. I haven't even had a chance to dry my hair. I mean, this is a fine little rocket. But there's nothing special about it—not by your standards. You could have built this in your sleep."

"If you're finished," said Amanda crisply, "let's prepare to launch."

She punched in a code on a keypad. A door the size of a manhole cover retracted nearby on the roof, exposing the silo that led down to Amanda's lab. Amid a whirr of hydraulics, a nose cone appeared, rising out of the silo. Amanda pressed a button, and the rocket's burners ignited, sending smoke rushing out of the silo and into the air. The four friends could feel the vibration through their feet now, as the thrusters powered up for takeoff.

"It's not the rocket that's special," Amanda finally explained. "It's what's inside it. I put the alien bio-controller in the nose cone. It's about to go where no one can ever find it."

"That's what you think!" growled a voice from the shadows behind them.

They turned to see a figure stepping out of a Gothic archway. Even in the twilight, Amanda could see that the skin of the tall, hunched figure was grey and waxy.

"Professor Thorne!" she exclaimed.

"In the flesh," he replied, his lips curling into his fish-hook grin.

Derek looked bewildered. "But you're . . . dead!"

"Wrong. I just appeared to be," he snarled. "I'm a biologist. Do the math, Einstein. The quidprey outbreak gave me the perfect cover. They were an opportunity in disguise. You see, after I killed the last of them in my lab, I manipulated my own DNA, slowing my metabolism down to a point that created the outward appearance of death. At least to someone as ignorant about biology as Snootman. I placed myself in a temporary state of deep hibernation, like a bear. A grizzly bear, waiting for spring. And spring has sprung, kiddies. I have been reborn as a free man. You see, I realized that once Snootman thought I was dead, I wouldn't have to worry about my gambling debts any more. I knew he would pay them off, just to keep anyone from coming around here looking for me and finding out about his hideous, vain, freak of a daughter."

"Can't say I disagree with you on that last bit," said Derek. "But then, why didn't you just leave?"

"Because I knew that Amanda was on to something!" he replied. "And when I couldn't stop you from continuing your work, I got desperate. Then I had an idea. A wonderful, awful idea! I realized that any number of rogue governments and corporations would pay me millions of dollars for the secret to creating a vast army of human-alien hybrids. Imagine what an unstoppable military force they would be! So, without further ado, hand over the bio-controller."

"Sorry, but I've got bad news for you," said Amanda. "That bio-controller is in the rocket, heading to where you'll never be able to use it to cause harm."

With the ignition sequence complete, she hit the launch button. An orange glow shone from the silo, lighting the sky above, as the rocket rose slowly out of the hatch and into the air. Thorne just smirked. He made no effort to stop the launch.

"Do you think I'm an idiot?" he asked. "I planted a listening device in your lab before I ever sabotaged the zero-g chamber. I've known about this rocket project since the first day you discussed it with your little friends here. So I know all about this touch-screen control that lets even someone with no experience redirect the rocket to anywhere in the world. Very clever. And very, very convenient for me."

Thorne reached into his pocket, pulled out a pistol and pointed it at Amanda.

"Now, if you and those three other kids will step aside, I've got some rocket redirecting to do."

He strode to the touch-screen monitor, shielding the view so Amanda and the others couldn't see where he was pointing to on the map. Then he tapped it lightly. The monitor bleeped.

Thorne laughed. "There. With just a touch of my finger—courtesy of the brilliant software devised by you and that fool Bill Snootman—your precious cargo has been redirected to a location that only I know about. Soon, I'll have more money than any casino in the world."

Amanda looked surprisingly calm.

"No, you won't," she said.

"Oh, really?" snarled Thorne derisively. "And why is that, smarty-pants?"

"Because there *is* no touch-screen navigation system on the rocket," replied Amanda. "I only told my friends that because I suspected that someone would try to take the bio-controller once they knew of its existence. I had to develop a cover story so no one could interfere with me launching the rocket with the bio-controller in it. See?"

She pointed to the monitor screen. It showed the rocket clearly continuing on its original path, not the least bit affected by Thorne's interference.

"Now, why don't you put that gun away before someone gets hurt?" said Amanda. "Mr. Snootman's security guards are on their way here."

"You have no idea how much trouble you've caused me," snarled Thorne. "Now I don't have the bio-controller to take over the world! I'll have to flee the country and find a job doing biological-warfare research in some crummy Third World rogue state."

"Yeah, it must suck to be you," replied Amanda.

Then, to their amazement, Thorne raised his arms and took a running leap off the roof.

The kids gasped at what looked like an act of suicide. But as Thorne hurtled toward the cemetery below, a cable attached to a hook shot out from his belt and clamped onto the gutters, breaking his fall. Amanda and the others raced to the edge of the roof, getting there just in time to see Thorne jump onto the back of a dirt bike hidden behind a large tombstone. He turned and shook his fist at Amanda, gave her one last sneer, then revved the engine and disappeared at high speed behind the hedges beyond the graveyard.

"Something tells me we haven't seen the last of him," said Sanjay.

"Never mind. Let's see how your rocket's doing!" exclaimed Derek.

Amanda looked up, her eyes following the rocket's progress as it climbed higher and higher into the evening sky. She squinted to follow its trail as the projectile ascended into the darkening heavens. As the rocket became too small for her to see anymore, she turned her attention to the monitor, which, with the help of Derek's observation satellites, provided a clear image of it. Amanda could see that it was now on the outer edges of the atmosphere. Then, achieving escape velocity—the speed at which an object is able to break free of Earth's gravitational pull—it slipped into the blackness of space and disappeared from sight.

"Okay, probably a dumb question, but that wasn't a suborbital weather rocket, was it?" asked Derek.

Amanda smiled. "No. Sorry I couldn't tell you before, but after the incident in the zero-g room, I realized that someone might be listening to our every word. The weather rocket was part of my cover story."

"Absolutely brilliant," said Sanjay. "I don't know why I ever doubted you."

"Probably for the same reason I doubted you about the aliens last year," said Amanda. "It was just too fantastical. Anyway, I'm glad you doubted me. I'm glad all of you did. It made my deception that much more convincing. If Thorne had suspected that this rocket was heading for space and couldn't be stopped, he'd never have waited to snatch the DNA bio-controller. He hesitated only because he thought I was going to make it easy for him by giving him a vehicle in which to conveniently smuggle it out of the country. But the truth is, this rocket is hardwired to fly to only one destination."

"And where might that be, if you don't mind my asking?" inquired Derek.

"The only place the bio-controller is safe," said Amanda. "The planet it came from."

"That's sixty light years away!" exclaimed Evelyn. "How can a conventional rocket possibly make it that far?"

Amanda kept one hand in her pocket, touching the star map that the real George had given her the previous year.

"There's a very interesting shortcut that a certain someone once told me about," she replied. "I've programmed it into the rocket's guidance system. If it works, it should knock a good 59.99999 light years off the trip."

"But how do you know that the shortcut will work?"

"I don't," replied Amanda. "But even if it doesn't, at least the alien DNA can't be misused by anyone here on Earth. Once the bio-controller is out there in space, the only beings who can find it will be too advanced to have any use for it."

"And if your shortcut *does* work?" asked Derek.

"Then we just might hear from an old friend someday."

She gazed up at the stars and planets, which were now appearing one by one in the deep indigo sky, then looked back at her friends.

"Now come on, we don't want to miss the party, do we?"

274

For further adventures at the STAR Academy:

Jim Panou

EDWARD KAY is the author of *Star Academy* as well as a writer and producer on CBC's *This Hour Has 22 Minutes* for four seasons. He was also producer and head writer of *The Itch*, a darkly humorous Canadian cult TV classic and a contributing writer to Rick Mercer's *Talking to Americans*. He is the co-creator of the award-winning kids' animated series *Olliver's Adventures* and the international hit animated comedy *Jimmy Two Shoes.*